SHOW NO WEAKNESS

Joyce M. Holmes

Contemporary Sweet Romance

Secret Cravings Publishing
www.secretcravingspublishing.com

A Secret Cravings Publishing Book
Contemporary Sweet Romance

SHOW NO WEAKNESS
Copyright © 2012 Joyce M. Holmes
Print ISBN: 978-1-61885-342-4

First E-book Publication: June 2012
First Print Publication: October 2012

Cover design by Dawne Dominique
Edited by J.B. George
Proofread by Ariana Gaynor
All cover art and logo copyright © 2012 by Secret Cravings
Publishing

PUBLISHER
Secret Cravings Publishing
www.secretcravingspublishing.com

Dedication

This book is dedicated to Julie Cohen and Jaquelin Bduard. Thanks, ladies, for all the years of handholding, sage advice and the occasional strategic kick in the butt.

Thanks also to Scott & Ginger for giving me a place of refuge while I worked on this book. And Andy, for your continued help and support.

Special acknowledgement to Sgt Peter DeVries of the North Vancouver RCMP detachment, whose knowledge, generosity, and charming wit were so very appreciated as I sent email after email full of questions, which he patiently answered every time. Any errors or liberties are mine alone, and may have been done intentionally for the sake of the story.

To Tasha,

First one was a reader, this one is a keeper. Love you.

Aunty Joyce

SHOW NO WEAKNESS

Joyce M. Holmes

Copyright © 2012

Chapter One

"Hey, Mom, I'm home," Taylor yelled as he exploded through the garden gate.

Joely Sinclair's troubled thoughts scattered like the old fall leaves beneath her son's feet. "My gosh, you startled me. How about closing the gate without—" Taylor aimed a sneakered foot at the outside corner of the gate and booted it closed "—slamming it."

"Sorry." Mischief sparkled in his bright blue eyes, contrasting with his apologetic expression. He lowered his lanky frame cross-legged onto the ground and pushed back his long, dark blond hair. "You look kinda stressed. Tough day?"

"Tough? Yes. I spent most of it with a pregnant sixteen-year-old."

Joely loved her job as a counselor for troubled teens. She took her responsibilities seriously and dedicated herself to helping the children she worked with make the best possible choices for themselves, because she knew firsthand how overwhelming it could be when life unexpectedly threw you a curve ball.

Taylor squinted against the late afternoon sunlight. "Same age as when you got pregnant with me."

"It was different back then." Joely reached for the glass of iced tea on the table next to her and took a slow sip. She continually struggled to keep her emotions detached from the situations she encountered at work, and those feelings took a real battering today because of her own experience being sixteen, pregnant, and scared.

"There's no reason this girl can't graduate with her friends, while I had no alternative but to drop out of school."

Taylor stretched out his long legs and crossed one size eleven over the other. "And then you and Dad got married."

If Taylor wanted a sentimental trip down memory lane, she'd have to disappoint him. Yes, she ended up marrying Brad Mills, the handsome and irresponsible father of her child, but the ill-fated marriage ended badly. The only thing Joely didn't regret about that time was the gift of her son. Taylor—her life, her sunshine, her very reason for being.

"Yes, that's when we got married, and I loved your dad at the time, but we were so young, it just couldn't last."

"I guess." His tone, rather than his words, told her he didn't buy her explanation. "Umm, about Dad. Can I call him after supper?"

"Of course you *may*," she corrected, sitting up straighter in the rocker. Because her perpetually broke and often inebriated ex had yet to enter the world of texting, email, and social networks, Taylor's interaction with his father was limited to phone conversations and the occasional visit, making it easier for Joely to monitor their contact. Sad as it was, she had just cause for her vigilance. "Did you have something in particular you wanted to speak to him about?"

"Yeah, I want to go over our plans for this summer. He said maybe I could go see him in Edmonton when school's out."

A tiny icicle of apprehension tinkled down Joely's spine as she studied her son. What was Brad up to? "You've already discussed this with your dad? He said it'd be okay for you to go up there?"

"Yeah, last week, when he called." A perplexed look crossed his face. "You got a problem with that?"

Ah, yeah, I have a major problem with that and your dad darn well knows why.

As usual, Joely kept those troubling thoughts to herself and instead took the time to carefully line up some potential pitfalls. "Did your dad say what you'd do all day while he's at work? Uncle Rick works fulltime too, so does Aunt Karen and Grandma. You might get bored without any friends to hang out with. Then again, you could always offer to baby-sit Cindy and Stephie for Aunt

Karen. I'm sure she'd appreciate the help."

Taylor pulled a face, as Joely knew he would.

"Dad'll probably take some time off work. Maybe he could even help me find a job."

Joely stifled a sigh. "You know your dad just started a new job." She managed to refrain from adding, "—again". "He won't be entitled to take time off for quite awhile. Besides, I thought you planned to work at Mr. Ning's vegetable market this summer. And everyone's counting on you to do the yard work around the condo."

As much as she ached to, she didn't dare voice her most pressing concern. Taylor couldn't stay with Brad because a standing court order prevented them from being alone together. Taylor didn't know how his boozing dad had taken his frustrations out on him when he was a small child. Because Taylor loved his dad, and Joely wanted to keep his happy childhood memories intact, over the years she'd maintained an uneasy silence about their past life in Edmonton. The older Taylor got, the more he wanted from his relationship with his father, and he'd also questioned why Joely wouldn't see Brad, why she refused to allow him in her home.

Taylor thumped his shoes together. "Mr. Ning can find someone else. And some other dude living here can do the yard work while I'm gone. You're just being mean!"

She swallowed down her despair and forced a calm, reasonable tone to her voice. "No, honey, I'm not. I'm really not. But I'd rather you didn't speak to your dad until I have a chance to go over this with him. He shouldn't've brought the matter up without talking to me first."

Taylor's obvious disappointment tugged at Joely's heart. Somehow she had to fix this. "Tell you what, I'll check with Grandma and Uncle Rick to see if either of them can take you for a week or so. You can get together with your dad after Uncle Rick's off work."

Taylor scrambled to his feet, heading for the condo door. "It won't be the same. You're trying to ruin everything."

Joely stared blankly into her glass of iced tea, then took a halfhearted sip. The ice had melted, but she barely noticed the diluted taste.

Damn Brad, she cursed silently. Damn him for raising the hopes of her son when he knew she'd never agree to the arrangement, and now she had to play the bad guy.

* * * *

Joely glanced at the sign saying *Royal Canadian Mounted Police* as she climbed the steps in front of the North Vancouver detachment Friday morning. She shifted her briefcase to her left hand and pulled the glass door open.

"Good morning, Nora," she called out, giving the civilian clerk behind the counter a friendly smile.

"Any morning without rain's a good morning far as I'm concerned," Nora Mercer replied as she ambled slowly over to the counter. "The way my old joints are acting up, rain's not far off."

"I hope you're wrong this time. We could use a sunny weekend for a change." Opening her briefcase on the countertop, Joely withdrew a file. She glanced quickly through the contents before handing it to Nora. "Here you go. The last of the paperwork on the runaway pregnant teen you referred to us on Monday."

"Another happy ending, judging by the smile on your face." Nora placed the file in a tray on the side counter. "I do love a happy ending, especially when young folks are involved."

"Me too, and I'm relieved to say that after a long and shaky week, the situation couldn't have resolved itself better. I have every confidence the young lady has her life back on track."

Joely derived a great deal of satisfaction from resolving matters this neatly for her clients. Sometimes it didn't go as well, and her heart always broke for the people involved.

Taking advantage of the unusually quiet detachment, she stayed to exchange pleasantries with Nora for a few minutes. While she spoke, a man entered the reception area from the offices behind the counter and, mid-sentence, Joely forgot the conversation. Without even glancing in her direction, his male ambiance captivated her completely.

His white T-shirt clung to the wide expanse of his shoulders, a pair of faded jeans molded naturally to his narrow hips and muscled thighs. Thick black hair held a hint of curls, and although his face was in semi-profile, Joely got the impression of dark eyes and a strong jaw.

She leaned against the counter and whispered to Nora, nodding in the man's direction, "Now, something that good oughta be illegal."

Nora glanced at the man before smiling back at Joely. "You mean Corporal Dennison? He sure does seem to be the new attraction around here."

"He's a *cop*?"

"Yup. Cole Dennison is all cop. And I have to say, the female attention he gets around here is downright comical, not that it seems to get the ladies anywhere."

Joely sighed, sinking onto her elbows, her gaze following his rugged frame as he retrieved a file from the back counter. He studied the contents of the folder, oblivious to the admiring glances being cast his way.

"Cole Dennison," she pronounced his name out loud, tasting the sound of it with her lips. "He doesn't look like the shy type."

Nora laughed. "I wouldn't say he's shy exactly, more of a loner. Quiet, polite, keeps to himself. He's been here a couple of weeks and no one knows him very well yet. I imagine you'll find out for yourself soon enough. He's the new head of the Youth Intervention Unit."

As Joely absorbed this interesting piece of information, the man glanced up, meeting her inquisitive stare with an intense black-eyed gaze. She drew in a sharp breath and glanced away, then instantly looked back at him. She caught a flash of frank admiration before he turned and strode from the room. Her pulse throbbed fast and furious in response.

How ridiculous and completely out of character to allow one short look from an undeniably handsome man to reduce her to a quivering mess. Giving her head a shake, she ended her conversation with Nora and turned to leave before she thoroughly embarrassed herself with further schoolgirl behavior.

* * * *

Joely returned to her Edgemont Village office late in the

afternoon, almost missing the weekly staff meeting with her coworkers, Maggie Lapage and Stella Carson.

"Sorry, I'm late," she said as she slid into her seat at the conference table. "You wouldn't believe my day. First, a stop at the RCMP detachment. Then, four meetings at three different schools and two home visits."

"What's not to believe?" Maggie asked. "I had six meetings at three different schools, two home visits, plus I had to hold hands with a client and her parents during the girl's restorative justice hearing."

"Okay," Joely laughed. "You win. But did you come across any hunky new cops during your travels?"

"Whaddaya mean—hunky new cop?"

Maggie's ears practically perked up. The baby of this trio of women, Maggie completed her social worker's degree less than a year ago, and she brought a great deal of youthful zeal to her job. The only time she showed more enthusiasm was at the mention of an interesting man.

Still recovering from the effects of her fleeting encounter, Joely briefly mentioned the handsome officer from the detachment, then fell silent as she glanced over at Stella who was doing her best to start the meeting. As office manager, Stella's unenviable tasks included keeping all the paperwork and electronic files current. These weekly meetings gave them the opportunity to go through the pending files together to ensure they were up to date.

"Did he speak to you?" Maggie persisted. "Does he have a sexy voice? I love a man with a sexy voice."

Stella rolled her eyes and closed the file in front of her. "I spoke to Corporal Dennison on the phone. He sounds intelligent and mature. I think he'll make a valuable addition to the juvenile department." She looked pointedly at Maggie, then at the trays of files on the table in front of them.

Maggie chuckled and tossed her waist-length red hair over her shoulder. "Not quite what I asked, but I can take a hint. Check him out on my own time."

Quitting time came and went before all the files were updated to Stella's meticulous standards.

"You want to grab a quick bite to eat, Joely?" Maggie asked as they prepared to leave.

"Thanks, but I better pass. I'm going to pick up some pizza to take home to Taylor. I'm not on his A-list right now, so I better spend some quality time with him."

Stella glanced up, concern creasing her forehead. Small, dark and maternal, she had a tendency to dole out helpful advice, regardless of whether the recipient wanted it or not.

"What's going on with Taylor?"

Stella, Maggie, and Joely habitually discussed the ups and downs of their lives with one another, and her friends knew all the details of her past. She sighed with frustration as she thought about this particular dilemma.

"Brad's the problem, actually. He had the audacity to invite Taylor to spend time with him this summer, without getting my okay first. He has the kid all excited about going and, of course, I had to be the one to tell him it wasn't happening."

"Now that Taylor's almost grown up, don't you think he'd be okay visiting Brad?" Maggie asked.

Joely's anger rose, not so much at Maggie's naïve question, as at Brad. "As long as I have any say in the matter, that man will never be in the position to hurt my son again. I'm not actually worried Brad might physically harm Taylor. It's his other problems I want to shield Taylor from. I phoned him last night to find out what plans he'd made. It was still early in the evening and he was already bombed. The ugly truth of the matter is Brad's an alcoholic, Maggie. And when he drinks, he turns nasty. Taylor has no idea his dad has a drinking problem, so how can I risk subjecting him to that? Even though he's a big boy physically, he only turned fifteen last month. He doesn't need to deal with a mean, drunken father he hardly knows."

Stella hugged her around the waist and gave a reassuring squeeze. "You've got that right. I don't know why you've protected Brad all these years. I understand you don't want to destroy the illusions of Taylor's childhood, but maybe you're borrowing trouble by not telling him the truth."

Stella's point sounded valid, but things weren't always as black and white as they appeared to someone on the outside. "It would devastate Taylor to learn the truth about Brad. He loves his father, and I believe Brad loves Taylor too. When he's not drinking, the man can be quite human. So far, he has managed to stay sober while he's with Taylor, but if they're together for any length of time, he might not be able to."

"I'm sorry if I upset you, Jo," Maggie apologized. "I guess I didn't realize the situation was so bad. And I agree, Taylor doesn't need to be around someone who can't control his drinking. Let me know if you want to do something this weekend. Maybe we could take Taylor bowling."

"Thanks, Maggie. I'll check, but don't count on it. He'll forgive me sooner or later, but I have the feeling I'm in for some more cold shoulder before that happens."

Instead of finding a sulking boy when she arrived home, complete silence greeted her. No music, no TV or video games blared from the living room. A cursory search through the condo confirmed Taylor wasn't there, and the note he'd left on the kitchen table explained why.

Spending the weekend at Nelson's. Call you later. T.

Nelson Baldwin was Taylor's best friend, and his family had lived here in their building until three months ago when they moved to West Vancouver. Taylor had been at loose ends ever since Nelson left, and Joely figured it'd do the boys good to spend some time together. Getting a note instead of a phone call asking permission didn't impress her, but she'd call the Baldwins' later to check up on him and say goodnight. Perhaps, Taylor might behave a little more civil after a weekend away, and the time alone would give her a chance to sort out this vacation fiasco Brad had dropped in her lap.

* * * *

Joely dabbed some mascara on, critically surveyed her appearance in the mirror, then added a little more to her lower lashes.

The first Monday in April meant she had to go to the RCMP detachment today with the progress reports on her clients doing community service. This was her regular routine on the first Monday of every month, but today her visit seemed to hold more significance than usual.

She dropped the mascara into her cosmetic bag and picked up a tube of pale pink lipstick, lightly skimming it over her lips.

The practical side of her mind taunted her about taking greater pains than usual with her appearance for her meeting with the handsome Corporal Dennison. Why else would she bypass her usual casual shirt and trousers, choosing instead a sleeveless, buttercup-colored turtleneck, navy jacket, and matching knee-length skirt?

Not the case, the other side of her brain denied vehemently. Cole Dennison had nothing whatsoever to do with her extra effort. She simply wanted to fuss because she felt happy.

"Hey, Mom." Taylor poked his head into the room. "I'm leaving for school now."

Joely placed the lipstick back in the cosmetic bag and turned to smile at her son. She had cause for her good mood. Taylor's sunny disposition had returned with him from Nelson's house last night, and she'd also managed to sort out his holiday situation. He'd stay with her mom for a week at the end of July and her brother, Rick, agreed to supervise the visits with Brad. While not the vacation Taylor originally had in mind, he'd accepted the new arrangements without too much protest, much to her relief.

"Don't forget your lunch."

"Got it." Taylor hefted his backpack to one shoulder and pointed a finger at it.

"How about your homework?"

"Got it, too." He patted the bulky pack again. "And it's even done."

"Good lad. How about a kiss for your mom?" She offered him her cheek.

Taylor moved further into the room and gave her a rib-cracking hug as he dropped a loud smack on her cheek. "You all duded up for something special?"

"Nothing out of the ordinary," Joely denied and mentally crossed her fingers. "You better hurry before you're late. Have a nice day, sweetie."

You're way too obvious if even the boy picked up on it, the pesky part of her brain piped up. No way, she denied once more, refusing to admit she'd go to such lengths for the benefit of a man she'd never even met.

Well, she grinned with satisfaction at her reflection, that minor detail would be rectified in approximately fifteen minutes. She gave her hair one last flip with the brush, then went off in search of her briefcase and purse. She hummed under her breath as she double-checked the briefcase for the community service file.

It must be the return of the sunshine after a rainy weekend and the scent of spring flowers in the air making her this cheerful, she decided, as she stepped into her car and pointed it in the direction of the police detachment.

She smiled a good morning at Nora Mercer and waited with reigned-in impatience for a uniformed member to arrive and usher her through security to the back offices. They entered the large open area with its maze of desks and turned into a short hallway. Joely increased her pace as they approached the office of the Youth Intervention Unit. She spotted Cole Dennison through the open door, and anticipation set her heart beating faster. She gave her escort a quick smile and word of thanks, then stepped into the office without waiting to be announced.

Swallowing hard, she resisted the urge to smooth a hand over her hair, lifting her chin instead as she approached the corporal's desk. He slid the keyboard tray under his desktop and glanced up at her. Joely found herself staring into a pair of sharp, dark eyes, totally observant and completely unreadable, like opaque panes of glass.

"Sorry to disturb you, but my name's Joely Sinclair, and I have an appointment with the head of the Youth Intervention Unit."

"That's me," he said. "I'm Corporal Dennison. Please…have a seat." He motioned to the chair beside the desk and made a polite half-standing gesture as she seated herself. "How can I help you?" His voice was neutrally courteous, one brow lifted in question. He had a cop's expression—detached, alert, and intelligent.

A face that revealed nothing about the man behind it.

She shifted the chair closer to the desk, wondering how she'd misunderstood the approving glance she caught from this man the first time she saw him. He showed not the slightest bit of interest in her today.

"I'm with the Youth Action Outreach agency, and I have the community service reports for the month of March. Three of our clients have now completed their required hours, one has recently started, and two more are partway through their course." She stumbled over her words, feeling cotton-mouthed and awkward. Opening the briefcase on her knees, she handed Cole the file she had prepared for him. "I think you'll find everything in order."

He took the file from her and placed it on his desk, without looking at it. "Youth Action? I'm new to this detachment, and I'm afraid I'm not acquainted with what you do exactly."

"I'll tell you what she does, Corporal," a loud, abrasive voice cut in on their conversation.

Joely winced. Great. Just great.

Chapter Two

Cole's head tilted in the direction of the intrusive voice. Joely turned to look as well, although she didn't have to. She knew exactly who had spoken.

Constable Trip Wilson. The obnoxious officer who took every opportunity to voice his negative opinion of Joely and of social workers in general. His brawny bodybuilder's frame stood braced against the doorjamb. A nasty scowl creased his face, and his huge arms crossed defiantly over his massive chest.

"She's one of those pain-in-the-butt do-gooders. You know the type, Corporal. Whenever we nab some little bugger for doing something he has no damn business doing, Ms. Sinclair here, or one of her cohorts, comes along and tells him, 'It's okay, honey, you didn't mean it'. Then before we can say, 'What the hell?' all our hard work is flushed down the toilet and the snot-nosed brat is back on the street, ready to break the law all over again, knowing next time he won't get so much as a 'bad boy' for it."

He sounded just like the schoolyard bully who had no fear of the teacher. His challenge was coolly sarcastic, meant to hurt, and it would've if Joely hadn't already heard it too many times to count.

She forced herself to smile diplomatically. "That's quite the speech, Trip. Although I hardly think you've given Corporal Dennison any accurate facts. There's a great deal more to my job than merely being a nuisance to the police force, and I'm certain I've never had any hardened criminals released onto the streets to reoffend."

Joely turned to Cole to explain further. She would've loved to see a glimmer of warmth or understanding in those dark, watchful, eyes, but there wasn't any.

"My agency deals with a multitude of problems today's youth come up against. Most of which, incidentally, are not of a criminal nature. However, when a good kid breaks the law, for whatever reason, he or she needs an impartial person on their side to liaison for them. That's where we step in."

"Oh, *puh-leeze*. That's her answer for everything, but us cops who gotta work in the real world know different, eh, Corporal?" Trip Wilson sneered and recrossed his arms, the movement emphasizing the bulge of muscular biceps.

"Thanks for your input, Constable. Now if you don't mind I'd like to finish this conversation with Ms. Sinclair alone. And please close the door behind you." Cole spoke with the quiet authority of someone accustomed to being obeyed. He watched silently until Trip heaved his bulk away from the wall and closed the door, before turning back to Joely. "You were saying?"

She met his gaze with a steady one of her own. Cole's expressionless face gave her no clue to his thoughts. The work she did in the community was far too important to let it be slandered by the likes of Trip Wilson, and she was prepared to do whatever damage control necessary.

"Contrary to what Constable Wilson thinks, our objectives are not to coddle these kids, or to let them off easy. Just the opposite is usually the case. We work through the Restorative Justice system to resolve minor issues in an expedient manner that's in the best interest of *all* parties involved." She grabbed a quick breath before hurrying on with her explanation. "My agency, and others like it, act as mentors to these young offenders. We offer them counseling and encourage them to take responsibility for their lives and their actions." He didn't show so much as a flicker of interest, she thought with frustration, and she wondered if she was just wasting her breath.

* * * *

Cole let Joely speak uninterrupted even though he remembered after a few words that he had already communicated with someone from her agency, and he knew exactly what they were all about. He agreed that their work was an integral and meaningful part of the juvenile Restorative Justice system. But he didn't stop her because he enjoyed watching the color rise in her cheeks while she spoke passionately about her work.

It also gave him time to shore up his shaken composure. He'd taught himself at a young age to hide his feelings, and the discipline served him well now. When he first saw this woman in the lobby of the detachment last month, he'd given a small prayer of thanks that she was walking out of his life, not into it. He could barely believe she was back again—and she looked even better up close. He gazed with pleasure at her fresh, attractive appearance. Bright blue eyes dominated her heart-shaped face, and her generously curved mouth hinted at an easy smile. Her shoulder-length hair was the color of melted butterscotch, streaked with sun-kissed highlights.

As much as he liked the look of this tawny-haired temptress with the face of an angel, he preferred to steer clear of female distractions. Truth be told, he didn't want too many people in his private world, period. It got too crowded in there once before, and he swore it'd never happen again. He'd do well to remember that vow.

Joely had run out of steam and now waited for a response. Cole leaned back in his chair and patted his fingers on top of the folder. He didn't allow his smile to show on his face. Although he preferred to dally with her for a while longer—make that a great deal longer—he chose the wise course of action, removing himself from the temptation of her presence as quickly as possible.

"Thank you for setting me straight, Ms. Sinclair. I'll look over this file and let you know if I have any concerns. I appreciate you dropping it by."

"Just doing my job, Corporal. And *thank you* for your time."

Did he catch a trace of sarcasm in her voice? Cole pressed his lips together in amusement as she snapped her briefcase shut and rose from her chair. For a moment, they studied each other, then she deliberately turned her back on him and left the office with a free-swinging stride. Cole's gaze cruised down the length of her as she walked away. Leggy and slim, she moved with a casual grace, her posture revealing her self-confidence. The tightening in his belly confirmed that he liked what he saw. She was dynamite both coming *and* going.

She had the kind of body that could make a man ache just looking at her. And he had the ache to prove it.

* * * *

"So, what's he like?" Maggie asked Joely before she'd stepped completely through the office door.

"What's *who* like?" she shot back perversely, knowing full well who she meant. She crossed the reception area and pushed through the door to her office, with Maggie in close pursuit.

"You know, that new cop. The hunk you were raving about. You met him, didn't you?"

Joely dumped her briefcase onto the desk, resisting the urge to slam it down. "I don't particularly remember raving about anyone, but if you mean Corporal Dennison, yes, I met him. And I've changed my opinion. He's not so hot."

She probably sounded snippy, but that darn superior attitude of the corporal's had her temper simmering out of control. Not that she needed him to stick up for her against Trip Wilson and his constant putdowns. When it came to defending what she did for a living, she stood on her own two feet just fine. But he didn't need to sit there with such arrogance, while making her explain her position as though she was nothing more than an inexperienced job applicant.

And then, to top it off, there was that unholy gleam she spotted in those brown eyes of his, right before she left, the one that said he was enjoying himself at her expense. She had no use for anyone who took pleasure in another person's discomfort.

Maggie slid into the chair beside Joely's desk, cupping her chin in her hand, elbow on the desk. "He's not as cute as you thought?"

Joely glanced toward the ceiling and shook her head with exasperation. "Oh, there's absolutely nothing wrong with Cole Dennison's looks." She held up a hand to tick off his many attributes on her fingers. "Deep dark eyes, heavily feathered with jet black eyelashes, great bone structure, strong jawline. Tall and powerfully built, with wide shoulders and a flat belly. Thick, dark, wavy hair. One of those sexy kind of napes that begs to be caressed..."

"All right, already. I get the picture." Maggie thumbed a loose strand of hair off her shoulder and laughed breathlessly. "Sounds like you've checked him out pretty thoroughly. And I haven't heard anything but perfection so far. What's not to like?"

Joely reached for her phone to check for messages. "He's too darn self-assured for one thing, almost patronizing. And those gorgeous dark eyes hold no emotion whatsoever, unless of course you count the nasty gleam of amusement I saw lurking there after Wilson pulled his usual 'do-gooder' speech. Then he outright dismissed me! Instead of reviewing the reports with me the way old Corporal George used to do, he simply dismissed me. Made me so darn mad."

Too distracted to concentrate, she chucked the phone back onto the desk, voicemail unchecked. "I don't like how he made me feel all insecure, or incompetent, or...or...something." She abruptly stopped trying to explain her attitude toward him. She didn't quite understand it herself.

It irked her to have placed such importance on a meeting with a man based on his physical appearance. Since when had she become so shallow? And the crushing disappointment she'd felt ever since realizing Cole Dennison wasn't as wonderful as she'd imagined, only added to her irritation.

Stella appeared in the doorway with a cup of steaming coffee in her hand. "I couldn't hear your conversation, but the pitch of your voice told me you needed a coffee to calm yourself down." She stepped into the room and handed the cup to Joely. "Did something happen at the police detachment?"

"Thanks, Stella. You're the greatest." Joely took an appreciative sip of the dark brew, closing her eyes for a second to savor the rich flavor. "Umm, this is perfect. I was just telling Maggie I don't think Cole Dennison is a very pleasant person."

Stella crossed her arms and frowned. "Why's that? Was he rude?"

Joely took another swallow of coffee while she considered this for a moment. Technically, he hadn't been rude. Patronizing—yes, infuriating—definitely, but rude...not so much.

"Not where you could tell," she admitted with reluctance. "He comes across as being terribly polite."

"Oh, well then, I know what you mean." Stella shook her head in mock disgust. "The nerve of the man. Terribly polite men never fail to get me going."

"Me too," Maggie agreed. She fanned the fingers of one hand out in front of her to study the perfection of her flawlessly manicured nails. "I hate polite men, especially really, really good looking, terribly polite men. I say they should be outlawed." Her nose wrinkled comically. "Is it possible to outlaw a cop?"

Although Joely knew they were just poking harmless fun at her, she refused to be teased. "I so don't find this amusing, you two. Everyone's entitled to their own opinion, and I happen to think Cole Dennison is a cold man—he didn't even smile once. You guys go ahead and decide for yourselves. Now if you'll both excuse me, I have phone calls to make."

* * * *

A week later, Joely spent the day in downtown Vancouver attending Government Ministry meetings. Because she hated to battle the cross-town traffic, she usually left her car parked in a lot at the foot of Lonsdale Avenue and rode the Sea Bus across Burrard Inlet.

On her return home, as she stepped out of the Sea Bus Terminal, she noticed a group of boys gathered outside the burger joint. She wouldn't have looked twice, except for one of them had the same build and hair color as Taylor. It couldn't be Taylor though, because he'd promised to rake the lawn at the condominium this afternoon. A quick check of her watch told her he couldn't have had time to finish the job and make it down to the quay already.

She slowed her steps while she examined the boys more carefully. She didn't recognize any of them. Maybe the one standing with his back to her just bore a remarkable resemblance to her son from behind. Then he tipped his head back as he laughed at another young man. It was definitely Taylor. She'd recognize his laugh anywhere and even though she was annoyed with him, her mouth curved up in response to the infectious sound she loved.

She waited until she was almost beside them before calling out. Taylor's face showed momentary surprise, then he gave his familiar easy smile that acknowledged he'd been found out.

"Hey, Mom," he answered casually, tossing his head to get the hair out of his eyes. "S'up?"

"Aren't you supposed to be doing something else right now?"

The other boys started hooting and jeering, one kid punched Taylor in the arm, telling him he was busted. Taylor grinned back at their gibes before shambling over to her. "How'd ya find me?"

"By accident. I spotted you when I got off the Sea Bus."

Taylor tilted his head closer to Joely's, turning away from the boys watching them. "Don't embarrass me in front of my friends, okay? I'll get the raking done after dinner. I want to hang out here some more."

"I'm terribly sorry," she told him facetiously. "I didn't realize my presence was such an embarrassment to you. Since when are these boys your friends? I don't know any of them."

Taylor shot a quick glance over his shoulder, then replied quietly, almost hissing, "They're new friends. They're cool guys, and I want to stay longer, okay?"

Joely looked over at Taylor's *cool* new friends. There were six of them. Their faces were closed, the frivolity of before erased from their expressions. She gave them a friendly smile and not one of them returned it. A blatant lack of respect showed in their postures and in the looks they directed her way. She'd dealt with enough hostile teenagers to know these boys considered her the enemy—someone to avoid at all costs.

"No, it's not okay, Taylor. You know I don't like you just hanging out. I want you to come home with me now, and we'll discuss this further when we get there."

"Mom! Stop treating me like a baby." His whiney voice and sulky expression were anything but grownup.

Joely shifted her purse strap on her shoulder and crossed her arms. "Then I suggest you stop acting like one. Let's go. Now."

Taylor's mouth compressed into a stubborn line, and Joely wondered if he'd actually defy her. She kept her face calm, but uncompromising. A few long seconds ticked by while they stared each other down.

Finally, Taylor sighed and looked back over his shoulder at his friends. "I have to go, Lionel. I'll see ya tomorrow."

They walked silently over to where Joely had the Mustang parked. Taylor, hands in his pockets, head down, kept half a step behind her, and she didn't try to start a conversation until they reached the car.

"Want the top down? The car's been parked here all day, and it'll be like an oven inside." When Taylor gave an ambiguous shrug, she lowered the top on the convertible anyway, hoping the fresh air would invigorate her. After a long day of tedious meetings, she wasn't in the mood to deal with a difficult teenager.

As they drove up Lonsdale, Joely tried to get Taylor to open up. "So, you've made some new friends. What are their names?"

Taylor looked out his side window. "Lionel and MJ," he mumbled.

"Lionel and MJ who?"

"I don't know."

"You don't know your friends' last names? Who were the other ones?"

Taylor shifted with irritation, still staring out the window. "I don't know. I only know Lionel and MJ."

A strong breeze caught Joely's hair and whipped it about her face. She pushed the strands out of her eyes and rolled up the side window, before continuing with her questions. "Did you meet these boys at school?"

"No."

"Do they go to your school?"

"No."

Another one word answer. This conversation was really going places.

"Which school do they go to?"

"I don't know."

"Sounds like you don't know much about these new friends."

Taylor shoved his long hair away from his face and turned to confront her. "Cut me some slack, okay? They're real cool, and I like hanging with them." His tone warned her he wouldn't put up with any more interrogation.

Joely kept silent while she concentrated on the left-hand turn off Lonsdale onto West Fifteenth Street. She knew from experience if you pushed kids too hard, they closed their ears off from the inside, and you might as well be saying, "yada, yada, yada".

"I'd like you to peel the potatoes and carrots right away for supper, please," she told Taylor when they got home.

"I thought you were in such a big hurry for me to rake the lawn."

Joely blinked at the sharpness in his voice. "*Taylor*! You watch your tone." His unusually abrasive attitude pushed her patience to the limit. She took a calming breath and said, "Come here, honey. Come on, let's start over, please. Give me a hug."

She held out her arms, and Taylor moved into them, returning her hug. "I'm sorry," he said. "I'll help with supper and then get right on the yard work."

Joely looked up at him, brushed the hair back from his face and kissed his cheek. "You need a haircut." She decided the rest of the conversation could wait until after supper. She changed from the business suit she had donned for the day's meeting into some comfortable jeans and an oversized Tee, then headed out to the serenity of her backyard sanctuary.

Without a doubt, the feature she loved best about her condo was the small garden patio. Her carefully nurtured bushes and perennials promised a show of glorious color to compliment the riot of spring bulbs already putting on a vibrant floral display.

The tulip and daffodil blossoms drooped sadly under the weight of raindrops from the afternoon's short, heavy shower. Kneeling on the damp lawn, Joely went to work, salvaging the flowers she could, deadheading the ones she couldn't. Pulling weeds and digging in the dirt served as excellent therapy whenever life's stresses threatened her peace of mind, and she plugged away without stopping until Taylor popped his head out the door.

"I've finished with the vegetables, Mom, and I'll start the raking now."

Joely stood and brushed her hands against her knees. "Okay, sweetie. Supper will be in about half an hour. I'll call you when it's ready."

Taylor lacked his usual animation during dinner, and even though Joely had a hunch why, she couldn't help but question him about it.

He slouched back in his chair and stared at her, his face a

study in stone. "Don't you know how embarrassing it is to have your mother track you down and give you crap in front of all your friends? They probably think I'm some little dweeb, having to go home with Mommy."

He'd obviously been stewing over this while he worked in the yard.

"You're being unfair. I told you I accidentally bumped into you on my way home from work. I didn't give you heck, I simply pointed out you were supposed to be home raking the lawn, not hanging out, talking trash with a bunch of strangers."

"If you don't know what we were talking about, don't call it trash," he snapped back at her. "Besides, it rained this afternoon. I thought it'd be better to wait and rake the lawn this evening."

"I'm sorry, you're right, I don't know what you were talking about. How about you fill me in?"

"I'm not one of the delinquents you work with, so stop giving me the third degree." He pushed away from the table. "I'm not hungry anymore. Besides, I've got yard work to do."

"Taylor! Please stay here and discuss this with me," Joely called to his retreating back.

When he didn't respond, she rubbed at her throbbing temples and wondered desperately what was happening with her son. He had always been a good-natured and affectionate boy, if a bit too determined and independent. He followed house rules and rarely rebelled. Lately, he was becoming more tenacious than ever, exasperating and, at times, downright defiant. She'd made a successful career out of helping troubled teens, so why couldn't she communicate with the one who meant more to her than life itself?

* * * *

"Hi, Ms. Sinclair, this is Brennan Peters. Remember me?"

"Of course, Brennan. How are you?" Joely asked her young client.

"Not so good right now. I'm at the North Van police detachment. Can you please come and help me? It's all a mistake, Ms. Sinclair, but you can fix it."

The boy sounded terrified and Joely promptly forgot her plans to get home early. "Hang tight, I'll be right there."

Joely left a brief voicemail for Taylor, then drove directly to the police detachment. It was her first time back since meeting Cole Dennison almost two weeks ago, and she hoped she didn't run into the handsome corporal. The memory of his annoying superior attitude still irritated her, so the less she saw of the man the better.

The simple misunderstanding her client referred to turned out to be a case of mistaken identity already resolved before she arrived. She took the time to speak with the shaken boy for a few moments until he regained his composure. After Brennan left the interview room, she quickly scribbled down some notes she would add to his file at the office.

A movement at the door caught her attention and she glanced up to see Trip Wilson standing there, the width of his massive shoulders blocking the doorway from jam to jam. He grinned cagily and stepped into the room.

"Is there something you wanted, Trip? I'm about finished here, and I'd like to get home." She stood and put the pad of paper back into her briefcase, aware of his gaze tracking her every move, like a cat sighting its prey.

"Was that another one of your juvenile delinquents I saw leaving?"

Tired and in no mood for his games, Joely raked her fingers through her hair, combing it back from her face. "As usual, you don't know what you're talking about. That boy did nothing wrong." When she made a motion to go past him, he stepped in front of her, blocking her path.

"Hey, what's your big hurry?" He reached out a beefy hand and captured her arm.

She shook herself free. "Don't touch me."

He didn't make another attempt to grab her, but he didn't get out of her way either. Alarm bells sounded in her head, and she instinctively moved again toward the door. Trip stepped closer, forcing her back, and she bumped up against the wall. He swiftly closed the distance between them, trapping her with one arm on either side of her body, his hands propped against the wall. Joely pressed herself flat, shrinking as far back as she could.

She glared up at him, narrowing her eyes into two angry slits. "I don't know what kind of game you're playing, but you better back off right now."

That appeared to amuse him and his smile held a predatory quality. A tiny finger of fear touched the back of Joely's neck. She doubted he'd actually hurt her. He just wanted to intimidate her, to show her who was stronger.

"I know all about your type," he drawled. "Little Miss Do-Good. Someone needs to give you a lesson on reality's nasty side, and I'm just the guy for the job."

Joely shoved hard against Trip's arm, but it was like trying to dislodge a tree trunk. Even though her heart hammered, she held her head high, refusing to reveal her fear.

"Let me go, Trip. This is wrong."

Trip sneered. "Not so righteous now, are you?"

She drew a calming breath, but her voice still came out with a shrill tremor. "I don't know why you're doing this, but you have to stop. Now."

His mouth twisted into a cruel line. "You come around here, thinking you're so special, making your demands, never once caring that you're trampling all over our hard work, like it means nothing. Time someone knocks you off your pretty little pins."

Joely stiffened, pushing with all her strength against his chest, unable to budge him. "Stop it this instant, or you'll regret it. You're acting like an animal," she hissed, refusing to give in to the impulse to scream for help. "And I find you completely contemptible."

He lowered his face, placing his mouth mere inches from her lips. "Oh, I'm an animal all right. But then, when you get right down to it, aren't we all animals?"

She twisted her face away and from over Trip's shoulder, she caught a glimpse of Cole Dennison standing in the doorway. She should've been relieved to have this awkward episode come to an end. Instead, a wave of pure mortification washed over her. Why did it have to be Cole, of all people, to walk in on them? What would he possibly think was going on?

Chapter Three

"Oh, excuse me. The door was ajar, and I didn't realize the room was occupied." Cole cleared his throat, embarrassed to have walked in on an intimate moment. He turned to leave, then stopped, his instincts telling him something wasn't right.

Trip Wilson had the woman, Joely Sinclair, pinned to the wall like a specimen butterfly, in a display of superior male strength. The patrolman didn't immediately back away from her, but his hands dropped to his sides as he glanced at Cole from over his shoulder.

Something fiery and primitive stirred in Cole's stomach—a male protectiveness he hadn't realized he was still capable of feeling. Taking in how warily Joely stood, so delicate, slender as a reed compared to Trip's massive bulk, Cole's chest squeezed shut, making it difficult to breathe.

"Ms. Sinclair, are you all right?" He stepped further into the small room. "Stand down, Constable Wilson." His voice held a low warning he hoped he wouldn't have to act on.

Trip stood nearly as tall as Cole and outweighed him by a good number of pounds, but he hesitated only an instant before turning to face Cole, an ingratiating grin on his far-too-smug face.

"We were just having a little fun, Corporal, that's all."

Without saying a word, Joely sprang away from the wall, snatched her briefcase from the table and rushed for the door. She paused in the doorway to glare at Trip with undisguised loathing, before turning to stare at Cole. Her lips trembled slightly, then she raised her chin and straightened her shoulders. With obvious effort, she moved calmly down the hall.

"I don't know what was going on in here, Wilson, but I sure don't have much respect for a guy who uses physical domination to get what he wants, especially from a woman half his size."

Conciliatory though he might've been at first, Trip's brashness quickly returned. "Oh, c'mon, Corporal, I didn't lay a hand on her.

If anything, she pawed me."

Cole shook his head with contempt. "You didn't have to touch her to intimidate her and you know it. I doubt Ms. Sinclair wanted any part of you, and I swear, if I ever come across you bothering her or any other women in this building again, I'll personally see you busted for it."

Stepping closer, he drilled the patrolman in the chest with one finger. "You behaved real stupid, Trip, real stupid. If you even think of speaking to the lady again, it better be to apologize and nothing more—you got it?"

Trip's big, broad nose offered too easy a target, and Cole left the room before he acted on his impulse to punch it. As he made his way down the hall, he noticed Joely Sinclair waiting near the elevator. Instead of her usual shoulders-back posture, she was slumped against the wall, her arms crossed protectively in front of her, eyes doggedly staring at the floor. Protocol required she have an escort from the building, and he decided to volunteer for the job. It was the proper thing to do professionally, he told himself.

Having grown up under the controlling thumb of a father who didn't give a damn about anything except his own rigid code of conduct, Cole had been raised to believe gentleness was a sign of weakness. Despite this, Cole grew up an innately gentle man. To be successful at work meant learning to play the role of a mean, remote man. And he'd assumed the posture so well it became engrained in all aspects of his life.

That self-restraint didn't prevent the overpowering compassion from surging through him as he watched the shaken woman, a reaction so unexpected, so intense, it tightened his throat and tangled his breath. With it came a flash of resentment for these unwanted emotions. It disturbed him to be this drawn toward her when he had no interest in initiating any sort of relationship, regardless of the strong physical attraction.

Everything about Joely Sinclair sent out danger warnings to him. Her physical appeal, her steady determination, with the underlying hint of vulnerability. These were a risky combination of feminine traits, and he wanted no part of it.

He sensed that she knew he was watching her, although she didn't betray her awareness with a single glance. She straightened her stance and picked up her briefcase, but it wasn't until the elevator doors slid open that she finally turned to face him with obvious reluctance.

He took a step closer, his demeanor a careful blend of good manners and restraint. "I didn't mean to disturb you, Ms. Sinclair. I just wanted to make sure you were all right."

He put a hand out to hold back the elevator door until she entered, then followed her in.

"I'm fine," she replied shortly, pressing the button for the main floor.

Her lips trembled and a dazed expression haunted her eyes. She looked on the edge of losing it, but was trying her best to be strong, and Cole had to admire the way she handled herself.

"I'm sorry you were put in such an awkward position by Constable Wilson."

She waved off his apology. "It's not your place to apologize. And although I appreciate you stepping in to help, I could've defended myself. Trip has a high opinion of himself and wanted to prove his male animal superiority, that's all."

"All the same, he had no right to force himself on you. There's a huge size difference between you, and it had to be frightening, yet you stood your ground admirably."

She searched his eyes and apparently reassured by what she saw, she relented and gave a wobbly little movement of her lips, not quite a smile. "I guess you had good timing. Thank you."

Cole smiled back, encouraged by the slight thaw in her attitude. The elevator door rumbled open and he moved aside to let her exit first. "I'd like to escort you to your car, if you're ready to leave."

She brushed a strand of hair away from her face with fingers that were still not too steady. "I can make it to my car by myself, Corporal Dennison. Thanks anyway."

"That would be Cole."

"All right, Cole. And please call me Joely."

For a second, nothing else existed as their gazes locked. And he abruptly plunged into free fall. His senses swam, blood banged inside his head, he forgot to breathe. He couldn't remember the last time he'd felt this real, this alive. As he opened his mouth to speak, the PA system came statically to life, breaking the spell twining itself around them.

"*Corporal Dennison, attend lock-up. Corporal Dennison, attend lock-up, please.*"

"Damn. I have to go." He tugged irritably at an earlobe. "Let me find one of the uniforms to accompany you outside."

Joely headed for the exit, and Cole kept pace.

"Thanks for the offer, but it's not necessary."

"You sure?" When she gave a definite nod of her head, he decided not to push it, although he didn't like letting her go off by herself while still so obviously shaken. "Please excuse me then, I'm needed elsewhere. Goodnight."

"Goodbye. And thanks again." This time, the smile she gave him looked more genuine.

You were saved by the bell on that one, old boy, he cautioned himself, as he watched until she left the office area. *She might be a pretty package, but she's not for you. Don't ever forget what a mistake it is to let a woman get inside your defenses.*

Dark thoughts of another beautiful woman, and the ensuing marriage from hell, scuttled busily through the back of his mind, but he abruptly pushed them out. He couldn't stand here all evening, daydreaming about Joely Sinclair and reliving the nightmare of his marriage to Debra. They needed him in lock-up.

* * * *

"Taylor," Joely called as she entered the apartment. "I'm home, honey. Sorry I'm late. I hope you found yourself something to eat." She kicked off her shoes and padded barefoot down the hall. "Taylor!"

"I hear you, Mom. I'll be right there."

Taylor stepped out of his bedroom, and Joely stopped dead in her tracks. For a split second, she almost didn't recognize him. His long, dark blond hair had been transformed into a short buzz cut, with the longer layers on top styled higher in the front.

He gave her his young, easy smile. "You said I needed a haircut."

"Indeed I did," she admitted ruefully as she circled around

him, surveying the haircut from all angles. "Those are great sidewalls, sweetie. I, uh, the faux-hawk might take some getting used to." She poked a finger tentatively at the gel-shellacked spikes. "I'd avoid open flames if I were you."

Taylor laughed at her jest. "You want to see the coolest thing. Look, I got my ear pierced. Up here." He leaned forward to show her where a small stud pierced through the cartilage three quarters of the way up his left earlobe. "Lionel says this is the coolest place for an earring. When I get to take out this stud, I'm gonna put in a silver hoop. Lionel says silver's the sweetest." He explained all this in an excited rush, his words piling up on one another in his haste to get them out. "Whaddaya think? Is it rad or what?"

Joely warily guarded her expression, but she didn't quite manage to keep the dismay from her voice. "A pierced ear, really, Taylor? Don't you think maybe we should've discussed this first?"

Taylor's animated disposition evaporated in a flash. "I shoulda known you'd hate it. Figures. You neg everything I want to do lately." He whirled on his heel and fled into his bedroom.

"Taylor, wait." The bedroom door stood open, so Joely entered without asking permission. Taylor sprawled belly down on his bed, facing the wall. "Taylor." She perched on the edge of the bed and rubbed his shoulder softly. "Please look at me. Come on, roll over, and let me see your gorgeous mug."

She waited for him to respond, but he ignored her. "I'm not angry with you. I'm a little shocked, is all. I honestly don't mind the earring. It's no big deal. I just wish you had let me in on your plans beforehand."

She smoothed her fingers over his freshly shorn neck. The soft delicate skin reminded her of when he was a baby. She used to blow tickling kisses against the downy softness of his nape, and he'd giggle so hard he'd soon have her laughing helplessly along with him. Somehow, she didn't think she'd get the same reaction out of him tonight.

"All right, if you won't talk to me, I'm not about to sit here talking to myself. Get some sleep. I love you."

Joely paused at the doorway and looked back at her son. He had rolled over onto his side with his knees pulled up to his belly, still facing the wall. She wanted to go back and hug him, but she didn't. It had been a long time since frustration or sadness caused her to dissolve into tears, tonight she felt perilously close. The rollercoaster of emotions she'd experienced in the past few hours depleted her reserves, and she couldn't handle another rejection from Taylor, so instead she quietly closed his door.

* * * *

Makeup did nothing to hide the ravages of Joely's sleepless night. Both Stella and Maggie readily picked up on her shadowed eyes and subdued manner when she arrived at work the next morning.

"You should've stayed home if you didn't feel well, Jo. You look awful," Maggie offered helpfully.

"Thanks, I needed that boost to my morale just now," Joely threw over her shoulder as she escaped into her office.

The other two women followed on her heels. "What Maggie meant to say is you aren't your usual self, honey," Stella said, her Mother Hen instincts on high alert. "Are you ill? It looks like you didn't sleep a wink last night."

Joely set her briefcase down beside the desk and ran her fingers through her hair, irritably lifting it up from her neck and dropping it again. "That's because I *didn't* sleep a wink last night. I'm not sick, I just have a lot on my mind."

"You gonna share?" Maggie prodded, making herself comfortable on the corner of Joely's desk.

She didn't want to rehash, let alone remember, last night's events, but she knew her friends weren't about to let this go. So she decided it'd be less hassle in the long run if she just told them the whole thing straight out.

"Okay, only this has to stay between the three of us, all right?" Joely eyed Stella and Maggie sternly and when they nodded their agreement, she continued. "Last night, as I was leaving work, I got a phone call from Brennan Peters, you remember the young fellow from last fall? He was at the RCMP detachment and wanted my help."

She reached down for her briefcase and emptied it out while she spoke, then went into the reception area to pour a cup of coffee. Stella and Maggie dogged her into the other room. Instead of returning to her office, Joely curled up in a corner of the comfortable couch they had set up for clients to use while waiting for their appointments. Stella and Maggie crowded in next to her.

"What then?" Maggie demanded. "What happened when you got to the police detachment?"

Slowly, awkwardly, speaking in a monotone, Joely poured out the events of the previous evening. She kept her gaze on her coffee cup, which was easier than watching the alarm build in the eyes of her friends. Both women were clearly shocked by her story. Maggie constantly interrupted with outraged questions and suggestions about what she'd like to do to various parts of Trip Wilson's muscle-bound anatomy.

Stella's face burned indignantly while she listened, but she kept quiet until Joely finished talking. "You have to report this, Joely. It is inexcusable behavior. I'm going to phone the staff sergeant right now." When she started to rise from the couch, Joely placed a restraining hand on her arm.

"No, you aren't. You said you'd keep quiet, and I'm holding you to it. I'm more embarrassed than anything by the whole thing. You'd think with my training, I would've had better control of the situation."

"And you'd think with your training, you'd know the victim often feels guilty without cause. You *are* the victim here," Stella pointed out. "That man was clearly in the wrong and he deserves a reprimand for his actions."

"I thought hard about this all night. Yes, Trip was wrong and yes, at the time he frightened me, but I'm positive that was his sole intention. There's no way he would've gone any further. He's an oversexed male with veins swimming with undiluted testosterone, and we all know that type doesn't always use the muscle between his ears to do his thinking. It's best if I don't give him the satisfaction of knowing he upset me. If he ever again makes so much as an offensive suggestion in my direction, I'll report it instantly, I promise."

Maggie muttered more slurs against Trip's character, then reluctantly agreed not to maim the man the next time she saw him. Because Stella proved harder to convince, Joely decided to distract her with Taylor's latest escapade.

"And if that wasn't enough to deal with, another interesting surprise waited for me at home. Taylor, my precious son, has gone high-fashion. Or something. He got an extremely short haircut, complete with faux-hawk, and a pound of hair product to keep it glued in place. To top that off, he's now sporting an earring— here." Joely grabbed her own ear to show the location of the earring.

"Cool," Maggie gushed. "I bet he looks adorable."

"You don't sound like you're too crazy about this, Joely." Stella searched her face. "What do you think of his new-found fashion sense?"

"I honestly tried not to overreact. I mean it's just his ear—it could've been somewhere a lot less appropriate. What bothered me was he didn't mention a word to me first. He's made a new friend, this Lionel character, and all I ever hear anymore is Lionel says this and Lionel says that. I'm not sure this boy is a good influence on my son."

"Taylor's a smart kid, Jo. He knows the difference between wrong and right," Stella reassured her, Maggie bobbing her head in agreement. "He's always had a strong independent streak, it probably didn't occur to him to ask you. How old were you when you pierced your ears?"

Joely touched the delicate gold hoop in her right earlobe. "About twelve."

"Did you check with your mom first?" Maggie asked.

"No, but..." Joely gave up with a frustrated shrug. The fact that, back then, her mother would've been more concerned about her latest date, than whether her daughter pierced her ears, was beside the point. "All right, maybe I could've dealt with the whole earring thing better, if I wasn't already upset. But you know, Taylor isn't acting like himself either. He gets angry over the least little thing and he refuses to talk to me about it. It's like he doesn't want me around anymore. I can't help thinking this Lionel is part of the cause. And I know nothing about the boy. If he's from North Van, why haven't I come across him at one of the schools or somewhere?"

"Maybe his crimes don't fall under our jurisdiction," Maggie suggested, then shrugged at the dirty look she got from Stella.

"You're not helping, Maggie. Joely, is it possible in your concern for Taylor, you're reading too much into this? Fifteen's a tough age for a boy. Hormones are kicking in, he has conflicting emotions tugging at him from every direction. It's only natural for him to want to withdraw from parental influences. Maybe because the two of you are extra close, Taylor's having more difficulty pulling back, and this makes him all the more confused and cranky. Be patient with him and he'll come around. He's the sweetest kid I know."

"Yeah, except when he's not," Joely retorted dryly. "You make it sound reasonable and logical, but it doesn't feel that way when you're trying to live with those raging hormones. I'm looking forward to seeing how you cope with teenagers—girls yet, and two of them," she added, referring to Stella's adorable young daughters. She giggled at the look of pretend horror on Stella's face, and it made her feel much better.

The phone rang and Maggie bounded off the couch to answer it. "Good morning, Youth Action Outreach. This is Maggie," she sang into the receiver. "She sure is. Hold for a second, please." She punched the hold button and offered the phone to Joely. "It's for you, Jo. A man, with a give-me-shivers kind of voice." Her eyebrows waggled meaningfully.

Joely elbowed her aside and took the receiver. "Joely Sinclair. May I help you?"

"Good morning, Joely Sinclair. Cole Dennison here. I'm calling to make sure you weren't experiencing any adverse effects after the altercation last night."

"Corporal, uh, Cole, yes, hi." Joely turned her back on her inquisitive coworkers. "I'm fine, thank you for asking." A pleasant and tingly case of those shivers Maggie mentioned skittered up her spine. Not adverse in the least, actually.

"I'm glad to hear it. I won't take up anymore of your time, then. You have a nice day." His tone was cordial, yet impersonal. Disappointment rapidly replaced the tingles.

"Thanks, I will. You do the same." She replaced the receiver in the cradle and turned a casual face toward Stella and Maggie, not wanting to reveal how easily that man knocked her off stride.

"Corporal Cole, would this be the infamous Cole Dennison?" Maggie asked, her mouth hanging open.

"The same. Now close your mouth before you let flies in."

Maggie snapped her mouth shut, only to immediately open it again. "And what did *he* want?"

"He called about what happened last night. Probably testing the waters to see if I plan to file a sexual harassment suit."

As she voiced the thought, the truth of it hit her like a jolt of electricity. That's exactly why he called. The image of his profession obviously concerned him more than her welfare. A feeling she wouldn't admit to as dejection crept into her chest, and she made a futile attempt to beat it down.

"How did he know what happened?" Stella asked.

"He walked in on us and ordered Trip to lay off. I felt completely mortified, but he was quite nice about the whole thing." Her sentence finished on an uncertain note. Actually, he'd been impeccably behaved. Very likable, in fact.

Regardless of her previous opinion of him, his behavior last night had certainly been beyond reproach. After she'd escaped from the interview room, she'd intended to get the heck out of there and crawl into the nearest hole to hide. But a sudden attack of nausea and dizziness hit her as she walked toward the elevator, some kind of delayed reaction, no doubt.

She'd had to lean against the wall for a moment to settle herself, the entire time praying no one would approach her. Her prayer went unanswered, but the encounter with Cole turned out better than she'd thought it might. At the time, she had barely been able to comprehend his grim look of concern was actually on her account. She thought she'd caught something else in the way he looked at her, something poignant, tinged with a hint of respect, revealing a glimpse of what lay behind his usually unreadable facade.

And then he'd smiled at her. A perfect smile that made her heart somersault abruptly, and she'd been totally won over.

Only now, she had cause to suspect his motives.

"Nice, is he?" Maggie jumped on her words, not her tone. "Lemme see, we have good looking, polite and now nice. I definitely have to meet me this man."

The telephone rang again and saved Joely from having to answer Maggie's gibe. While she spoke on the phone, a mother and daughter came in for their nine o'clock appointment. Another busy Friday.

* * * *

Taylor ambled down Lonsdale Avenue. He didn't mind the long hike to the quay. He liked people-watching along the way and anyway, he had plenty of time before meeting up with Lionel and the others. He'd left a note for his mom about eating out with friends. Her reaction to his earring last night still bugged him. Lionel said she wanted to run his life, and Taylor was starting to believe him.

He stuffed his hands into the pockets of his baggy cargo pants. Lionel said he might know about a party, and as badly as Taylor wanted to go, he felt rotten about not letting his mom know the truth. She'd worry if he got home late. Then again, if she'd let him have a cell phone like he deserved, she could reach him any time she wanted.

When he told his friends his mom's new favorite word was 'no', Lionel suggested if he was going to get hassled about it anyway, he might as well wait and get in trouble later rather than sooner. Made sense to Taylor. Besides, he smiled at the thought, a party meant girls, and although he didn't have much experience with girls, he intended to learn.

He swung off Lonsdale onto Esplanade and headed for the fast food place by the Sea Bus Terminal, where he usually met up with the other guys. No one was there yet, so he went inside to order some food. He took his cheeseburger and wandered over to the quay market. It was a warm afternoon and the square was crowded with people, some hanging around, enjoying the sea air and sunshine, others rushing to shop for their evening meal.

Taylor snagged a bench by the water, where the breeze was cool and wet. He munched on his burger and watched a container freighter ply its way through the inlet on the Vancouver side. The screeching seagulls, circling overhead, caught his attention. He tore off a piece of bun and tossed it in their direction, just for the fun of watching them squabble over it.

"Yo, Taylor, my man." Lionel slid onto the bench next to him and slapped his outstretched palm. "Momma let you out tonight, after you went and pierced your ear like a bad boy?"

"I didn't stick around to get her permission. Did you line us up a party?" Taylor tried not to appear too interested. He didn't want to come across as uncool. Most of the other guys were at least seventeen or eighteen years old. He didn't think any of them knew his real age, and he didn't want them to find out.

"I sure did," Lionel said. "It oughta be a rockin' time with lots of hot chicks. But the action don't start 'til the sun goes down. You got any money ta buy me one of those burgers?"

"Sure." Taylor flipped the last of his bun to the greedy gulls, and they made their way back to the restaurant. By the time Lionel polished off a burger, large fries, and a chocolate shake, MJ and another guy named Ned had arrived.

"C'mon, dudes. I got jest the thing we need for a Friday night buzz," MJ said, motioning for Taylor and Lionel to follow them away from the Sea Bus Terminal. He gave a loud hoot. "It's some sweet stuff. I'm higher than a giraffe's toupee right now."

He laughed again, and Taylor laughed along with him even though he didn't have a clue what MJ meant.

They stopped at an empty corner, and MJ pulled a baggie from his pocket. Taylor could see skinny little hand-rolled cigarettes inside it, and he finally figured out what was going on. Cold sweat broke out on the palms of his hands, and he wiped them on his pants as he glanced nervously up and down the street.

He suddenly didn't want to be here, didn't want to have anything to do with this.

Chapter Four

Taylor stepped back as MJ shoved the bag in his direction. "No thanks, man." His throat tightened, and the words didn't come out easily.

MJ shrugged and lit one for himself. "Okay, cool."

The other two guys shared the joint with MJ, then they lit another one. A smelly cloud of smoke formed above them, burning Taylor's eyes, making him feel dizzy. He squinted and waved a hand in front of his face.

Lionel laughed at him. "Look dudes, the cherry's 'fraid he'll get a buzz just breathin' the air." He shoved Taylor in the shoulder, and the other two giggled as though Lionel had said something really funny.

Taylor didn't see the humor, but he laughed too, giving Lionel a shot back. Lionel stumbled backward a few steps, then landed on his butt. Taylor's smile faded quickly, and he reached down to help Lionel up. Instead of the anger he expected, Lionel began laughing so hard Taylor couldn't haul him to his feet. With their concentration on Lionel, none of them noticed the police cruiser turn onto the street, until the *WOOP WEE YOOO* blast of the siren jerked them to attention.

"Damn," Lionel moaned from his prone position on the sidewalk. "This is not good, man."

"Evening, fellas," the constable called as he climbed out of his cruiser. "What's going on here?" He stepped up next to them on the sidewalk, sniffed a couple of times and then said, "Okay, which of you guys is holding?"

MJ showed him a cigarette package. "This is all we got on us, Officer. We was jest hangin' out. We ain't doin' nuttin' wrong. We ain't hurtin' no one."

Lionel hurried to his feet, no longer laughing. "What's your problem, Officer? You got no right ta hassle us. Like my friend says, we're not doing nothing wrong."

The constable nodded his chin in Lionel's direction. "I stopped because I saw you on the ground and assumed a fight was in progress. The smell of pot is quite strong, guys. And last I checked, it's still illegal to smoke marijuana on the street corners of North Vancouver. If you want to hand it over, we can all be on our way."

MJ and Ned exchanged glances, and Ned gave a small warning shake of his head.

"But we ain't got no dope, man, I tole ya that already," MJ insisted.

Taylor wondered why MJ didn't just hand over the joints. He had the sinking feeling maybe these guys had something more serious to hide.

"Yes, you do," the constable argued. "You can either empty your pockets now, or you can empty them over at the detachment."

"Look, Officer, we had one skinny little stick and we smoked it already. No harm, right? We're not holdin' nothing else," Lionel told him defensively.

The constable studied each of them, one by one. They all stared back. None of the others looked as scared as Taylor felt. The constable clicked his tongue and slapped his baton on the palm of his hand. "If that's the way you want it, you've just won yourselves a free ride to the detachment courtesy of the buffalo cab." He opened the back door of the cruiser. "Hop in, and get comfy."

* * * *

"May I speak with Ms. Sinclair, please?"

Joely didn't recognize the crisp, efficient voice of the man on the other end of the phone. "I'm Joely Sinclair."

"Are you the mother of Taylor Mills?"

Joely's knuckles tightened over the receiver. "Yes, I am. Why are you asking about Taylor?"

"My name is Constable Martin Poplich, and I'm with the North Vancouver RCMP detachment. We have a young man down here who says he's Taylor Mills. Do you know where your son is this evening, ma'am?" The man's professional voice didn't hold any accusation, he was simply looking for the facts.

"I, um, he left a note saying he was getting something to eat with his friends. What's this about? Is my son okay?" The words came out sharper than Joely intended, a reflection of her fear for Taylor.

"Your son is fine, ma'am, but I can't discuss the situation over the telephone. Are you able to come down to the detachment?"

"Yes, of course. I'll be right there."

Without bothering to turn off the lights or put away her plate of food, Joely grabbed her purse and car keys and left. When she entered the RCMP detachment a few minutes later, she gave her name to the large brunette behind the counter, a police officer Joely wasn't acquainted with.

"A Constable Poplich phoned and said my son, Taylor, uh, Taylor Mills, was here."

"The officer will see you in a moment, if you'll have a seat." The woman motioned to the seats skirting the windows of the reception area, then turned away to speak into the phone, leaving Joely no choice but to cool her heels.

She paced the length of the reception area about a dozen times, back and forth, back and forth, her mind bursting with the worst kinds of dire scenarios. Finally reaching her wits end, she was about to demand someone bring her to her son immediately, when the security door opened and Cole Dennison stepped through it. Even though she had a greater distance to cover, she beat him to the counter.

"Cole, hi." He acknowledged her with a distracted nod, while his eyes scanned the busy lobby area behind her. She went up on tiptoe, leaning forward across the counter to force herself back into his line of vision. "Listen, I could really use some help locating a young man who's being detained here."

Even in her distraught state, a part of her reacted to the slow, almost boyish smile that curved Cole's mouth when he focused back on her. His eyes were so brown, they were closer to black, and tonight they were warm and friendly.

"Joely, good evening. Was one of your clients part of the group of teenagers brought in earlier this evening?"

"I'm looking for my son. I'm not sure why he's here. Please confirm for me he's okay."

Confusion showed on Cole's face. "I was told a mother of one of the boy's was waiting out here, but we didn't bring in anyone with your last name."

"Mills, Taylor Mills."

"Taylor Mills is your son?"

"Yes, oh please, Cole, just tell me what happened."

"Of course, sorry for sounding dense. I had no idea you had a teenager. Come on, let's go to my office, and I'll fill you in." He ushered her through to the back and down the hall to his office.

"Have a seat." Cole waited until she perched herself on the edge of a chair before he sat down. "One of our uniform patrol members picked up four young men at the foot of West First Street. There were indications they'd been smoking marijuana, so he brought them in."

"Oh, Taylor, no. I can't believe he'd do that."

"Apparently, he wasn't. The other three corroborated his story that he wasn't using drugs. He didn't even know they were carrying, until they brought the marijuana out."

"Thank God. May I please see him? The poor kid must be scared out of his wits."

"Actually, I think he could stand being a little more scared. I had a chat with him and while he's polite enough, he's getting by on bravado right now." He cleared his throat and glanced down at his report, before looking back up at her. "There's one other thing I'd like to mention."

"What? What is it?" She leaned forward, her hands kneaded themselves together in nervous abstraction.

Cole scratched at his ear and grimaced. "Is Taylor really only fifteen?"

"Yes, he turned fifteen in February. Why?"

"I think it'd be wise for you to discuss his choice of friends with him. Those other youths are considerably older than he is, and they're known to the police. In fact, they all have juvenile records. One boy was holding a fairly substantial amount of crack cocaine on his person this evening." His tone of voice changed abruptly, becoming hard and brittle. "They aren't the kind of friends I'd want my child to associate with, if I had a child."

Shock lingered for a moment, before a blaze of anger and edgy defensiveness took over. Joely scanned his face to check whether

Cole was judging her, but his eyes were black enigmatic pools of darkness, making it impossible to read anything there. It took enormous effort to control her temper and the volume of her voice when she was finally able to speak.

"You *do not* have a child, yet you feel you have the right to tell *me* how I should raise *my* son?"

She didn't understand the expression that flickered across his face, it disappeared too quickly. His eyes remained emotionless as they returned her searching look, yet she felt seared as though a wild fire raged behind that ebony gaze.

"I meant no offense in what I said." His voice held the careful note of someone watching his words. "I'm sorry if you thought I implied anything about your parenting skills. I merely wanted to warn you about the other youths, in case you didn't already know. Now, I guess you're ready to take your boy home. I'll go and get him."

Joely realized she should be the one apologizing, but without another word, he pushed out of the chair and left the room. While she waited, she wondered why she tended to overreact to everything Cole Dennison said and did. If Stella had offered her the same warning, she would've thanked her for her concern and acted on the advice immediately.

She heard the sound of shuffling feet outside the door and sprang from her chair, anxious to see for herself if Taylor was all right. He stepped through the doorway alone. The whiteness of his face told her he was frightened, but when he saw her standing there, his features assumed a closed expression.

"Let's go home," Joely ordered, resisting the urge to either hug him or shake him. "So we can discuss why you ended up at the police detachment tonight."

Taylor shrugged without answering, as though it didn't matter, and silently followed Joely from the building.

Joely waited until they were in the living room before she asked for an explanation.

"It's no big deal. I didn't do anything wrong." He started for the hall, and she lifted her hand to stop him, then pointed at the couch.

"Sit."

He scowled, but did what she asked.

"This is serious, Taylor. I just picked up my fifteen-year-old son from the RCMP detachment. I've been told the other boys were doing drugs. Drugs, Taylor! Those boys are much older than you and they all have juvenile records. I don't find any of this even remotely amusing and you aren't leaving this room until you tell me what you've been up to. Why did you put yourself in that position? I thought you knew better."

He pressed his lips together in a mute reply.

"The silent treatment won't work this time. You're going to talk about this even if we have to sit here all night. Corporal Dennison has assured me you weren't doing drugs, but I still find this situation very scary. Haven't I taught you what a dangerous waste of time drugs are? Even marijuana. Was Lionel doing drugs?"

Taylor's baby blues rolled. "It wasn't Lionel's pot."

Joely tilted her chin at him, fed up with his evasiveness. "That's not what I asked you, Taylor. Does this so-called buddy of yours do drugs?"

Suddenly all the fight slid from his body, like straw from a scarecrow, leaving him limp against the back of the couch. He sucked in his breath noisily in an obvious attempt at control. "I guess he does," he admitted softly. "I've never seen him smoking it before, but he looked like he knew what he was doing."

Joely lowered the pitch of her voice to match his. "Why were you there with them while they were doing drugs?"

"I didn't know they were going to, honest. We were on our way to a party and MJ goes something about getting a Friday night buzz. I didn't even know what that meant, so I went along with them. Then MJ pulled out this bag of joints and they started smoking, and I'm, like, 'no' and they're, like, 'that's cool'. Then they were laughing their heads off and Lionel fell down, or I guess I pushed him over and I was trying to help him up."

Joely frowned with the effort it took to follow his rambling explanation. "Slow down a bit, Taylor."

But the words kept tumbling out. "Then the cop was there and Lionel was mouthing off and we were all put in the cop car and then—I was, like, totally scared." His jaw trembled so badly he had to clamp his teeth shut. He swallowed hard and tears rushed to his eyes. He couldn't speak for several seconds. "I guess I won't be hanging around so much with those guys anymore."

"I guess you won't," Joely confirmed quietly, knowing he had almost reached the limit of his emotional endurance. A cauldron of feelings bubbled up inside her as she watched him struggle not to cry. She was still angry and disappointed, but he was her child and she loved him so completely. "Do you need a hug as badly as I do?"

Taylor immediately slid across the couch and wrapped his arms around her, hiding his face in her neck. His body trembled against her shoulder and her eyes filled with tears of relief and compassion. When he lifted his head, she turned away, blinking back the tears and pretending to be unemotional.

"We have one last thing to discuss," she told him as she moved back into the corner of the couch. "Why were you going to a party without asking me first? You know you aren't allowed to go out unless I know where you'll be."

Taylor drummed his feet against the coffee table and refused to meet her eyes. "Lionel said not to tell you."

"Since when do you follow the advice of someone else when it's in direct opposition to what I've taught you?"

"I don't know, Mom," he stammered amid lots of squirming and shrugging. "It was a bad decision and I'm sorry. I won't let it happen again. Can I go now?" His face flushed with mortification and he looked as if he was about to be ill.

"All right, for now. This conversation isn't finished, though." She called him back before he left the room. "How long should you be grounded?" It was a ritual they always followed. Whenever he needed to be reprimanded, he had to come up with a suitable punishment.

"Three days?" he suggested hopefully.

"I'm thinking more along the lines of two weeks."

"How about one?"

"Deal. One week, no phone, no leaving the house except for school."

"Right." His mouth hiked up in a crooked half-smile and he returned to the couch to kiss her goodnight.

* * * *

Cole twisted the cap off the beer bottle and tossed it at the small garbage can by the back door. It balanced on the edge for a moment, teetered and fell to the deck. *Damn, that should've been a sure shot.* Thinking he must be losing his touch, he debated hauling his carcass out of the hot tub to try again. It ended up being a short debate. It was only a beer cap after all, and what did it matter if he made the basket or not?

He tilted the bottle back and chugged a long swallow of ice cold beer, and another one, then eased back in the water. He felt great. Totally relaxed.

He straightened back up and balefully eyed the beer bottle. Who the hell was he trying to kid? He felt restless and edgy. And he could pinpoint the exact moment it all started. That fateful day when he'd looked up from his paperwork and saw Joely Sinclair standing beside his desk. His hottest dream and worst nightmare all rolled into one tempting little package. Relaxed? He didn't know the meaning of the word since she walked into his life.

Drawing hard on the beer bottle, he emptied most of it in one long pull. He set the bottle aside and smiled, even though nothing was remotely funny. His grin quickly faded.

For the better part of two weeks he'd tried to forget Joely Sinclair existed, but the encounters with her in the last couple of days proved he'd only been fooling himself. He had it real bad for the lovely Miss Sugar and Spice, and she was one huge distraction he didn't need. Didn't want. Correct that, he wanted her all right. He just didn't *want* to want her, and it made him jumpy, this combination of wanting to be near her and wanting to be rid of her.

Hard to believe someone who looked like her could have a teenaged son. A teenaged son headed for delinquency if he didn't shape up. But as long as the boy didn't end up back in police custody, he wasn't Cole's concern. When he'd tried to warn Joely about her son's choice of friends, she'd jumped on him with both feet. Who needed the hassle?

With his mood rapidly turning sour, he drained the last of the beer and deliberately turned his mind away from thoughts of Joely

Sinclair and her son. He should get out of this hot tub and spend an hour or so unpacking. After a month in this house you'd think he'd be good and tired of looking at boxes stacked a mile high in the dining room.

He slouched low in the water, letting it lap over his chin and around his ears. On second thought, those boxes could stay right where they were. They contained nothing but memories. Memories best kept forever sealed away in cardboard.

* * * *

On Taylor's first night of freedom after his week of grounding, he talked his mom into letting him go out for awhile to get some fresh air and pick up a slushie. Instead of going to the convenience store, he started off for the quay, curious to see what he'd missed all week. He wasn't very far down Lonsdale when a black sports car pulled up to the curb beside him.

"Yo, Taylor. Hop in, dude," Lionel called from the front passenger seat.

Taylor walked over to the car and leaned through the open window to see inside. "Thanks, man, but I think I'll pass. I'm just going down to the quay for awhile."

MJ sat behind the wheel. "C'mon, Taylor, don't be a tool. We'll give ya a ride."

Taylor thought it over quickly. It was a long walk to the quay, and he had to be back soon. If he caught a ride one way, it'd save a lot of time. "Okay, I guess I'll catch a lift with you."

Lionel got out of the car to let Taylor climb into the back seat with Ned.

"Mom's still not very happy about having to haul me home from the cop shop, so I gotta keep on her good side 'til she cools off," he told the other boys. "Did you guys get in trouble for the dope thing?"

"Nah, I snitched the joints from my old man's stash, so what could he say ta me?" MJ's wild laugh made Taylor nervous.

"I might have ta spend some time in Juvy, for havin' the crack," Ned drawled nonchalantly. "Can't be any worse than the crummy foster home I'm in now. Timing's good, if it happened next month, I'd be in adult court."

It stunned Taylor how they casually admitted all this. He realized he really didn't know anything about these guys. He had a feeling he should stay as far away from them as possible.

Lionel peered back at him from the front seat and smiled slyly. "We're heading over ta Stanley Park, maybe cruise for chicks along the way. You're in, right?"

"I don't think so. If you can pull over, MJ, I'll get out."

MJ turned onto West Thirteenth Street, ignoring Taylor.

"Seriously, MJ, I don't want to go with you guys. Let me out, all right?"

Lionel grinned at him over the seat. "C'mon, Taylor, now's not the time ta sprout little yellow chicken wings. We're gonna have some fun!"

Their hoots and hollers drowned out Taylor's protests. As they entered Marine Drive, MJ picked up speed, switching lanes and darting in and out of traffic. His driving became crazier as he increased his acceleration and the boys hung from the open windows, yelling swear words and making rude gestures at strangers as they drove by. Taylor slouched lower in his seat and tried not to be afraid.

A police siren wailed behind them, and Taylor turned in disbelief to see the whirling gumballs flashing from the roof of the cruiser closing in on their car.

"Shit, it's the Mounties," MJ yelped. "I'm gonna try ta outrun 'em."

They came to an intersection just as the light turned red, and MJ roared through it, the cruiser staying on their bumper. Taylor closed his eyes and held his breath, bracing for the collision that didn't happen.

"MJ, you're gonna kill us, dude," Lionel yelled. "C'mon, we're busted. You gotta pull over."

MJ twisted hard on the steering wheel and with screeching tires, he pulled onto a side road and came to an abrupt stop. Taylor's heart pounded so hard, it hurt to breathe. How could he ever explain this one to his mom?

* * * *

Cole should've been off shift, but he'd stayed late to clean up some dreaded paperwork, so he was still at his desk when young Taylor Mills was brought into the detachment for the second time in the span of a week. Cole scanned the arresting officer's report quickly before heading into the interview room where the boy waited.

He found Taylor pacing nervously about the room. A white line of strain showed around his mouth, his lips pressed tightly together. Tears glimmered in the kid's eyes.

"Grab some wood there, bub. You and I are going to have a little talk, and I want some honest answers." He settled back in his seat, studying the boy as he arranged himself restlessly on the other chair. He was a good looking kid, straight and tall, and one day he'd be a big man, but at fifteen he still had a lot of filling out to do.

No mistaking this was Joely's kid. He had the same combination of candid directness and sweet vulnerability shining from his blue eyes that Cole noticed in Joely's. The generous mouth was shaped like Joely's and in different circumstances, Cole could picture a good-natured grin on it. At the moment, the boy's mouth looked anything but happy, the corners were turned down, and he worked hard to keep his lips from quivering.

"Driving without a license, reckless driving, running a red light, driving under the influence, and possession of a stolen vehicle." Cole ticked the offenses off on his fingers as he listed them. "Last week drugs, this week stolen vehicles. Those are *some* friends you hang around with."

Taylor's eyes grew larger in proportion to the seriousness of each offense. When Cole said the car was stolen, he jerked forward in his seat, shaking his head in disbelief. "No way. I mean, no sir, I didn't know they stole the car."

"And where did you think those kids would get a car like that?" Cole intentionally raised his voice, lifting a brow before letting his face settle into a practiced scowl. He intimidated many people with that scowl, and he could see it had a tremendous effect on Taylor.

"MJ," Taylor started, then grew silent as his voice threatened to break. He took a deep breath and tried again. "MJ has an older brother. I met him once, he drives a black sports car. I thought it was his. And I didn't know MJ didn't have a license. There's no way I would've gotten in the car if I knew they stole it."

"What if I told you your buddies say it was your idea to peel the car?" There was no truth to this, Cole deliberately fabricated it in order to alarm the boy further.

Taylor shook his head again in swift denial. "No way. I didn't know anything about it—I didn't! When I found out we weren't going to the quay, I wanted to get out, but MJ wouldn't stop." He stared at Cole for a moment, his lower lip trembling dangerously. His voice dropped to a hoarse whisper and his gaze searched for the floor. "I can't believe this is happening. I'm so stupid, I am just so stupid."

Something about his openness touched Cole and against his best intentions, a wave of sympathy for the boy washed over him. He suddenly didn't have the heart to finish the charade. This inexplicable compassion irritated him and as he continued to gaze at Taylor, his own face tightened, freezing out all emotion.

"I'm taking you to a holding cell now, where you'll have some time alone to contemplate your fate."

Taylor came out of his chair as if jet-propelled. "I want to see my mom. Can't I call her first?"

Cole kept his tone gruff. "No, you can't see your mom just yet. I'll phone and explain to her where you are, so she won't worry. Now let's go."

As they left the room, Taylor touched Cole's arm diffidently. "Sir, when you call my mom, will you tell her I'm, like, real sorry?"

Cole couldn't stop the smallest suggestion of a smile from crossing his lips. The boy's candor was hard to resist. "I can manage that for you."

When they got to lock-up, Cole motioned Taylor into the cell the guard held open. "You sit here and think about the circumstances you find yourself in and consider what you could've done differently to avoid this. I don't think you're a bad kid, Taylor, and I might agree to waive all charges, if you can show me any reason why I should. I'll speak to you again later."

Cole didn't look back as he walked away. He didn't want to see the boy sitting there, huddled in fear. Now he had to phone this kid's mother and tell her that her son was once again a guest of the RCMP. He remembered the alarm and concern that marred the beauty of Joely's features last week, and he didn't look forward to witnessing it again.

The lump in his chest caught him by surprise. He knew Joely was protective of Taylor and that this would upset her. But he didn't get why it mattered so much to him. Who was she to him? He'd wasted far too much time thinking about her these past couple of weeks, and he knew it'd be unwise to become drawn into Joely Sinclair's life any more than he had to. But her son was in trouble, and it was beyond him not to offer whatever help he could give. Nothing hurt a parent more than a threat to their child's well-being.

His mind tripped suddenly on the image of a small girl with dark, corkscrew curls. His daughter, Sarah. Her huge, pain-filled eyes flashed through his head. Then she was gone. But the voice accompanying the vision stayed longer, floating back to him on the currents of memory.

It hurts, Daddy. It hurts bad. Make the hurt go away, please, Daddy, make it go away.

He thought he'd walled all his memories of her away in a corner of his mind he never intended to enter again, but the pain came anyway, sharp, swift, and deep. He should've been long past all this emotional backlash, yet here he was as wrapped up in the agony as he had been four years ago.

With careful deliberation, Cole slammed the door on those memories. Some things time couldn't ease, and dwelling on them only made the heartache worse.

His hands were shaking and he needed a minute, as he slid onto his desk chair, to pull himself into a better state before he reached for the phone to call Joely.

Chapter Five

Joely turned on some music and poured herself a glass of wine to celebrate surviving an entire week of Taylor's constant company. After being together all evening, every evening, she needed a respite from him for an hour or so. Not that she didn't enjoy having him around, but the strain of his forced confinement was starting to wear on both of them and they deserved the break.

The phone rang as she wrestled the cork back into the wine bottle.

"Joely? It's Cole Dennison. I have a situation here, and I wonder if you could please come down to the detachment right away?"

The severity in his voice instantly put her on edge. "What's this about, Cole?"

"It's Taylor. He was brought in again."

Shock held her rigid. "*Taylor*? How can that be possible? He hasn't even been out of the house for an hour."

"Believe me, he's here. He's all right, but this is serious, and I'd like to discuss it with you in person."

"I'll be right there."

When Joely got to the police detachment, Cole was waiting in reception and, with a grim demeanor, he took her straight through to his office.

"Where's Taylor?"

"I put him in a holding cell."

Her eyes widened with outrage. "You did *what*?" She choked on the words as they came out. "*A cell*? Why would you put a boy in a holding cell? My God, what could he have done to deserve that kind of treatment?"

"He was picked up with the same group of youths as last week, joyriding in a stolen vehicle. A uniform patrol member spotted the vehicle driving erratically down Marine Drive toward West Vancouver. When he ran an RO on the plate, it came up stolen. Taylor swears he didn't know the car was hot or that the driver wasn't licensed. Your son's a lot more frightened this time around."

"Of course he'd be scared. Who wouldn't be? Why did you have to put him in a cell, for goodness sakes?"

They were both still standing and Cole pointed to a chair. "Why don't you sit down?"

Joely continued to glare at him. "I don't want to sit down. I want to see my son."

"Sit, please, Joely, and I'll explain my position." Cole waited for her to seat herself, then he drew a chair up close to hers. He leaned forward, forearms resting on his knees, his face earnest. "Taylor can handle sitting in a cell for awhile longer. He's alone and he's safe. Being a little afraid won't hurt him and maybe the shock of finding himself in jail will do some good. In fact, I think he should stew there for a couple hours, I just need to make sure we're working from the same page, you and I, before I proceed."

He reclined in his chair and waited while she tried to absorb what he'd told her. Desperation burned through her body and her thoughts beat about in her head like the wings of a terrified bird. What in the world was going on with Taylor? She thought they'd made great strides toward understanding one another this past week. He said he would stay out of trouble and away from those boys, and she'd believed him. Now, his first night out of detention and he landed right back at the police detachment. What was she doing wrong? And what would be the right course of action to take with him?

Cole cleared his throat, interrupting her racing thoughts. "Hey, Joely, tell you what. I'm off duty now. How about to help the time pass, I buy you a coffee. You could probably use someone to talk to."

Joely had to force her shock-numbed mind to work rationally. Surely his offer was simply a polite gesture, which he expected her to refuse. "That toxic waste you cops guzzle around here? No, thanks." She forced the joke past stiff lips to let him know she didn't take him seriously.

"No, not detachment coffee. I'll spring for the real thing. There's a little cafe right around the corner, across from the hospital. What do you say?"

Joely looked into his endless brown eyes and to her absolute amazement—she agreed.

* * * *

Cole ordered their coffee while Joely located an empty table. When he sat down, their knees touched out of necessity under the small table. She flicked a glance at him to see if he was as aware of the intimate pressure as she was. Their gazes tangled, and her pulse hammered unevenly under the steady regard of his dark gaze. Chemistry was definitely working overtime.

"Joe-lee." Cole's white teeth flashed as he emphasized the pronunciation of her name. "I've never heard that name before. It suits you. Pretty and unique, just like you."

Joely fussed with her coffee cup, her face warm in response to his gentle flirting. "Mom named me in honor of my father, Theodore Joseph. He died in an industrial accident shortly before my birth."

"How clever of your mother to give you such a lovely name in his memory."

She pulled a face. "Better than Teddy, I guess."

Cole laughed. "Much better. I like your son," he added, changing the subject unexpectedly as he shifted in his chair. "I think you've done a great job with him. He's a respectful boy, and he sure is attached to his mom."

Joely started with surprise at those words. "You think so? Because although I hate to admit it, his behavior lately hasn't been terribly respectful or affectionate."

"I'm serious. He was very anxious to call you, and he said to tell you he's real sorry."

"Thank you for saying that. And, Cole, I also want to thank you for the advice you gave me last week about those other boys. At the time I may not have seemed very grateful, but believe me, I was. I appreciate everything you've done for my son." She picked up her mug and toasted him.

"Just doing my job, ma'am," he drawled with a slow smile. "As I said, Taylor seems like a good kid. So, why did he get mixed up with that bad crowd?"

There was no judgment in his voice, and Joely found herself responding to his kindness. Worry about Taylor consumed her to point of making her ill. Perhaps this man, another professional, could give her some insight on how to deal with her son. Heaven knows nothing she'd tried so far had worked.

"I don't even know when or where he met them. I imagine that sounds terrible, it's just that Taylor has become secretive and defiant lately. We used to do lots of things together, now the mere sight of me anywhere near him in public embarrasses him. I'm sure the change happened gradually, yet it seems like overnight he's turned into a mother-hating, back-talking, totally alien creature I can't even recognize as my own son. I feel like he's gone to some scary place that I can't get to."

Cole leaned forward, his elbows on the table, strong fingers wrapped around his mug. "Have there been any changes in his life recently that he might be having a difficult time dealing with?"

Joely took a thoughtful sip of her coffee. "I think it all started a few months ago when his best friend, Nelson, moved away. Taylor stopped chumming with his other friends and started hanging out at the Lonsdale Quay. I'm sure that's where he ran into these boys. He wants so badly to fit in with them that he keeps making bad decisions. Anything I try to do to help only makes matters worse."

Cole nodded his understanding. "Kids tend to think they're invincible, and it's easy for them to forget there's a tomorrow. As a parent, you can only do so much. Even though you want to protect your child, you can't guard against everything. Sometimes it's impossible to shield them from harm."

Joely watched as an incredible sadness came over him. It started with a downturn of his mouth then grew to include his eyes. Muscles worked along his jaw line, controlling whatever emotion churned inside him.

"Cole, are you all right?"

Her question appeared to jerk him from his thoughts, and he focused back on her. The eyes surveying her beneath thick black lashes were dark with secrets. "My coffee's about gone. Ready for another cup?" he offered as though nothing had happened.

"Maybe we should get back. I'm anxious to see Taylor."

Cole glanced at his watch. "We should let him sweat for a while longer. I'll get some refills."

His long legs brushed against hers as he stood up, once again making her aware of his many physical attributes. She watched as he got the coffee, appreciating the strength and ease of his well-made male body.

Wait one darn moment, she caught herself up guiltily. How could she possibly enjoy the company of an attractive man while Taylor remained locked in a jail cell a few short blocks away?

Cole sat down and pushed her cup across the table, his knees pressing firmly against hers. "Here you go, one black decaf."

Joely didn't touch the cup. Shame knotted her stomach painfully, making her feel reprehensible. "I can't do this anymore. I have to go see Taylor now. It's too heartless to sit here chatting over coffee while he's locked up and probably more frightened than he's been in his entire life."

Cole tilted his head and gave her a sympathetic smile. "Even though it's difficult, it's better if you don't coddle him. Your son has some tough decisions to make, and he'll have a better chance of making the right ones if he's scared and uncomfortable. Try to relax, okay?"

He reached his hand out as though he might touch hers, then stopped short of actually doing it. Joely found herself wishing he hadn't stopped. She had a hunch those big fingers could be as tender as they were strong.

"You know something?" His finger traced along the edge of the table, his eyes watching the movement of his finger. "When I first met you, I didn't want to like you, but I did."

Joely eased back in her chair, enjoying the irony. "That's funny, because when I first met you I really wanted to like you, but I didn't."

He sent her a twinkling glance and they smiled. She knew he understood what she meant without any further explanation.

"How did Taylor end up with such a young mom anyway?"

"The usual way, I guess. After my dad died, my mom bounced from relationship to relationship, and my older brothers and I were often left to fend for ourselves. In fact, I spent much of my formative years on my own. I needed someone to pay some attention to me and make me feel special, and I fell for a man with more charm than character."

She shrugged and her finger took up the movement along the table edge that Cole had abandoned. "I was fifteen when I met Brad. He was nineteen. He was a big strapping fellow, real good looking, and he completely dazzled me." She snickered, soft and humorless.

"By the time I turned sixteen, I was pregnant. I became a child bride at seventeen, married to an adult-sized infant with chest hair, with a real live baby doll to take care of as well. That marriage was the biggest mistake I've ever made. Before I hit twenty-one, it was over." She heard the bitterness in her voice and stopped talking.

"That had to be rough, but isn't it time to stop beating yourself up about it? At least you had enough sense to get out."

The compassion, the offer of understanding in his voice almost overwhelmed Joely. She wondered if he'd be as sympathetic if he knew she had left her precious little boy with her alcoholic husband while she worked. And it took four years and a serious injury before she clued in to the fact her toddler didn't get all his bruises from being overactive and clumsy.

No, Cole had it wrong, she didn't have a whole lot of sense when she was younger.

He pushed his coffee cup aside and leaned forward in his chair to stare sharply at her. She realized he must be very good at his investigative work. Those dark penetrating eyes would intimidate anyone into telling the truth when they flashed as fiercely as they were right now.

"You're upset. I didn't mean to do that," he apologized. "I wanted to make you feel better."

"Oh no, hey, I'm not upset with you. I actually appreciate your effort. I can't remember the last time I had a conversation with a man who cared about how I felt about myself. Men are usually much more concerned about how I feel about them."

"You already told me you didn't like me." He smiled brilliantly, his eyes crinkling. "Whaddaya say to giving me a chance to change your mind?"

For just a moment, Joely saw beneath the laughing, self-confident grin to the flicker of loneliness in his eyes. He was new to the area, she remembered. He probably didn't know many people and here she was monopolizing the conversation. She ignored his question and posed one of her own.

"Why did you choose law enforcement for your career?"

His gaze unexpectedly turned cold. His features revealed no emotion, nothing to indicate why he suddenly shut down. The pause grew a little too long, giving Joely the impression he preferred not to answer.

"I take a lot of satisfaction out of my job, especially working with the kids," he eventually replied, his voice back to that aggravatingly polite, neutral tone. "But it wasn't a matter of choice so much as of doing what was expected."

"Your parents said you had to become a cop?" Joely wanted to keep her mouth shut and let him do the talking, but stunned disbelief made her blurt it out before she could stop herself.

Cole smiled tightly. "My grandfather was a cop, same with my father. As far as they were concerned, there was no other suitable job for a Dennison, and they presumed I'd follow their lead. My mom didn't get a say, she died when I was five."

Joely let out an involuntary gasp of sympathy. "Oh, I'm sorry. How sad for you to grow up without a mother." Not having a father had left a gaping hole in her childhood and even though her mom would've never won mother-of-the-year, she'd always given freely of her hugs and kisses. She was important to Joely, and Joely couldn't imagine growing up without her.

Cole lifted a shoulder casually. "I survived. You don't miss what you never really had."

"Yes, you do," she retorted fiercely. "You miss it and you want it terribly. At least I did. I wanted a father more than I wanted anything else. It was the defining reality of my childhood. How can you say you didn't miss your mother?"

Something hard and acrid flashed in his eyes, and he didn't acknowledge her words. He pushed out of his chair abruptly. "We should get back to the detachment. Your son's waited long enough."

The quiet walk gave Joely an opportunity to contemplate the past hour spent with the too-silent man beside her. He presented an intricate paradox. On one hand, he was charming and warm and darn right sexy, on the other hand, he could suddenly become distant, brooding, and secretive. More than once tonight he'd shut down for no apparent reason. She sensed a pain, a darkness, inside him crying out for help, although she doubted he'd ever ask for, or accept, the help he needed.

Cole held the door open for Joely as they entered the building and spoke for the first time since leaving the cafe. "Wait here and I'll get your son."

"Couldn't I go with you?"

"That's not possible. Besides, I'd like to speak with him alone before I release him."

"Be kind—please." She pleaded with her eyes as well as her words.

"I will, but when I bring him out here, don't let him off the hook too easily, okay?"

Unexpected tears tightened her throat, and she could only nod her head mutely. She wanted to hold onto her son as tightly as she could and protect him from all of life's dangers. But as painful as it'd be to follow, she understood the wisdom of Cole's advice.

* * * *

When Cole entered the cell, Taylor bounded to his feet and then immediately put on the brakes. He fidgeted nervously, twisting and turning the ring on his pinkie finger.

"Can I go now, sir?" he begged hoarsely.

"In a moment. I thought we should finish that chat we started earlier. Did you use your time constructively while you were detained? Or have you decided you like being locked in this little room?" With each step Cole took toward the boy, Taylor retreated a step. "Don't be scared of me. I'd like to help you put this trouble behind you, but only if you show me you're willing to make the effort."

Taylor bobbed his head and started blinking rapidly, as though he might cry. Cole's first impulse was to tell him to buck up and act like a man. Words from his childhood echoed through his mind. *Be a man. Men don't cry.*

He placed a hand on the boy's shoulder and gave it a squeeze.

"Don't be ashamed to cry. It doesn't make you any less a man." The words surprised Cole more than they did Taylor, even though they came out of his mouth.

Taylor pawed at his eyes clumsily. "I don't wanna cry. I just want outta here."

Cole gave an easygoing shrug. "So, don't cry, then. I only wanted you to know I wouldn't hold it against you if you did. I was never allowed to cry, you see, when I was a boy and that's quite a weight for a kid to carry."

Where the hell did all this come from? It was true, whenever he'd been hurt or scared his father had clenched his teeth and warned, "Don't you dare cry!" He didn't even recall how to cry anymore. But why have this heart-to-heart with a mere boy, a stranger? He didn't discuss his emotions with anyone. It was unnerving to catch himself doing it now, and his instincts told him to turn this kid over to his mother and get the two of them out of his life for good. He ignored the gut feeling and pointed at the sleep bench.

"Why don't you park it and tell me what decisions you've come up with."

Before Taylor's butt hit the bench, the boy had rushed into speech. "I never want to see those guys again. I know they're bad news, and they were only using me because I always had pocket cash to spend on them."

Cole perched on the bench beside him. "What does your dad have to say about this?" He recognized this as a cheap tactic on his part. Joely was no longer with the boy's father, but Cole was curious to find out whether the man still played a part in their lives or not.

"My dad lives in Edmonton. That's where me and my mom lived when I was little. She hardly ever lets me see him," Taylor answered with a slight edge to his tone.

It was obviously a touchy point between them, and Cole felt a curious need to defend Joely. "She must have good reasons. I know your mom only wants what's best for you. I also know sometimes a guy needs another guy to talk to."

Taylor gave a soft snort and ducked his head. Cole pressed a finger against the underside of the boy's chin, making him look back up. "There are some things you can't discuss with a mom, aren't there? Not even with an understanding mom like yours. I want you to feel free to call me, whenever you need a guy to consult with. I think you'll do just fine, but if at any time you're unsure about the path to take, please, I'm here. I'm willing to help." He fished a business card out of his shirt pocket, scribbled his cell phone number on the back and handed it to the boy. "This is my card. Hang on to it and use it any time you want to reach me."

He briefly scanned the information on the card, then looked back at Cole. "Thank you, Corporal Dennison."

"I'm letting you go now and I want you to keep your nose clean from here on out, because you've used up the last get-out-of-jail-free card I'm giving you."

Cole caught himself leaning forward, staring into unblinking sky-blue eyes. The same sort of sky-blue eyes he'd just had coffee with, except these eyes were bloodshot and hero-worship reflected from them. Against his will, he could feel himself being pulled in emotionally, and he didn't know where this concern for the boy's welfare came from.

He flinched and pulled back.

"Let's move it," he ordered more gruffly than he meant to.

Cole could tell Joely didn't even notice his approach. Her gaze went over his shoulder to her son, a fiercely maternal protectiveness overshadowing the anger on her face. He turned back to Taylor. "Your mom's sure worried about you. I think you owe her a huge apology and a sincere promise to shape up." And he hoped this time the promise stuck, for both the boy's sake and his mom's.

* * * *

To Taylor, the large man standing in front of him seemed so smart and so understanding. He looked over at his mom and realized the corporal spoke the truth, and it made him feel awful. His eyes filled with tears, and he wiped them on his sleeve. "Thank you, sir. I will. Thank you."

"Go on, boy. She's waiting for you."

Corporal Dennison hung back and Taylor had to walk the last

few feet around the counter by himself. He couldn't get up the nerve to say anything to his mom until they were seated in the car. It worried him that she didn't say a word to him either.

"I'm real sorry, Mom," he apologized as he pulled his seatbelt on. "I didn't know they stole the car."

"Save it, Taylor. I'm very angry right now, and I don't want to hear any excuses. I hope this incident scared the hell out of you," she warned him, without any sympathy in her voice. "Because if anything like this happens again, it won't go as easily for you. You have no more chances."

Taylor dropped his head and started to shake. His mom used a swear word and she never swore, so she must be real mad. He didn't mean for any of this to happen, but he sure blew it this time. She'd probably never trust him again. His lungs hurt and he swallowed with difficulty, trying to ease the tightness squeezing his throat.

"I'm sorry, Mom."

She didn't answer him or even look his way.

His tears came in a rush, burning his face as they splashed down his cheeks. He cried so hard he could barely breathe. He hated it when he blubbered like this, but no way could he calm down. He cried because he was scared and frustrated, embarrassed and angry. There were also tears of relief because he'd survived something really scary and was now safe. And he bawled even harder because his mom didn't seem to care in the least if he was upset.

By the time they pulled into the parking area behind their building, his tears had just about stopped, he sniffed and gasped for air. He stayed in his seat when his mom opened her door to get out.

"Coming?" she asked, nicer now.

"I love you, Mom," he said, rubbing his eyes hard. "And I really am sorry." The interior car light was harsh and he blinked painfully. His eyes ached and his cheeks were wet and sticky with tears.

His mom leaned toward him and held his face in her hands. She kissed him under each eye before hugging him. "I love you too, sweetie, and I know you're sorry."

He started crying again, but this time it felt better.

* * * *

Neither Joely nor Taylor had said goodbye when they left the detachment, and Cole should've been relieved by that. He should've been damn relieved, instead, he found himself wondering if he'd ever see them again. He very much wanted to see both of them under better circumstances.

An idea clicked in his head and deciding to act immediately, he took the time to make a phone call before leaving for home.

"Perry, it's Cole Dennison here. Sorry to bother you at home on a Friday night, but I'm calling about that basketball program you were telling me about. I've changed my mind and would like to get involved. Do you know when and where the next game is?" Cole talked briskly, not giving himself a chance to change his mind. "Sunday morning at nine? Perfect. Let me grab a pen to write down the address. Uh-huh, I know where that is. All right, see you then. Thanks."

Perry Schwartz, an officer who worked youth detail with Cole, had been encouraging Cole to join a volunteer unit called Diversion, the purpose being to divert young people away from crime. One aspect of the program involved a group of adults getting together with some at-risk teens to play drop-in basketball a couple of times a month.

Up until now, Cole had strongly resisted the concept, not wanting to mix his work life with his leisure time. He worked in a rough business where bad things happened to good people, and he didn't like to form attachments to anyone he came into contact with on the job. Far better for his sanity if he stayed detached.

Now this beautiful young mother had entered his life, with a teenage son in dire need of positive male reinforcement and suddenly he found himself eagerly volunteering for the job. What happened to not getting involved, to not caring?

A notion came sneaking across his mind—was he interested in helping Taylor as a way of getting closer to Joely? Was he capable of using a vulnerable kid that way? He laughed at himself and firmly brushed the pesky thoughts aside. That couldn't be it because he didn't want the woman. Not that way. He *never* wanted another woman, not in any type of committed arrangement anyway. His long and miserable marriage ensured he'd never willingly repeat that experience.

There had been lovers since his divorce, of course, brief transient affairs of the flesh. But none of them had ever been allowed entry into his deeply guarded inner recesses. Never again would he surrender himself to a woman's control.

* * * *

While working in the garden, Joely heard the buzzer announce someone at the front door of the building. Instead of tracking dirt into the condo, she popped out of the gate and stuck her head around the fence to see who was calling on them at ten o'clock on Saturday morning. The huge cedar tree on her side of the building blocked her view of the entranceway.

"Hello!" she cried out. "Over here, I'm in the yard."

"Joely?" She did a double-take as Cole came strolling around the cedar. "Oh, there you are. I thought I heard you calling."

The closer he got, the more acutely aware Joely became of the snug fit of his black polo shirt and how it emphasized every well-toned muscle in his upper body. She was also painfully aware of her own disheveled state, with her hair tied up in a haphazard ponytail and her hands grubby with soil. She didn't have a speck of makeup on.

Completely mortified, she could only stare at him like an idiot, with her eyes wide and her mouth hanging in a silly little O. Cole stared back, starting at her face and slowly working his way south. Joely couldn't do anything to prevent the rush of blood to her cheeks, overly conscious of the way his dark-eyed gaze roamed appreciatively over her entire body. Her pulses throbbed in response, and she grew lightheaded with the sensations running through her. When he reached her bare toes, he smiled slowly and started the journey back up.

His inspection eventually returned to her face, and her flushed cheeks must've conveyed how shamelessly he'd ogled her, because his gaze darted away, settling on a neutral point a few feet to her left. He frowned and clamped a hand on the back of his neck.

"Sorry for showing up unannounced. I had to attend to something at the detachment and because you live close by, I thought I'd take a chance you'd be home. I hope you don't mind I looked up the address in Taylor's file."

Clearing her throat softly, she searched for her voice. "Not at all. Is there something more you needed to know, about last night, I mean? Oh, excuse my manners, please come in."

She stood aside to let Cole enter the yard through the gate. They brushed shoulders as he passed, and the physical contact sent another disturbing wave of sensation through her body. How crazy was it that he should be able to cause this kind of reaction in her?

"I did come here to talk to Taylor, it's not about last night, though. He's not in any trouble."

"I'm relieved to hear that. He's still asleep, I'm afraid. I could get you a coffee or something cold to drink if you wanted to wait? If Taylor doesn't wake up soon, I'll get him up."

"Coffee sounds good." An amused smile curved his lips.

"What's so funny?"

Cole moved closer to her, his eyes focused on her cheek. He wiggled one finger in her direction. "Uh, you have dirt, there, on your face."

Joely's hands flew to her cheeks, flapping self-consciously. "Where?"

The smile turned into a chuckle. "You're making it worse. Here, let me." He took another step in her direction.

Joely watched wide-eyed and dry-mouthed as he stopped in front of her. His left hand settled on her shoulder, turning her slightly. His fingers were gentle against her skin, and her stomach constricted sharply at the contact of his hand to her bare skin. With his right hand, he brushed the tips of his fingers across her cheek and down to her mouth, his thumb lingering for a tantalizing second next to her lips.

His touch generated a warmth crawling up from under her skin, the lazy heat enveloping her. He leaned in, his gaze moving from her cheek to her lips.

He's going to kiss me, she thought dizzily, and swayed toward him.

Chapter Six

With Joely's mouth mere inches away from his, Cole felt, as well as heard, the ragged catch to her breath. If he leaned in a little closer…

He stepped back, dropping his hands to his sides. "There you go, dirt's all gone."

Joely ducked her head as hot color flooded her face. "Thanks. Coffee—" she stammered. "I'm going to put the coffee on now." She fled into the condo.

Cole didn't follow her. He couldn't have if he wanted to. He remained rooted to the spot, trying to retain an aloof cool he was nowhere close to feeling. The near proximity of this woman completely stripped him of all reason—his intense longing to kiss her left his body aching. And it annoyed the hell out of him because he didn't want or need this kind of complication in his life. It frightened him to both resent something and want it so badly at the same time.

If only she hadn't looked so unbelievably perfect this morning. With her hair up, her bare neck beckoned, long and desirable. With that first glimpse, he'd fantasized trailing kisses along her slender throat. Touching her had threatened his considerable self-control, tempting him to follow through with his fantasy right there in the yard.

"Cole, coffee's on." Joely's voice called from inside the condo. "Come on in and get comfortable, it'll be ready in a moment."

Cole closed his eyes and took a couple deep shuddering breaths before stepping into the condo. Joely's hair now flowed in a soft swirl of butterscotch about her bare shoulders. Any evidence of her reaction to their powerful connection had been removed from her face along with the remnants of dirt. Her hands mesmerized him, long supple fingers rubbed lotion onto her skin, triggering yet another X-rated fantasy.

"I'm afraid you caught me with dirt on more than my face this morning. I've been working in my garden."

"I noticed the beautiful flowers," Cole lied. His innate observation skills had deserted him, and he'd barely noticed anything in the yard besides Joely. If pressed, he wouldn't be able to name a single plant out there, but he could say with certainty that Joely's skin was softer than any flower petal in creation. Realizing he was rudely staring again, his gaze slid away and circled the living room. It had a welcoming feel to it, and Cole hoped it'd help him relax, because right now he needed all the help he could get. "You have a lovely home here, Joely."

"Thank you, I like it too. Sit down, please. You take your coffee black?"

Cole stretched his long frame out on one corner of the couch, crossing his legs at the ankles. "I'm told I'm not sweet enough, so make it black, one sugar. Did you manage all right with your son last night?"

Joely handed him a mug of coffee and took the armchair facing him, curling her legs under her. "The poor kid. He cried the whole way home. I took your advice and didn't baby him, but I felt like the most heartless mom in the world. He couldn't apologize enough times." She paused and took a sip of coffee, looking steadily over the rim at him. "The fact is, except for using bad judgment by agreeing to a ride, he really didn't do anything wrong."

A tinge of accusation showed in her gaze. Cole doubted anything he said at this point would make her feel better, so he remained silent and let her vent.

"Ever since he was small, Taylor's had to come up with his own punishment when he's misbehaved. It's a way for him to realize his actions have consequences and he has to take responsibility for those consequences. Last night he offered to go without TV and video games for an entire month. I told him a couple of hours spent in a holding cell was punishment enough.

"He then asked why it took so long to get him out, and I admitted I purposely left him in there to teach him a lesson. All the tears dried up in a heck of a hurry, and he became furious with me. He even accused me of not loving him. No matter how carefully I tried to explain my reasons, he wouldn't listen. During the night, I heard him crying out in his sleep and when I went into his room to comfort him, he asked me to leave. Do you have any idea what that felt like?"

Cole puffed his cheeks up and blew the air out noisily. "It must've been awful for you, and I'm sorry. But I still think you did the right thing. Did he promise he wouldn't associate with that group of youths anymore?"

"Yes, he made it clear he'd have nothing to do with them. He admitted he knew very little about them and the more he found out, the less he liked."

A door opened down the hall, and they fell silent as Taylor padded into the room in his pajama bottoms. Seeing Cole on the couch, he swung in panic toward his mom, his arms circling his bare chest.

"Is he here to arrest me?"

"No, honey. Corporal Dennison has something to discuss with you. Why don't you get dressed and hurry back, so we can find out what's on his mind."

Taylor returned to the room a few moments later, dressed in baggy shorts and a T-shirt. He perched on the arm of Joely's chair, bending down to give her a kiss on the cheek before turning to look warily at Cole.

Joely touched his chin with loving fingers. "You're not in trouble, pumpkin. Go sit down and listen to what the corporal has to say."

Cole found it almost unbearable to watch the easy affection and comfortable display of devotion between the boy and his mom. He'd been the recipient of such loving devotion at one point in his life. It seemed like a long time ago, but witnessing it just now made it all fresh again in his mind.

Images welled up before his eyes causing a jolting pain to explode at his temples. The ache had lessened over time, but still remained, increasing in intensity when the memories returned. Sarah had died more than four years ago, but he could see in precise detail her adorable little face, her mischievous smile, the incredible love he felt when she'd hug him. Grief caught him off guard and he tried to shut down, but he didn't quite manage to this time. Taylor and Joely were too poignant a reminder of what he'd lost, and it left him shaken.

Taylor ambled over to the loveseat across the room, distracting Cole from his painful contemplation. With ruthless discipline he wrenched his attention to the boy slouched low on the seat with his chin resting on his chest. Taylor watched him silently, twisting his ring around and round nervously, his expression cautiously curious.

Cole carefully cleared his throat, unsure whether or not his voice would work. "Good morning, Taylor. I came over here today to talk to you about a program I hoped you might want to join with me."

Taylor immediately sat up, a crooked smile breaking out on his face. "You wanna do something with me? Just the two of us?"

Cole smiled at the enthusiasm in his voice and glanced over for Joely's reaction. She didn't say anything, but she watched them thoughtfully.

"Actually, lots of people are involved. About twice a month, a group of adults and teens get together to play basketball. It's not overly structured, whoever shows up, shows up and they divvy up teams from there. An officer I work with has been involved with this program for years and he asked me to join. I figure I'll give it a try if you will."

Taylor's face sparkled with animation. "Play basketball with you? You really want me to?"

Cole found the boy's obvious pleasure touching, although the transparent tones of hero-worship scared him. He assumed a huge responsibility by initiating this friendship.

"Sure," he replied and knew there was no turning back now. For a man who avoided commitments, he had just committed his friendship to this kid. "I wouldn't be here if I didn't. Next game is tomorrow morning at nine. I'll pick you up at eight thirty, if you want to go."

Taylor turned to Joely. "Is it okay? Can I go?"

"Of course you may, if you want. Corporal Dennison made a kind offer, what do you say to him?"

Taylor got to his feet and offered his hand to Cole. "Thank you very much, sir. I'll be ready at eight thirty tomorrow."

Cole stood and solemnly gave the extended hand a firm shake. "You're welcome. I look forward to it." He realized how lonely he'd become, how lonely he'd made himself become, since Sarah died. This was his first step to reclaiming his life. "Now I should leave you folks to get on with your day." He turned to Joely and found himself inexplicably reluctant to leave.

* * * *

"Morning," Joely greeted Cole at his desk, a week later. "Thanks so much for taking Taylor out for brunch after the basketball game last weekend. You didn't have to do that, but he sure enjoyed himself. I think you've got yourself a fan."

"My pleasure. I had as much fun as he did. Your son's a good sport, and he's not too shabby on the basketball court, either."

"That's my boy." She faked a dunk shot. "I taught him everything he knows."

Cole's eyebrows lifted and he grinned. "I'd love to see more of your moves. Maybe I can talk you into playing someday."

His dancing eyes spoke of the double meaning behind his words, but Joely thought it best to ignore the innuendo. "No, thank you. That's Taylor's time to spend with the guys, and I wouldn't think of intruding. Say, Cole, I have my month-end reports for you, but can we push our appointment back a bit? It's been a crazy morning, and I've fallen behind on my paperwork. If I don't keep things up to date, Stella tends to get cranky."

"Paperwork." Cole gave an overly dramatic shudder. "The bane of my existence. Go ahead and take all the time you need. I'll be here all morning, barring some emergency. Come on, I'll find you a quiet place to work." He let her into an unoccupied interview room. "I'll be back in a little while to go over the file with you."

As he turned to leave, Joely placed her hand on his arm to detain him. Her fingers had to resist the urge to tighten around the strong, warm muscle beneath them. She couldn't help wondering what it'd feel like to have those powerful arms wrapped around her. Paradise, she decided, it would feel like paradise.

"I just wanted to thank you again for how great you've been with Taylor. You've made him happier than he's been in a long time."

"My pleasure. He's a good kid." His smile said he meant it.

She gave him a searching look, trying to discover what made this man tick. Evasive, mysterious, enigmatic. Strong, yet tender, perhaps a bit softhearted, despite the tough guy exterior. He was a walking, breathing dichotomy.

Belatedly, she realized her hand still lay along his forearm and she snatched it away.

"Thank you," she murmured hoarsely and backed away a step. It took concentrated effort to recover her self-possession. "I better get at this paperwork."

Amusement etched itself on Cole's face, but his eyes were full of promise. "See you shortly."

A rap of knuckles against the doorframe interrupted Joely a few minutes later. She looked up with a smile, expecting to see Cole. Her smile evaporated as she honed in on the man standing there. Trip Wilson once again took up the entire doorway, blocking her exit. Fear made the hair on her arms stand on end.

Just stay calm, she told herself, *you can handle this.* She paused and assumed an icy expression, forcing herself to relax and unclench her fingers from the table edge.

"I want you to leave right now, Trip. Corporal Dennison will be back any moment and this time, I will make trouble for you." Hoping she'd have more control if she didn't have to look up at him, she rose slowly to her feet.

"I'm not going to bother you. I saw you come in here, and I'd just like a few minutes of your time. I'll stay right here if it makes you feel better."

"You leaving right now would make me feel better."

"Just give me a chance to say what I need to say, then I'll leave you alone."

Joely's accusing gaze slid suspiciously over the entire length of him, noticing for the first time he wore street clothes, instead of his uniform. Small beads of sweat appeared on his forehead as she continued to stare unwaveringly at him. He shifted from foot to foot, looking about as uncomfortable as a man possibly could.

"I'm sorry for the way I behaved last time," he blurted out finally.

"It must've hurt your massive ego to say that," she answered mockingly. Anger made her feel better. "I'm afraid your feeble attempt at an apology won't make up for the humiliation and disgust I felt that night."

"That pinches, but I deserve it." He took a step into the room, his hands coming out in a gesture of appeasement.

"Stay where you are!" she ordered instantly.

"All right. I'm not moving. I'm sorry, Joely—Ms. Sinclair. I was way off base, but I wouldn't've hurt you." He ran a hand over his closely clipped hair. "Uh, well, I guess I probably did hurt you and I'm sorry. The very next day, I applied for a medical leave. I knew I was on the edge of burning out. But I'm a good cop, Ms. Sinclair. At least I used to be. I've busted my tail, worked long hours, without pay sometimes. I've lined up my case and presented the facts as best I could. And what happens? The perp walks. Over and over, the perp walks. Do you know what that does to a cop after awhile?"

Joely's defensive edginess subsided somewhat. She understood his exasperation. "But Trip, you've blamed me, and it's not my fault. I work with kids who have shoplifted or vandalized a piece of property in a fit of frustration. I don't have anything to do with the kind of people you're referring to. I agree our justice system needs an overhaul and I can even commiserate with you. No matter how thwarted you feel, though, you can't use that as an excuse to treat people the way you treated me."

"I realize that and I've sought help. I'm seeing the detachment shrink a couple times a week to learn how to deal with my anger in a more positive way. And now a situation has developed in my own family that has me rethinking my opinion of the work you do."

Rubbing a meaty finger along the side of his brow, he cleared his throat noisily a couple of times, obviously having difficulty with what he wanted to say.

"The thing is, you see, my sister has this girl. Janine's her name, she's only thirteen. The past few months, Janine's gotten into all sorts of trouble. She stays out late and won't listen to her parents. She got caught shoplifting and even disappeared once for an entire weekend. Rosie, that's my sister, she doesn't know what to do with her anymore. She asked for my help and my first impulse was to give the brat a good spanking and then ground her for the rest of her life."

"That won't work."

Trip smiled bashfully. "I know. That's when I thought of you. Maybe Janine could use someone like you to talk to. I know I'm eating a lot of crow here, but I don't mind. This is my sister's kid. I'll do whatever I can to help them out."

Joely had no desire to say, "I told you so". She could never turn down a request to help a child. She reached into her briefcase and took out a business card. Using one finger, she slid the card down the table as far as she could reach, then left it there. "Have your sister phone me, and I'll recommend her to someone in her area."

Without stepping further into the room, Trip stretched out his arm to pick up the card. He gave it a quick glance before tucking it into his pocket. "Thanks a lot. I'm glad I got the chance to talk to you." He made a small coughing sound. "I have one more favor to ask." He cleared his throat again and stared down at the floor for a long moment, before raising bleak eyes to meet Joely's. "If you could tell me you'll try to forgive me at some point, maybe not right now, but some day, then maybe I can start respecting myself again."

For a stunned moment, Joely was speechless. This oversized, brawny cop, who had tormented her for years with his arrogance and insolence sounded as though he might cry. She didn't get a chance to formulate an answer, because Cole arrived at that moment and when he noticed Trip inside the room, he stiffened alertly. His gaze swung over to Joely. She was still shaken by Trip's unexpected vulnerability, and it must've shown on her face because Cole's anger flared spontaneously as he turned on Trip.

"What the hell are you doing in here, Wilson?" he demanded. "I told you to stay away from Ms. Sinclair. If you've upset her in any way, I swear—"

"No, Cole," Joely interrupted quickly. "It's all right. Trip stopped by to apologize. He acted very polite, even when I didn't." She turned back to Trip. "I hope you're able to return to work real soon. We need all the good cops we can get. And thank you for explaining your circumstances to me. Tell Rosie I'll be waiting for her call."

Trip nodded his head and rubbed a finger under his nose as he sniffed loudly, then cleared the emotion from his throat. "I appreciate you saying that. It couldn't've been easy." He eyed Cole anxiously for a second, then reached out his hand to him. "I want to thank you, sir, for pointing out what a jerk I was that night. You'll be relieved to know I'm taking steps to work out my problems. I apologized to Ms. Sinclair and now I also offer you my regrets."

Cole glanced over his shoulder at Joely, before grasping the extended hand. "Take care of yourself, Trip. We can use you back here." After Trip left, Cole closed the door and turned to Joely. "Are you sure you're all right? You had to have been frightened."

His gentleness and concern touched her deeply and Joely swallowed down a lump in her throat. The conflicting emotions inside her completely confused her. She'd never experienced such compassion and caring, and it attracted her. After a lifetime of being self-sufficient, she didn't know how to cope with this surprising inner weakness. She wanted this man's comfort and protection. She yearned for his kisses…his caresses...

She lowered her head, not letting him read her face. She wasn't ready for Cole to know her feelings.

"Joely, what is it?"

She peeked up to find his dark eyes boring directly into hers. How on earth had he come to be standing right beside her? She glanced down at the file on the table, trying to maintain her equilibrium. He was too close, way too close, and his proximity robbed her of the ability to think straight.

* * * *

Cole continued to study her, his chest aching with an indescribable want. Two minutes around this woman was all it took to find himself tangled up in knots. He warned himself not to touch her, to just back away. His body, however, decided to act independently of his mind.

"You're so pale," he whispered, stretching out a hand to brush his fingers across her cheek.

At the touch of her satin skin, his groin tightened painfully, taking away his breath. His hand lowered to her shoulder, drawing her toward him. His fingers captured the fragile bones of her shoulders, then moved up to slide into her silky soft hair, tilting her head upward. Her lower lip was pouty and undeniably kissable.

"God, you're beautiful."

The firestorm of desire exploded inside him, and a rasping groan dragged across his lips as he lowered his mouth onto hers. His lips moved restlessly against hers, and Joely's lips parted in willing submission. His tongue teased the inside of her mouth. Her tongue met his with soft stroking thrusts that left him needing more. His hands moved down her shoulders, gliding over her spine to bring her tightly against him. She moaned softly in her throat, and heat roared through him in response to the sound.

With his breath coming in short pants, Cole tore his mouth away from hers. He released her so quickly, she nearly fell backward, and she reached out a hand to the table edge for support.

"Cole? What's wrong, why did you push me away?"

He dragged the back of his hand across his mouth, then raked his fingers through his hair. "What's wrong?" he echoed harshly. "I don't know what the hell I'm doing here. I'm behaving no better than Trip Wilson."

"How can you say that? This is completely different."

"Different how? I wanted to kiss you, so I did. I didn't check first to see if you wanted it too." He swung away from her, putting some needed distance between them. The treachery of his emotions infuriated him, and he crushed down the remnants of his passion with brutal determination.

"Did I protest? Did I ask you to stop? I wanted that kiss as much as you did." He heard her take a couple of steps in his direction, then stop, waiting for him to react, but he remained impassive, his back still turned to her.

The silence stretched his nerves to the breaking point, but he couldn't speak, couldn't explain how wrong this was, even though it felt so right.

"You know, Cole, there's been this crosscurrent of attraction—of sexuality—between us since the day we met. I wasn't sure until now if you felt it as strongly as I did. This kiss, this—this—whatever it is—was inevitable. If it didn't happen today, it would've happened another time. Maybe it wasn't appropriate here where you work and maybe we didn't even have to act on it, but we can't deny the attraction is there."

Cole pivoted back to face her. While she spoke, he managed to wall himself off completely. He didn't like turning off his emotions around Joely, but he had to regain control of the situation before it got completely out of hand.

"We should go over those reports now," he said evenly, instead of acknowledging her words.

Frustration furrowed Joely's brow, her eyes blinked with hurt. "No, thanks. I'll leave them with you. If you have any questions, please call the office and speak with Stella Carson." She made a studied effort not to walk anywhere near him as she swung out of the room.

You really blew that one, he told himself maliciously as he followed a few steps behind her down the hall. *She'll probably never talk to you again. But that's what you wanted, wasn't it?*

No, it's what he needed. It came nowhere close to what he wanted.

Chapter Seven

"Joely Sinclair," she chirped into the receiver. The phone call came as a welcome distraction. For almost an hour, she'd tried to concentrate on updating files into the computer, but her mind kept wandering. She couldn't get Cole out of her thoughts. Or rather, she couldn't get the sensation of Cole's lips, hands, and body moving against hers out of her system. An unyielding restlessness existed inside her that she couldn't shake. "How may I help you?"

"By agreeing to have dinner with me."

"Cole?" Joely's eyes widened with surprise, and her heartbeat quickened. "I didn't expect to hear from you."

"I want to apologize for my behavior yesterday. I'm sure you know by now all men are idiots when it comes to beautiful women, and I'm no different. I'd like to start fresh. Go slower, get to know you. Will you have dinner with me tonight?"

"I appreciate the offer, but I can't have dinner with you. Not tonight."

"Not tonight means some other night," he persisted. "When are you free?"

"I have a son, remember? I don't go out for dinner during the week when he's home." She thought quickly. "Tell you what. Taylor's going to the movies Friday night with some friends from school. I planned to use the opportunity to join a coworker, Maggie Lapage, for a bite out. If she doesn't mind me bailing on her, I could have dinner with you then. Would it be okay if I get back to you later?"

"Sounds good. Tell Maggie if she's willing to forego your company for me, I'll buy her the coffee next time." On that cryptic note, he hung up.

Joely held the receiver in her hand for a moment, unsure how to proceed. Private to the point of being remote, Cole either couldn't or wouldn't share anything about himself, so completely opposite to her own transparent character. And this aspect of his personality gave her just cause for concern.

To his credit, however, he was sensitive to her feelings, he was an understanding listener, and he appeared to want to take an active part in Taylor's life. That was important to her. It pained her to admit it, but Taylor craved male attention. When he got home from brunch the morning they'd played basketball together, he'd worn a smile a yard wide. All she heard the rest of the day was Cole, Cole and more Cole. He was definitely turning into a positive role model for her son.

Just thinking about their kiss, the warmth of Cole's hands roaming over her body, sent a thrill shooting straight through to her toes—not to mention other places. No other man had ever aroused this level of sensual excitement in her. Her marriage had left its mark, stolen her innocence. Time slowly replenished her faith in love, but the emptiness Brad created inside her lingered.

Until Cole came along.

Her mind made up, she replaced the phone and went down the hall to Maggie's office. The door was ajar, indicating she didn't have a client inside. Joely rapped lightly, opening the door at the same time.

"Hey, do you have a moment?"

"What's up?" Maggie slid the computer keyboard tray under the desktop and gracefully stretched the kinks from her back. "You look guilty. Are you about to pawn a case off on me that you don't want?"

Joely slipped into the client chair. "Nothing like that, although I do have a favor. Would it hurt your feelings if I begged off having dinner with you on Friday?"

"You got a better offer?" Maggie joked.

Joely actually blushed and before she could explain, Maggie jumped in with enthusiasm. "I don't believe it! You did get a better offer. Who is he? With a blush like that he must be hot."

"It's Cole Dennison," Joely admitted, her face still embarrassingly warm. "He just called and invited me out to dinner. Because he's spending time with Taylor, I think it's a good idea to get to know him better. I told him we already had plans, and I'd have to check with you first. He said to tell you he'd buy the coffee next time if you agreed to postpone our evening out." She paused to see if Maggie would volunteer the reason why she'd bought Cole a coffee, without Joely having to come right out and ask.

"Wow! Joely has a date with Corporal Sexy Ebony Eyes! Here—" She lifted the phone off the hook and handed it to Joely. "Use my phone. Call him right now. Say yes, before *he* gets a better offer. Oh—" She wrinkled her nose in apology. "That didn't come out quite how I meant it."

Joely returned the receiver to its base. "It's okay, I'm sure a guy like Cole has had plenty of better offers. And thanks, but I'll use my own phone. I'm nervous enough about calling him without you eavesdropping."

"You don't have anything to be nervous about." Maggie tapped her front teeth with a long fingernail. "Now that I think about it, Cole did seem awfully interested in you when I talked to him the other day."

Joely did an abrupt about-face two feet from the door and hurried back to Maggie's desk. "What do you mean he sounded interested in me? Why didn't you tell me this earlier?"

"Because I didn't think you were interested in him. You as much as said so. I wanted to check him out, and thank him, you know, for what he's doing with Taylor, so I picked up a couple coffees and tracked him down at the detachment. Before I met him, I couldn't imagine why you'd socialize with the man, Jo, while poor Taylor was stuck in the slammer. But now that I've finally laid eyes on this Cole Dennison, I can definitely see his appeal." Maggie twirled a strand of long red hair around her finger and grinned salaciously.

"My decision had nothing to do with his looks," Joely protested, although a small part of her worried that perhaps it had. "I simply bowed to his professional judgment."

"Yeah, right, tell it to the judge. But it's not your fault, Jo. You couldn't help yourself. Cole's the kind of man women desire, and he achieves this simply by being in the same room as them. The man is absolutely divine. Such a dreamy smile. And those dark eyes!" Maggie gave a dramatic shiver. "Perfection! You've changed your mind about him, haven't you? You do think he's nice now, right?"

"Hmm." Joely nodded. "He appears to be a good person, very

compassionate, but there's something about him..." She didn't know how to verbalize her intuition about his hidden intensity. It still bothered her the way he could shut himself down as easily as turning a switch. "I guess he's just private," she decided. "He doesn't share much."

"I don't know about that, he had all kinds of nice things to say about Taylor. He's quite taken with our boy. And come to think of it, he got me to tell him all sorts of things about you without directly asking me anything."

"Like what sort of things?" The thought of Maggie spewing all her personal little foibles to Cole Dennison left Joely with a sick feeling in the pit of her stomach. And what business did he have checking her out in the first place?

"Don't look so peeved. I didn't tell him anything private. Just stuff like you don't have a boyfriend and how you don't even date very often." Maggie slapped the top of her desk and shook her head in mock disbelief. "Hot damn, that guy's got sneaky detective skills."

Before Joely could offer her opinion about the use of Cole's detective abilities, Stella stuck her head in the door.

"Sorry to interrupt, but Joely, you're wanted on the phone again. Sounds like the same guy who just called."

"If he's calling to cancel, the next coffee I buy him will end up in his lap," Maggie vowed loyally to Joely.

"Cancel what? Who's canceling what?" Stella asked as she stepped into the room.

"Cole Dennison asked Joely out on a date for Friday night. Come on, pick up the phone, Jo. The man's waiting."

Joely stared at the flashing red light with dread. He must be calling to back out. Why else would he call this soon? Her throat went bone dry and she tried to stem her disappointment, her annoyance with his nosy impertinence practically forgotten and completely forgiven. She hadn't realized until this moment just how much she looked forward to going out with him.

"Did you want me to take a message, Joely?" Stella prompted when she continued to watch the phone without moving.

"No, I've got it," she replied and finally reached for the receiver. "Hello?"

Show No Weakness   85

"Did you ask her yet?"

Joely started laughing, more relieved than she wanted to admit. "You only called five minutes ago."

"Well, did you ask her yet?"

"I'm in the process of doing that. She's agreed to a rain check, so if you still want to go out, I guess we're on for Friday night."

"Great. I work until six, so I'll pick you up around seven. I thought we'd try this little place I've discovered off Marine Drive. Do you like Italian?"

"Italian sounds perfect. I'll see you Friday at seven." She smiled at Stella and Maggie as she hung up. "He didn't want to back out," she stated simply.

* * * *

Joely decided not to tell Taylor about her date with Cole. She was certain he'd like the idea of her seeing him, and she didn't want to disappoint her son if it didn't work out. She remembered the long succession of "Uncles" in her childhood, there one day, gone the next, and she vowed years ago never to put Taylor through the same ordeal. She didn't introduce him to her male friends until after the third date, although most of her relationships rarely lasted that long. Today's men, she discovered, were more interested in a noncommitted sexual alliance, rather than developing something serious that involved a child as part of the package.

It was with only a tinge of guilt that she let Taylor believe her plans with Maggie hadn't changed. She didn't tell him this in so many words, he assumed it, and she didn't bother to correct him. He was preoccupied with his own activities, or he would've picked up on her nervousness and how she'd changed her dress three times before settling on a little black number she would've never worn for dinner with Maggie. The soft silk of the dress concealed skin, but not curves, and was definitely designed to attract a man's eye.

Joely gave herself one last glance in the hallway mirror when the buzzer announced Cole at seven sharp. Her stomach muscles tensed with a thrill that was part excitement, part anxiety. The flattering attention Cole paid her as he led her over to the dark green vintage Mustang parked in front of the building went a long way to putting her at ease.

"Wow, this is your car?" She whistled, as she circled the impeccably restored muscle car. "It's a beauty. I drive a Mustang too."

"I know. A red convertible." Joely lifted her eyebrows in question and Cole explained with a smart-aleck grin, "I'm a cop. I'm trained to observe."

"Uh-huh. Would you mind letting me drive your car tonight?" She asked the question simply to wipe the smirk off his face and she succeeded.

"It's not that I don't trust your driving skills—"

"Oh, come on," Joely interrupted, giving him an offended look. "My car's gotta be forty years newer than this one."

"Exactly my point."

"I'll flip you for it. Heads, I get to drive. Tails, you let me drive. And I promise, if I put a mark on it, I'll pay for dinner."

"Okay, you win," he agreed unexpectedly and tossed her the keys. "She responds best if you double-clutch when you downshift. And remember, this old girl doesn't have power steering. Or power anything for that matter."

"I'm joking. I don't want to drive." She tried to shove the keys back at him, but he was having no part of it.

"Nope, you have the keys. You're driving." A childlike smile of satisfaction spread across his face and the devilish light in his eyes taunted her.

"All righty. I hope this sucker has seat belts at least, because I drive fast. Cops don't give speeding tickets to other cops, do they?" The flash of chagrin Joely spotted on Cole's face as she climbed behind the wheel and gunned the motor was almost worth the nervous anticipation curling in the pit of her stomach.

Contrary to their mutual, if carefully hidden, apprehension, they arrived at the restaurant without a single mishap, no dents and no speeding tickets.

"We have reservations, please," Cole told the hostess. "The name's Dennison." He reached for Joely as he spoke, drawing her closer. His hand rested lightly on her shoulder and where he touched, her skin tingled.

Their dinner conversation flowed smoothly as Cole, charming and attentive, asked her questions about her family and Taylor's activities. Before long Joely realized the exchange had grown one-sided. "Where did you grow up, Cole?" she asked, deliberately trying to draw him out.

"Toronto," he revealed indifferently, reaching for the carafe of wine. "May I top up your glass?" She nodded and he tipped the remaining wine into her goblet.

"Have you been in BC long?" She attempted again to get him back on the subject of himself.

"Tell me what Taylor's doing tonight. A movie with some school friends, did you say?" he broke in, making no effort to answer her question.

Joely put down her fork and pushed her plate away. "Why do you do that?" she objected with exasperation.

"Do what?" All of a sudden, those gorgeous eyes were dead serious.

"Change the subject whenever I try to talk about you."

His frown and the small restless movement of his head made it clear he disliked the direction of the conversation. "My life isn't terribly interesting. You'd be bored."

For a few seconds their gazes locked stubbornly, then Joely offered what she hoped was a winning smile. "Why don't you let me be the judge of that? Speak to me, please. How are we suppose to get to know each other if I'm the only one doing the talking?"

Cole clicked his tongue irritably, then returned her smile. "Okay. Let me see, where should I start?" He pretended to scratch his head and ponder the question. "I'm an only child. My father was a city-cop in Toronto until his retirement a number of years ago. I joined the RCMP instead, thinking it'd give me the chance to move around and see more of the country. I entered the Academy when I was twenty." He seemed about to add to this, then fell silent.

"Weren't you lonely," she probed hesitantly, "growing up without a mother?" In his face, she could read his reluctance to go back to that topic.

But then he surprised her. "Sometimes I felt as if she had

abandoned me, that she should've been there for me, because she was the one person in my childhood who loved me without condition."

"What about your father?" she persisted softly, afraid if she pushed him too hard he'd shut down again. "He must care a great deal for you. His only child."

A muscle twitched at the corner of one eye. He coughed, a ragged, self-conscious clearing of the throat. "I think I'm a disappointment to my old man. I've never quite measured up to his standards of what defines a man. You know all that macho stuff—stiff upper lip, never let them see you sweat, show no weakness. They're the credos he lives by. My father is a man in control—he always controls himself, and he completely controlled my mom and me. No weakness has ever been allowed in his world, only discipline and self-control. My childhood was very regimented. A certain code of behavior had been imposed on me, and it was rigidly adhered to."

The calmness in his voice didn't match the disturbing darkness brooding in his eyes. Joely regretted ever encouraging this conversation, but something lurking in his restraint struck an alarming chord in her.

"What did your dad do to make you listen?" she asked in a wavering voice.

"You're wondering if my father hit me? Well, he never did. He didn't even yell at me. He rarely appeared shaken or burst into an honest rage and sometimes that was scarier than if he'd lost his temper. But he never abused me." He quietly held her gaze for a long penetrating moment, then adroitly changed the subject. "I'm told the dessert here is spectacular. Have you saved room for something decadent?"

Joely's mouth opened, but she held back her words. There was no point. He'd obviously finished confiding.

"I'm going to pass, thanks anyway. I should get home before Taylor does."

"It's not that late yet, would you like a coffee?"

"I don't think so. Do you mind?"

"Whatever you want." He flagged down the waitress and requested the bill.

Cole eased his hand onto the small of Joely's back as they walked down the block to where they'd parked the Mustang, his touch causing little pinpricks of awareness to attack her lower spine. He opened the car door for her, then before she could get in, he tilted his face down toward hers. "Thank you for tonight," he whispered and kissed her lightly on the cheek.

Joely watched him walk around the car—a tall, handsome man, intelligent, strong and seductive. Dangerously close to tears, she touched her fingers to the spot his lips had just pressed against. How could anyone possibly think this incredible person didn't measure up as a man?

The somber drive home paled in comparison to the hilarious trip earlier in the evening. Joely stole surreptitious glances at Cole while he silently maneuvered the car through the late evening traffic. If his father taught him that showing emotion equated to weakness, no wonder he shied away from discussing himself. After losing his mother at a vulnerable age, he must've felt so alone with a cold, unemotional father more interested in control than in providing a nurturing atmosphere for his young son to grow up in.

But contrary to what his father may have told him, Cole Dennison was all man. Women would always be attracted to his potent male essence, and the attraction went much deeper than his raw sex appeal. His gentleness and sensitivity, when he allowed it to show through his hardened veneer, was simply irresistible.

"There aren't any lights on at your place. I guess Taylor isn't home yet," Cole commented without looking at Joely as he coasted to a stop in front of her building. His mouth barely moved when he spoke, and he kept both hands firmly clenched to the steering wheel.

Joely chewed uneasily on her lip and stared at his profile gazing doggedly off into the distance. She sensed his inner struggle, she could commiserate because she was struggling too. She should go directly inside, but she wasn't ready to say goodnight yet.

After a moment of debate, she yielded to the delicious temptation growing inside her and leaned across the stick shift to kiss him on the cheek. When he turned in surprise, she tenderly brushed his mouth with hers. She flicked the tip of her tongue across his lips before pulling away, and grinned as she leaned back. He tasted good, real good.

"I figured it was only fair to let you know, you've changed my mind. I like you now."

Cole caught his breath loudly. He undid his seatbelt and twisted sideways, reaching out a large hand to cup the side of her neck where her pulse throbbed madly.

"I'm trying real hard, you know." His voice took on a huskier, sensual note as he leaned even closer. "I can't stay away from you, if you do things like that. I want you too much."

Joely lifted her face to meet his. Their lips clung, their tongues touched and all sorts of crazy sensations leaped about inside her. Cole's hungry mouth moved restlessly, feathering kisses across her cheek, seeking the curve of her neck. Tiny shivers rippled over her skin in response to each exquisite nibble, and she tipped her head to one side, allowing him free access to her sensitive throat.

"Oh, baby, it's just not fair what you do to me." He pulled her tightly into his arms and kissed her over and over again, leaving her limp and at risk of losing all rational thought.

Regretfully she backed away from his embrace, her body buzzing and tingling from his sweet kisses. "Maybe you shouldn't kiss me so much, if we're supposed to be taking it slow," she teased, fanning a hand in front of her face.

In answer, his mouth came back down to bruise her lips in another ravenous kiss. When he finally released her mouth, he pressed her head tenderly against his broad chest. She could hear the reverberations of his heart hammering away in unison with her own.

He smiled into her hair. "I am way too old and too large to be making out in the front seat of the 'Stang."

Joely disentangled herself from his arms. "I agree. Besides I really do have to get inside before Taylor catches us out here necking like a couple of teenagers." She pressed her lips briefly to his and stepped quickly from the car, barely evading his greedy grasp.

She chuckled out loud at his moan of unadulterated, male frustration.

* * * *

Taylor was already up and on the phone when Joely got out of bed the next morning. She noticed he ended his call when he saw her coming down the hall.

"A little early for you to call your friends, isn't it? I thought you guys usually slept most of the morning away." Joely carried on into the kitchen to get the coffee going.

"Actually, I was talking to Dad." Taylor followed her into the kitchen and leaned against the counter.

"Oh, what's up?" She filled the reservoir with cold water as she spoke.

"Dad wants to come out here. He says he could fly out Friday after work and stay until Sunday evening." He stared steadily at her.

Without responding, she fitted a filter into the basket and measured coffee into it. She waited for the other shoe to drop because she knew he was building up to something.

"I told him he could stay here."

Joely wasn't sure she heard him correctly, she prayed she'd heard him wrong. "You said *what*?"

"He could stay here," he repeated clearly. "He can have my room, and I'll sleep on the couch."

Joely slammed the lid down on the coffee canister and shoved it forcefully against the wall. "No way, Taylor. There's absolutely no way." She started back to her bedroom. If she had to match wits with Taylor, she wanted to wash the sleep out of her eyes and get dressed first.

Taylor accompanied her down the hall, pleading with every step. "Why not? If he stays here, we can spend more time together, and it won't cost him so much money. C'mon, Mom! You never let him stay here. Why can't he?"

Joely turned at her bedroom door. "I'm going to wash up and put on some clothes. That'll give me a few minutes to calm down and then we'll discuss this rationally. But, Taylor, he will not be staying here."

When Joely reemerged from her room moments later, Taylor was nowhere in sight. She poured herself a coffee and called his

name twice without getting any answer. Then she noticed the door
to the patio gaping open. Sure enough, he was outside, sitting
cross-legged on the lawn, picking morosely at the grass.

She set her mug of coffee down on the patio table and sat on
the grass facing him. Drawing her legs up, she circled her arms
around them and rested her chin on her knees. "You ready to talk
to me, sport?"

Taylor tossed away a handful of grass and glanced up with a
scowl. Joely couldn't keep up with his mood swings from one day
to the next. Just last night, he'd sprawled belly-down on her bed to
tell her about his evening. She hadn't listened too closely, instead
she'd watched the expressions cross his face while he talked—his
blue eyes sparkling and full of zest, his wide, mobile mouth
stretched even broader in a happy grin. Times like those, she really
felt blessed to have him in her life. Now he looked as if he hated
her and she had no clue what to do with him.

"Why are you being so mean? Just because you don't like Dad
anymore, you can't stop me from seeing him. It's not fair." He
returned his attention to the ruthless defoliation of the lawn.

Joely pressed a hand to her forehead. She could tell this boy a
few things about fair. Such as, it wasn't fair for a full-sized man to
take out his frustrations on a small child. Nor was it fair for that
same man to then expect free access to that child, if he wasn't
willing to give up his drinking habit. Except, of course, she
wouldn't do that to Taylor. She didn't want him to hate his father
and she couldn't deprive him of what little time they spent
together.

"I can't explain why I don't want Brad staying here. I need you
to trust that I'm doing the right thing." She reached down and
stopped his hand from relentlessly plucking the lawn bare.

He jerked away from her touch. "I don't believe you. I think
you're being mean on purpose. You can't stop me from seeing my
dad—*you can't.*"

"Oh, sweetheart." Joely sighed and rallied her patience. "I'm
not trying to stop you from seeing him. If you want him to come
out and see you, then that's okay with me. Let me try and work
something out, and I'll let you know what I come up with. Okay?"

Taylor didn't answer, but he didn't pull away when she kissed his cheek before getting up.

The early morning chill had drained the heat from her coffee, so she poured it down the drain and got a fresh cup before phoning her brother.

"Hi, Harry, it's Joely. How's Carolyn?" She exchanged a moment or two of small talk with Harry before coming to the point of her call. "Brad wants to fly out here next weekend to see Taylor. So, I have a huge favor to ask of you."

"You want me to baby-sit Brad while he's with Taylor. No problem, Sis. Just tell me when and where."

Joely was forever grateful to Harry and her other brother, Rick, for willingly doing this necessary task for her so many times over the years.

"Actually, it's a bigger favor than that. Taylor told his dad he could stay here. Naturally, he's furious with me now because I said no. I'm hoping you and Carolyn will take him for the weekend, and Brad can stay at that motel a couple of blocks from your place. I know I'm putting you on the spot and I'll understand if you say you can't do it."

"I don't see a problem with that. We love having Taylor. You could probably use a weekend off too, after everything the two of you have been through lately."

Joely didn't realize she was holding her breath, until an explosive sigh of relief escaped her. "Thanks, Harry. Thanks so very much. I'll make it up to you somehow. I'll phone back in a day or two after Brad and I work out the details. Give my love to Carolyn."

Taylor came in as she hung up. "You called Dad to tell him he couldn't come?" he asked, his tone accusatory.

"No, Taylor. I never once told you your dad couldn't come out. I said he couldn't stay here. And you can lose the longsuffering expression. Uncle Harry agreed to have you spend the weekend with them and Brad can stay at the motel around the corner from their place. If the weather's nice, maybe you guys could do some golfing on Saturday."

Taylor loved staying with his doting aunt and uncle, and the plans pleased him, she could tell, even if he wouldn't give her the satisfaction of admitting it. "I guess I better phone Dad and tell him about the change."

"No, I'll phone him later. I have a few things to discuss with him."

Like why he kept trying to go against the court order, for instance. The last time she talked to him, he'd been too drunk to make any sense. This time, she'd make sure she got through to him. His blatant flaunting of the restrictions placed upon him and the encouragement he gave Taylor to do the same were tearing her and her son apart, and it needed to stop.

Chapter Eight

"Brad, this is Joely. We have to talk," she announced to her ex-husband without any preliminary pleasantries.

"Damn straight we do," Brad agreed. He sounded sober and worried. "What in blazes is going on down there? Why are you letting Taylor run wild? And who the hell is this Cole somebody-or-other Taylor can't shut up about?"

"Is that what's really bugging you? That Taylor has found someone he can actually look up to, someone with redeeming qualities he might want to emulate?" Joely asked pointedly. When his only response was an impatient sigh, she went on. "I hear you're coming out next weekend and Taylor's offered to let you stay here. You know that's not going to happen, don't you?"

"Look, my kid phones me and says he's met some guy at the police detachment while he's being busted for stealing a car, and then he throws in something about drugs as well, and you wonder why I want to go down there to check it out for myself? I'd appreciate you communicating with me once in a while about Taylor, especially if he's getting in trouble with the law."

"You lost all rights to Taylor years ago when you decided it'd be more fun to slap him around than to play with him." Instantly regretting her harsh words, Joely tried for a more reasonable tact. "I'm sorry, forget I said that. If I had known Taylor mentioned anything to you, I would've explained the entire situation. Taylor's doing just fine and he didn't break any laws. He started chumming with a bad group of boys, but that's over and he's learned a valuable lesson from it. As for Cole Dennison, he's an RCMP corporal, and he's been kind enough to take an interest in Taylor's welfare."

"He's a cop, big deal, that don't mean anything. Have you even met the guy?"

The image of Cole's handsome face, his dark eyes heated with desire as he kissed her to distraction flashed through her mind. Oh yeah, she'd met him all right. "No need to concern yourself in that regard. Corporal Dennison is an upstanding person. He's the head of the juvenile division here in North Van. I'm completely comfortable with Taylor spending time with him."

"I still want to come out."

"I don't have a problem with that. I do have a problem with the way you're trying to get around the court order forbidding you to be alone with Taylor. As long as he's a minor in my care, that won't happen."

"Taylor *wants* to be with me and I'd never hurt him. What happened before was in a different lifetime, when I was in a bad place. I've changed a lot since then. And you'd know that if you ever spent any time around me."

Joely closed her eyes and gripped the receiver tighter. She wanted so badly to believe him. "You're still drinking. Nothing's changed there. Don't you think it would hurt Taylor to see his dad stinking drunk and belligerent?"

"I'm thinking about joining AA and I haven't been in a fight for years." His voice had turned sulky, reminding Joely of Taylor when she called him on something he didn't want to admit to. "I have a good job now, and I want to hang on to it. And I want to spend time with my son without one of your gooney brothers breathing down my neck."

"We can have this conversation again after you've actually stopped drinking, and maybe then I'll be more impressed. And you should be thankful my brothers are willing to supervise your visits or you wouldn't have any access to Taylor. I've arranged for him to spend next weekend with Harry and Carolyn. If you want, I'll make reservations for you at the motel near their place, where you stayed last time."

"Fine," he replied curtly. "I shoulda known you wouldn't let me stay with you. When did you turn into such a cold fish?"

Tears stung her eyes and she impatiently blinked them away. What he thought was of no importance to her. "I just have a long memory, and I'll never forget the day I found out what you'd been doing to Taylor." She took satisfaction in slamming the receiver down hard.

The phone rang almost instantly and she jumped. If it was

Brad calling back, she had a few more choice words for him.

"Hello," she barked into the phone.

"Did I get you at a bad time?"

"Cole?" Joely's spirits instantly lifted. "Oh no, not at all. Good morning."

"I wanted to check to see if you got any more sleep last night than I did. For some reason, I felt restless."

Joely giggled, her conversation with Brad put firmly behind her. "Maybe you needed a cold shower."

"I'd like to see you again next weekend." His voice grew husky with meaning.

Joely picked up on his want, it matched the want inside of her. "Taylor's dad is coming out for the weekend."

"Your ex-husband is spending the weekend at your place?"

The flicker of possessiveness Joely thought she caught in Cole's tone unexpectedly pleased her. "No, Harry's taking Taylor for the weekend, and Brad will visit with him there."

"Who's Harry?"

"My oldest brother. He and his wife, Carolyn, live in Richmond."

"Right, I remember you telling me about them now. You lived with them when you first moved out here, while you went to school for your social worker's degree."

"That's them. They aren't able to have children, so they enjoy spending time with Taylor. It's lucky for me they're willing to help out whenever Brad visits."

"If Taylor is gone for the weekend, then you'll be free Saturday night, and I won't even have to get you home early." There was a pause, then a quick intake of breath. "I have an idea. We could have dinner here, at my place. I'll cook. And I have a hot tub out on the deck. What do you say to drinking a glass of wine, under the stars, while soaking in the hot tub?"

Joely thought it sounded like the perfect setting for a seduction and this made her nervous. She knew going slowly would be impossible for them. Their chemistry was too strong to resist. She took her time replying and she could hear his steady breathing over the phone line while he waited her out. For some reason she found it reassuring that he didn't try to press her into agreeing and she wanted to be up front with him.

"Are you looking for more than dinner and a hot tub? Are you counting on us spending the night together?"

The silence continued for a moment, then he volleyed in return, "Only if it's what you want."

Not the answer she expected. He'd put the decision squarely in her hands. "I'm not real comfortable with this. I don't fall into physical relationships with just anyone."

"I'm glad to hear that. Promiscuity isn't a flattering trait nowadays. Look, Joely, let's not worry about what might happen and just let whatever happens happen. I'm not planning to force myself on you."

He sounded so calm and reasonable that Joely found herself relenting. She wasn't fooling herself anyway. She wanted to spend time with this man. "Okay, it's a date. There's just one other thing. I'm not sure how to put this, but I'd rather you not mention to Taylor that we're seeing each other socially."

"Any particular reason?"

Joely gnawed on her lower lip. She couldn't very well say she wanted to see how serious things got between them first, so Taylor wouldn't get his hopes up. That sounded too pushy, too expectant.

"I just want to keep it private for now. I don't want Taylor jumping to any wrong conclusions. Okay?" She waited with bated breath, hoping he'd understand and accept her request.

* * * *

Cole didn't get why Joely wanted him to keep quiet about their relationship, maybe it embarrassed her that the boy might think they were sleeping together. Whatever the reason, he readily agreed not to say anything to Taylor. He would've agreed to nearly anything in order to see her again. She had completely blindsided him with the kiss she gave him last night. He couldn't remember ever being kissed so tenderly. It was an experience he intended to repeat and explore further at the first opportunity.

Joely was a sweet and caring person, and she made him want things he knew he shouldn't want. And what he wanted, more than anything, was to crawl into the comfort of her arms and lose himself with her, for just a little while. She had the ability to reach through all the darkness inside him and shine in a little light.

He liked being around her and wanted to explore the physical side of their friendship. He got the impression she felt the same. So why not? If Joely was willing, they could become friends and enjoy themselves together without allowing it to go beyond that. What did the young people call it—friends with benefits?

After hanging up, he thought about Joely's ex-husband coming out for a visit and wondered why he'd be seeing Taylor at her brother's place instead of hers. They mustn't be on good terms, he decided and found himself absurdly relieved. Something sharp and biting twisted in his gut at the notion of Joely with another man. *Son of a bitch!* he thought in disbelief—he was jealous. This was a new reaction for him and as much as he didn't like it, he couldn't shake the feeling.

* * * *

Saturday evening found Joely sitting in her car in Cole's driveway, staring through the windshield at his house, both nervous and excited about the evening ahead. It surprised her to discover Cole lived in a well kept, though modest house in a quiet family area of Lynn Valley. As much as Joely loved her condo, she dreamed of one day living in a neighborhood such as this, in a house with a backyard large enough for a garden and a swing set, with lots of room for the children she still hoped to have to run and play.

Cole appeared suddenly in the driveway, distracting her from her daydream. The sight of his rugged, masculine good looks tore at her senses and sent her pulse skittering out of control. She grabbed the bag with her swimsuit off the front seat and stepped out of the car.

"I was just taking a moment to admire your house. It's beautifully landscaped, and I love the neighborhood."

"I can't take credit for the yard. It looked like this when I moved in, and I haven't been here long enough to kill anything yet," he said, anchoring his arm around her waist and directing her to the side of the house. "If you're into Mother Nature, you gotta see the backyard. It's something else and maybe you can give me some pointers. I have zero experience when it comes to gardening."

Cole opened the gate for her and Joely paused to gaze in amazement. It looked like a private little park, beautiful with spring flowers. Everywhere she looked, she found another delight for the eye—flowers, shrubs, trees, and in the far corner, an enchanting water fountain tinkled.

A large ornamental plum tree was in full glorious bloom. Three rhodos, enormous and ancient, were covered in brilliant magenta blossoms. The numerous buds on the hydrangea shrub promised to deliver a spectacular showing in the days to come. Bamboo grew densely on one side of the yard, providing privacy from the neighboring yard. Clematis vines climbed the six-foot fence on the other side. All along the length of the sundeck, tulips, daffodils, lily of the valley and hyacinth put on a heady display of color and scent.

Joely clasped her hands together under her chin and turned to Cole. "I'd absolutely die for a yard like this. You don't know how lucky you are."

Cole's grin showed his mystification. He obviously didn't appreciate the attraction. "Feel free to come over whenever you want. I've been cooped up in an apartment ever since...well, for a long time, and I find it's a great stress-buster to come out here and putter around the yard, but I'm in way over my head. I could use any help you're willing to give me."

A buzzer started up a monotonous ringing inside the house. "That means the lasagna is ready to come out of the oven. After you."

Cole motioned for Joely to enter the house through the patio doors. They stepped directly into a bright, spacious and surprisingly barren kitchen.

Cole turned off the timer, then used oven mitts to remove the lasagna pan from the oven. "This has to sit for a bit. I hope you don't mind, I opted for a simple meal, just Caesar salad and French bread to go with the vegetable lasagna."

"It smells delicious."

"So do you," Cole told her as he moved in closer to plant a

casual kiss on her brow. "Why don't you grab yourself a chair, angel, and get comfortable. Soon as I open a bottle of wine, we'll be ready."

Joely's heart did a funny little somersault at the easy endearment. She smiled in appreciation as she watched the play of muscles across his broad back while he eased the cork out of the wine bottle.

"Is there anything I can do to help?"

"Nope. The table's set, food's ready. I apologize for the fact we're eating in the kitchen. I'm still living out of boxes and most of those boxes are sitting in the middle of the dining room."

"I don't mind. Taylor and I usually eat in the kitchen."

The meal Cole prepared tasted as delicious as it smelled, and Joely teasingly speculated out loud whether he had actually cooked it himself, or if he had ordered takeout. Rising to her challenge, Cole offered to share his recipe. They chatted easily throughout the meal on a wide range of topics, and eventually they got back to Cole's lack of expertise in the garden.

"Where did you live before you bought this place?"

"An apartment in Burnaby," he replied without much enthusiasm. "Tell me why you and Taylor have different last names."

"My, aren't you the crafty one. You just handily deflected the subject off yourself again," she said, unsurprised at his maneuver.

He smiled, showing lots of teeth. "Yeah well, not so handily. You weren't supposed to notice. You're just much more interesting to talk about than my old apartment. I really am curious why you have different names."

This irritated her, but amused her too. She found him hard to resist when he looked at her like that. "Okay, I'm willing to abandon the topic—for now."

She drank some wine, taking refuge behind the glass while she decided how much to tell him. She didn't see any reason not to be open about her past. Maybe knowing what she and Taylor had been through would help Cole understand why she tended to be overprotective of her son.

"When I left my marriage, I only wanted to keep Taylor. I wanted nothing from Brad, especially not his name."

"Was it a difficult divorce?"

"What divorce isn't? My marriage was a mistake from day one. I married too young and divorced too late. Brad liked to party, and he couldn't see why he should change his ways just because we had a baby. We fought all the time, over his drinking, and the money he spent, and the way he couldn't hold down a job. Every day found a fresh reason to argue.

"One day after yet another fight, I asked him whether he would've married me if I hadn't been pregnant, and he admitted he probably wouldn't have. Young as I was, I knew having a baby wasn't a good enough reason for two people to get married. But he was my husband, and I wanted to make the marriage work. That is, until I found out he was taking his frustrations out on Taylor."

Cole jerked forward in his chair as though someone had touched him with a live wire. "He hurt Taylor?" His voice was shot through with angry disbelief.

"I didn't know it for some time, but yes, he did. I was holding down two jobs, trying to make ends meet, and Brad took care of the baby most of the time. Taylor was an active child, Brad said he fell a lot and ran into things. Silly me, I believed him. One day, when Taylor was four, Brad phoned me at work. I could tell right away he was drunk. He told me Taylor fell off the couch and wouldn't stop crying.

"I rushed home in a panic to find Taylor lying on the floor by the couch. He usually flew happily into my arms when he saw me, that day he wouldn't even get up. I'll never forget how his tiny shoulder jutted out at an unnatural angle. The skin around it was all swollen and discolored." She had to stop talking and compose herself. Her throat hurt and her eyes burned with tears.

Cole reached over and squeezed her hand tightly. "What happened?"

"I carefully carried him out to my car and took him to the hospital emergency. The doctor took one look at my poor baby and told me he had a dislocated shoulder. He also let me know he didn't get it from falling off the couch. He said quite bluntly someone had jerked his little arm right out of its socket. He looked me in the eye and I read the accusation there. He thought I had hurt my own child!

"Suddenly everything fell into place and I knew the awful truth. Taylor rarely hurt himself when I was home, usually while he was alone with Brad. It made me ill to realize Brad was mistreating him. After I left the hospital, I brought Taylor over to my mom's place. Then I hurried home to confront Brad. Of course, he denied doing anything wrong. I was so furious, I wouldn't let it go. I kept yelling at him, calling him names, trying to get him to admit what he did, and finally he hauled off and slapped me across the face to shut me up."

Cole sucked in his breath noisily and his fists clenched tightly on the tabletop in front of him, but he didn't interrupt her. The careful, compassionate attention he paid to every word she spoke bolstered her spirits and enabled her to continue, even though she hated reliving that night.

"Brad had never hit me before, never even came close. I think the guilt of being found out, combined with the fact he was really hammered, pushed him over the edge. Anyway, I packed up all Taylor's things and my clothes, and moved in with my mom. I got a restraining order placed against Brad forbidding him from seeing either of us. Once he'd sobered up, he felt sick with remorse, but even though he begged me, I refused to take him back.

"I eventually agreed he could have short visits with Taylor if someone else was with him at all times. Not me. I couldn't stand to be in the same room as him. I moved out here after the divorce finalized, went back to school, got my degree and tried to build a better life for myself and my son."

"And you're doing a commendable job." Cole's face relaxed into an encouraging smile, then turned reflective. "It's surprising Taylor would want to continue a relationship with his dad. After going through all that, you'd think he'd be scared of him."

"Taylor can't remember anything. Either he was too young or he's blocked it out. I haven't told him what happened, and I don't want him to know. He loves Brad, and Brad loves him too. I grew up without a dad, and it's a hole I've never been able to fill. I don't want that for my son. I can't take away the small amount of time they have together. Wow." She smiled ruefully. "Sorry for dumping on you."

Cole got up from his seat and stepped around the table to

hunker down in front of her. He took her hands in his big, strong hands and pressed them to his lips. His dark eyes brimmed with understanding and kindness.

"I hate that you and Taylor went through such a terrible ordeal, but I'm glad you shared it with me. If I have any say, no one will ever hurt you again, neither of you."

Joely looked at his broad-shouldered frame, his determined jaw, the strength in his gaze, and she knew he spoke the truth. He'd protect her from any danger, except maybe the danger of falling in love with him too fast.

After they finished cleaning up the dinner dishes, which Joely had to insist on helping with, Cole brought their wine glasses into the living room. Joely found this room to be even more spartan than the kitchen. Not a single picture hung on the walls and while the furniture was of excellent quality, there were no personal items—no mementos, no framed photos—anywhere to be seen.

"How long did you say you've lived here?" she wondered out loud, and Cole laughed as he pulled open the adjoining French doors. The room he revealed was obviously the dining room and it was stacked high with boxes.

"I can't seem to get at these boxes. The majority of them were in storage for a long time, and I don't even know for sure what's in them. My last apartment was tiny and I didn't have room for everything, so I stored some stuff at a friend's place. Now, I dig through them to find what I need and ignore the rest."

Joely took another sip of wine, then set the glass down on the coffee table. "Tell me, did you live out of boxes at your apartment, too?"

"No, I actually didn't. Say, are you ready for a soak in the hot tub?" Cole scratched the back of his head and frowned. "Damn, I had planned to set candles out on the table during dinner and then move them outside while we went in the hot tub. Shows how rusty I am at entertaining because I completely forgot. Oh well, we can skip them."

Joely envisioned the romantic ambiance of flickering candlelight, steamy hot water, and crisp cold wine. Not to mention Cole's naked chest. She barely controlled a shiver. "Candles would be nice. I'll set them up outside, if you want."

"Okay, they're in one of those boxes." He pointed at a group of boxes stacked separately from the others. "Those came from the apartment. Take a look and see if you can find them, while I get the hot tub ready."

Joely wandered over to the stack of boxes and randomly selected one. She picked at a corner of the packing tape. It appeared to have been on there for a long time and it peeled easily. It surprised her to see children's belongings inside—books, a doll, hand-drawn pictures, some clay bowls obviously molded by the inexperienced hands of a young child. Taylor had made her similar treasures over the years. She smiled at the precious items, puzzled why Cole would have such articles in his house. There obviously weren't any candles in the box and as she went to close the lid, a framed photo caught her eye. She drew the picture from the box to examine it more closely.

In her suddenly trembling hands, she held a family photo—a man, a woman, and a young girl. The woman was beautiful in a cold, pale sort of way, with champagne blond hair and chill-blue eyes. Her expression was distant and rather haughty. The little girl was too darling for words. A beauty in the making, with huge chocolate brown eyes, a mischievous grin, and a long cascade of dark curls.

The man was Cole—younger and somewhat more innocent looking—but definitely Cole.

Chapter Nine

Joely distinctly remembered Cole telling her at the detachment, the first time Taylor was taken in, that he didn't have a child. Yet, here he was posing in a picture with a woman and a little girl who had to be his wife and daughter. There was no mistaking the resemblance between Cole and the child. Their eyes, their smile, their coloring, they were all the same.

Thinking back now, Joely remembered how Cole's mannerism changed when he said, "If I had a child". He became abrupt and there seemed to be a rage burning in his eyes. Joely thought at the time he was angry with her and had been trying not to show it. She'd been too busy being angry with him to give his demeanor much consideration. Now, she wondered why Cole had lied to her and what had caused him to be so upset.

"Any luck finding the candles?" Cole startled her as he came up from behind, setting his hands on her shoulders. Jumping nervously, Joely whirled to face him. He saw with a glance what she was holding and immediately snatched the picture away from her.

"That picture—you're married?" Somehow, she managed not to sound completely desperate and bewildered. She'd often wondered why Cole hadn't married. It didn't seem plausible that such a dynamically attractive man hadn't been snatched up before now. Yet, he'd never mentioned his marriage, not once in any of their conversations.

"Was. A long time ago," he confirmed shortly, his words clipped, his impatience obvious.

"You have a daughter?" She reined in her consternation because all at once she could see there was a genuine problem here. Beneath the surface of Cole's controlled expression lay a pain so intense he was unable to mask it, and her heart contracted with compassion at the poignant and powerful hurt lurking in the guarded darkness of his eyes.

"I forgot this was in here," he said instead of answering her question.

He made a gesture to chuck the picture carelessly back into the box. At the last moment, he gently placed it face down and closed the lid without looking at the contents inside. He watched her solemnly for a moment, then dropped his gaze to the floor and kept it there, not saying anything to explain his actions.

Finding the awkward silence more unbearable with each passing moment, Joely touched Cole lightly on the shoulder and smiled brightly when he looked up, hoping the smile didn't look as counterfeit as it felt.

"I should've guessed you'd been married. How long since the divorce?" She realized she'd made a mistake the moment the question was out. Even if she couldn't sense his withdrawal, which she could, the look on his face told her quite plainly she'd crossed some invisible line.

Cole shrugged finally, and his sensual mouth slanted back at her in a suggestion of a smile, but there was no humor reflected in his eyes. "It's a long story."

In other words, don't ask. It disappointed her, but his sidestepping the question hardly came as a surprise.

Cole eased in closer to her and reached out to circle her waist, drawing her to him. He rested his forehead against hers, his muscular frame taut as a coiled spring. Even now, with her brain a maelstrom of bewilderment, his touch sent a slow shiver of arousal through her. For several moments, they stood silently holding one another, as the tension slowly seeped from Cole's body.

He caught a lock of her hair, watching it slide through his fingers. "Let's make tonight about us, okay?" he whispered, his lips inches away from hers. "No one else, just you and me."

He kissed her, his mouth demanding possession, and any thought of resistance went up in flames. Her hands moved across his chest and over his shoulders. Her fingers threaded through his hair, and she stroked his neck, loving the feel of his hard body pressed against hers.

"You can use my room to change into your suit," he said as he slowly pulled away. "It's the last room on the left, down the hall. I'll find the candles."

* * * *

Cole paused as he stepped out onto the deck, a couple of thick towels in his hand. Candles glowed softly in the darkness, creating the perfect ambience. Joely, looking like a goddess, lounged back in the hot tub, bubbles from the low jets obscuring her best parts. She sat forward when she noticed him standing there. His gaze trailed over her body, taking in the way the candlelight reflected off her wet skin and the slow, pulsing heat in his groin burned with real fire. He set the towels near the edge of the tub and lowered himself onto the seat next to her. Leaning toward her, he kissed the moisture off her shoulder.

"Are you okay?" He wanted to know if he'd ruined everything with his stupid reaction to the photo of Debra and Sarah. It had shocked him to see it again, after all these years, and he had reacted badly. The last thing he meant to do was be abrupt with Joely, but he couldn't explain to her why he behaved as he did. No way was he going down that particular road tonight. All he could do now was hope she understood.

Joely tilted her head in his direction. She pressed close, kissing him on the mouth. "I'm fine. Everything's fine." She kissed him again, touching his lower lip with her tongue. The gentle kiss quickly grew hard and hungry.

Not releasing Joely's mouth from his, Cole effortlessly lifted her onto his lap, so her knees straddled his hips. His hands began a slow, delectable journey of discovery down her back and over her hips. She moved against him and the already unbearable weight in his groin became a persistent ache. He eased her off his lap and slid into the center of the hot tub, lowering himself onto his knees in the water.

"I haven't done this for awhile and if we're not careful, I might embarrass myself," he admitted. "You're quite the temptation."

She smiled at him, slow and sweet. "So are you."

Her grin turned wicked as she joined him, kneeling in the water, her body up against his in the confined space. Her lips found his, warm, soft, probing, and unbearably sensual. She ran her fingers lightly through the patch of hair on his chest, then moved over to his pecs, searching out and finding his flat nipples, rubbing and teasing them until they hardened in response to her touch. He groaned as her hand stroked his belly. She slowly inched her hand lower, ever lower, torturing him with her intent. Before she could continue with her quest, he pulled away.

"If we plan to go further, we should move this inside," he whispered against her lips. "It's up to you, Joely. Do you want to continue?"

Please, oh, please, please, please.

Sexual trysts had been few and far between since Joely's marriage ended. Being intimate wasn't something she took lightly, and she was usually so cautious and self-conscious that it ended up being difficult to derive much pleasure from the experience. None of that was an issue tonight. Her body was achingly ready for what came next.

She pressed her lips against his and whispered back, "I want to make love with you."

Cole helped her out of the water and then he enveloped her in a towel, holding her tightly against him. Once inside his bedroom, he gently and painstakingly dried her body with the towel, peeling the wet suit away as he worked his way lower.

Sensation buffeted Joely at every turn, and she could barely stand on her quivering legs, legs that suddenly had no more strength than licorice sticks. Cole knelt before her as he inched the swimming suit down her hips. She found herself helpless against the passion building inside her, and she sagged against him, no longer able to support herself. Rising swiftly, Cole lifted her onto the bed and with one impatient movement, stripped himself of his wet shorts before joining her.

Their bodies moved restlessly, searching for that exquisite pleasure of skin against bare skin. Hands roamed, pausing only long enough to excite, before moving on to the next delight. Lips met and clung, tongues touched in wanton exploration. The sensation felt like molten honey and its warmth spread throughout Joely's insides. Their movements quickened, together in total harmony, in a primal rhythm as old as love, yet thrilling and fresh, special and new.

* * * *

Cole rolled over onto his back, pulling Joely along with him. She contentedly nestled her head on his shoulder, enjoying the closeness and warmth of his naked male body. Her body tingled with leftover pleasure, tired and satisfied at last.

His hand drew absentminded circles on her bare back. "I don't want to move, baby, but I have to get up for a moment."

He called from the washroom seconds later, saying he was grabbing a shower, if she cared to join him. Not wanting to lose the warm, contented glow inside her, Joely stayed put, her body so relaxed, she wanted to stretch like a cat with the sheer pleasure of being inside her own skin.

But of course that wonderful languid feeling had no staying power and the afterglow ebbed away as reality spitefully reasserted itself. For several hours she'd allowed herself to be completely absorbed in the here-and-now, forgetting about the other world outside of herself and Cole. But another world did exist and it contained her son, who was in the company of her ex-husband—a difficult man who, at the moment, was upset with both her and Taylor.

Sounds of the shower echoed from the adjoining bathroom as she scooted off the bed and reached for the bag containing her cell phone. Her mouth went dry with nervous tension when she saw she'd missed a call from her brother's place.

What if something had gone wrong? What if Brad and Taylor had exchanged heated words? What if Taylor had tried to reach her and couldn't? She'd never forgive herself if anything bad had happened to him and she was unavailable to her son when he needed her most. She couldn't return the call fast enough.

"Mom?" It was Taylor's voice on the other end. "Where are you? I tried calling home first and there was no answer, then you didn't pick up your cell either. I was getting worried."

"Hi, sweetie-pie." Joely forced herself to sound natural. She couldn't outright lie to Taylor, she'd never done that before and didn't intend to start now, so she borrowed one of Cole's deflecting tactics. "Is everything okay there? What were you calling about?"

Taylor's easy laughter came over the line, dispelling most of her tension. "Man, I can't believe what a dope I am. I have to call Cole, and like, tell him I don't need a ride to basketball tomorrow but I forgot his card at home and he's not listed with 411."

"I'll let Cole know about tomorrow. Don't tell me you're having Uncle Harry drive all the way out here just to play pickup basketball for an hour?"

"Um, well, he said he wanted to. Dad's coming, too. Do you think maybe they could play with us?"

"I don't know the rules, Taylor. You can check with Cole tomorrow." Joely heard the shower turn off. "I have to go, honey. You remember your manners and have fun tomorrow, okay?"

"I will. Goodnight, Mom. I love you."

"I love you too. See you tomorrow night." Joely turned off the phone and reached for her clothes folded neatly on a chair. The missed call shook her up a great deal, telling her she needed to get home. Now.

A pair of well-muscled arms slid around her waist from behind, lifting her and drawing her back against the hard, warm length of Cole's body, still damp from his quick shower.

"Who were you professing your love to?" he quipped, nuzzling her neck.

With nothing but a towel slung about his hips, he was too appealingly naked, and Joely quickly twisted away before she lost her resolve. "I have to get dressed and go home."

Cole caught her arm before she could step away. "No, you don't. Come here and tell me what's wrong." His voice rose in concern. "Did something happen between Taylor and his father?"

Joely self-consciously started pulling her clothes on. "No, but that was Taylor on the phone. I'd missed his earlier call and he wanted to know where I was."

Cole's eyebrows shot up and his mouth twitched. "Oops. Busted, eh?"

"It's not funny. I told you Taylor doesn't know about us and this isn't how I want him to find out. Thankfully, everything's all right and he just wanted me to let you know he doesn't need a ride to basketball tomorrow morning."

Cole pulled her down onto the bed beside him. "Then why are

you rushing off?" His fingers trailed down the side of her neck, before slipping beneath the hair at her nape. "Lose the clothes and come back to bed. Stay with me tonight." He leaned against her and she tried getting up, only to be pulled back to his side, this time much closer. "Joely? Did I do something wrong? Give me another chance, and I promise I'll do better." A smile sounded in his tone, as well as some confusion.

Joely couldn't help laughing. She took up his hand and held it to her face, then turned the palm over and kissed it. She kissed each fingertip before releasing his hand. "You were wonderful, marvelous even. You made me feel like I've never felt before. I just can't stay overnight. What if Taylor tried to reach me and I wasn't home?"

"He'd call your cell phone again. You're allowed to have a life."

"It doesn't feel right, I'm sorry." She made an appeal for his understanding, but she could tell he didn't accept her reasoning. His annoyance, though well concealed, didn't escape her and she struggled to find a more acceptable excuse. "Besides, you have to get up early in the morning. Harry and Brad will both be there with Taylor." As she said the words, she realized that meant Cole would meet Brad. "Will you be okay with that? Meeting Brad, I mean, after what I told you tonight?"

"I'd never embarrass Taylor by telling his dad what a loser I think he is. Heaven help the man, though, if he ever raises a hand to either of you again."

He pulled her back into his arms, and she pressed her cheek against his chest, savoring the feel of him, the clean smell of him. She closed her eyes, knowing she didn't ever want to leave the warm shelter of his arms again.

Finally, she forced herself back away. "I have to go."

When she picked up her sodden swimming suit from the floor and stuffed it into her bag, Cole rose from the bed and slid his robe on. "I'll walk you out."

He held her to him at the front door, taking her mouth in one final kiss, so sweet and so long and lingering, when it ended she had to cling to him for support. After her head stopped swimming, she grinned up at him. "Thank you for a lovely dinner. I especially liked the dessert."

"Dessert? I didn't make—oh, dessert..." His sigh was shaky, and he ran a hand through his tousled hair. "If you don't leave right now, I'm not letting you go."

* * * *

Taylor was in a talkative state of excitement when he arrived home Sunday evening. He described every moment of his weekend right down to the tiniest details. He had gone golfing with Harry and Brad on Saturday, and Joely had to listen patiently to his reenactment of each swing and every putt.

His enthusiasm faltered when he started to recount the events of the day. "Dad didn't come with us to basketball this morning. He phoned to say he wasn't up for it. I called him when we got back to Uncle Harry's, but he sounded funny and he said he wanted to take a nap before we met for lunch. But he missed lunch and by the time he got to Uncle Harry's, we only had about an hour together before he had to leave for the airport. Do you think he was mad at me because I went to basketball, instead of doing something with him?"

Joely knew exactly what happened. Brad couldn't face the challenge of meeting Cole, so he begged off going to basketball, then he needed several drinks to bolster his flagging confidence. By the time Taylor called him, he was drunk and had to sleep it off. Joely was thankful Brad had the sense not to show up at Harry's while under the influence, but that didn't stop her from being furious with him for wasting his visit with Taylor.

"Maybe your dad wasn't feeling well. I'm sure he wanted to be with you. And there's no way he'd be angry with you."

Taylor nodded his head, apparently accepting her word as fact. "I wish he could've met Cole. It was so rad this morning, playing ball. Uncle Harry got to play with us and he'd get all red in the face after he ran for a while. Cole can play forever and barely even sweat."

"The comparison is hardly fair, sweetie. As a police officer, Cole has to stay in shape, while Uncle Harry spends most of his day sitting behind a desk. I hope you didn't give your uncle a hard time."

Taylor laughed with the pleasure of it, his blue eyes sparkling mischievously. "Of course I did. Uncle Harry told me afterward he thinks Cole's a real cool guy. I do, too. What about you, Mom, do you like Cole?"

Joely wouldn't get a better opportunity than this. "Come and sit beside me, Taylor." She patted the couch and when he sat down she took his hand in hers, nervously twining her fingers through his. She took a deep breath and moistened paper-dry lips. "Last night, when I talked to you on the phone—I was at Cole's house. That's why you couldn't reach me at home. I apologize if I misled you."

Taylor's head swung toward her, a genuinely dumbfounded look on his face. "What were you doing there?"

"We're seeing each other, uh, socially. Last night, Cole cooked dinner for me at his place."

"You and *Cole*? You're dating *Cole*?"

The animosity in his gaze surprised her. "Why would it bother you? You just said you liked him."

Taylor pulled his hand away from hers. "Cole is *my* friend, not yours. I don't want you having anything to do with him. Find someone else to go out with."

Joely didn't even try to contain her anger. "Why are you reacting this way? I thought you'd be happy for me. It's been a long time since I've wanted to spend time with a man."

Taylor swung off the couch and paced around. "Because— because one day you'll decide you don't like Cole anymore. Just like you did with Dad. Then you won't let me see him either. You can't do that to me again."

Joely exhaled tremulously and squeezed her eyes shut. A strong, hurtful moment of guilt jabbed her—like a quick, deep stab wound. Her anger dissolved immediately, only the pain and the guilt remained.

"That won't happen. What you have with Cole is between the two of you. It has nothing to do with Cole and me. Try to understand that."

"You're wrong," he concluded flatly and left the room without another word.

Guilt made Joely confess to Taylor that she had been at Cole's, and now guilt made her wish she could take back that confession. It never occurred to her Taylor would feel threatened by her involvement with Cole. Did growing up without his dad make Taylor so insecure he thought no relationship was permanent?

And what if he was right? What exactly was going on between her and Cole? Did she just risk her son's peace of mind for a flash-in-the-pan night of hot passion? Joely wasn't at all sure what last night really meant. No commitment had been made, no promises. Had it merely been an act of gratifying sexual urges? Or was it more than that? She found herself reluctant to examine it too deeply, worried it wouldn't hold up to what she wanted it to be.

The phone rang and Joely eagerly snatched it up, relieved to have her troubled thoughts interrupted. When she heard Cole's low voice in her ear, something tight and almost unbearable inside of her relaxed.

"How are you doing? I wanted to call earlier, but this is the first spare moment I've had all day."

Joely didn't know how to play games or act coy. She had to speak her mind. "I thought maybe you were mad at me."

"A little disappointed, yes. Angry, never. My bed felt so cold and empty last night, after you left. And the smell of your perfume on my sheets just about drove me crazy. I wanted to wake up with you in my arms this morning. Or maybe we wouldn't have slept at all, maybe we would've made love over and over and over all night long."

His husky tone and intimate words gave Joely shivers. "Ohh, you better stop talking like that, I feel bad enough right now. I don't need you rubbing in exactly what I've missed."

"What has you feeling bad?"

"I just had an unsettling conversation with Taylor. I told him I've been spending time with you. He likes you so much, I thought he'd be happy. Instead, he tried to insist I couldn't see you anymore. He thinks I won't allow him to continue spending time with you if things don't work out between us."

"You're not taking his advice, are you?"

"Of course not. Please don't hold it against him, Cole. I can't really blame him for feeling the way he does after what happened between his dad and me."

"He should be old enough to understand his friendship with me and my relationship with you are completely separate from each other. Do you want me to speak with him?"

Joely debated for just a second. She didn't want Taylor to feel embarrassed around Cole, nor did she want Cole to have to deal with Taylor's obvious resentment toward her. She'd have to work this out with her son by herself.

"Don't say anything unless he brings it up. I'm sure he'll come around on his own. For now, let's not push it."

"However you want it, but try not to worry. I'll call you after work tomorrow." Cole's voice dropped to an intimate pitch. "Have a dream or two about me tonight, the good kind, okay?"

That shouldn't be much of a problem. Dreaming about him was her new favorite pastime. She even did it while awake.

* * * *

Joely and Cole were sprawled out on his bed one lazy afternoon near the end of May, recovering from yet another ground-shaking round of lovemaking. Exhausted from her spent passion, her mind wandered aimlessly, while her body attempted to revive itself.

More than three weeks had passed since their first date and they had spent every available moment they could together. Despite the fact they occupied more of their time making love than they did talking, Joely found herself growing closer to Cole with each passing day and she knew her feelings for him were becoming serious—even though she had no idea what he thought of her. He continued to be sweet and romantic, kind and considerate, but completely uncommunicative about himself. He refused to confide his feelings and if she pressed, he usually brushed her attempts uncomfortably aside.

She sensed that Cole carried a heavy burden inside himself and because of his regimented upbringing, he didn't know how to share his pain. There were times when his eyes clouded over with some hidden thought he couldn't or wouldn't express, and she'd wonder if she really knew him at all.

He had a daughter, a little girl of his own, who he never talked about. The infinite patience he showed her son illustrated to Joely what a terrific dad he must be. This made it difficult to understand why he never mentioned his own daughter. But he had never again referred to his marriage or his daughter. Joely noticed the box containing the child's belongings and the photo was no longer anywhere to be seen. She had no idea where Cole's daughter lived or how often, if ever, Cole saw her. She couldn't imagine he wouldn't want to spend time with her. He wasn't that type of man.

Squirming into a more comfortable position against his shoulder, she scratched her fingertips playfully through the soft, springy hair on his chest. "Tell me about your little girl. How old is she?"

Cole took a sharp intake of air and his entire body stiffened beneath her. He didn't move so much as a muscle and something almost like violence lurked beneath his stillness. Joely expected his usual taciturn response, not this type of fierce reaction. She levered herself up onto an elbow, staring with alarm at his face. Deep within his eyes lived a raw, brutal pain, a pain so powerful he couldn't disguise it. She sensed the warring inside him as he fought for self-control.

"What is it? Doesn't your ex-wife let you see her?" She accompanied her anxious words with a soft touch to his arm.

Cole jerked to a sitting position and turned his back on her. Joely watched helplessly as he drew in deep, shuttering breaths, the heels of his hands pressed against his eyes. She knelt behind him, wrapping her arms around his straining body, not understanding what he was going through, but wanting to shield him all the same. Watching him withdraw into himself was nearly as agonizing for her as it obviously was for him.

"Cole, talk to me. Tell me what's hurting you so badly."

"My daughter died when she was eight years old," he revealed in a slow, hard voice as he pulled away from her.

Joely froze as shock iced its way through her. "Oh, Cole, no! I'm sorry." She began trembling, hurting, silently crying inside for Cole and for his little girl. She put a shaky hand to her aching throat. "How did it happen?" Tears slid down her face, unwanted, but unchecked, and she crawled to the edge of the bed beside him.

Cole pulled her up tightly against him, burying his face in her hair and she could feel the misery welling up inside him. "I can't talk about it. I'm sorry, but I just can't."

"I'm here for you, and I want to help. I think it'd make you feel better to discuss it."

"No, Joely. There are things in my past I need to keep there. It's over with and I won't dredge it all back up. I won't. So, let it go. Please."

"It's all right, sweetheart. If you'd rather not talk, I understand," she told him, although she didn't really.

She closed her eyes and held him tenderly, loving him more than she had ever believed it was possible to love a man. Her heart hurt for him and she wanted to shelter him, to comfort him. Nothing could be more traumatic for a parent to endure than to outlive a child. The natural order of existence was destroyed, and life could never be normal again. She couldn't even begin to imagine how she'd survive without Taylor.

Poor Cole. What a devastating ordeal. If only he'd talk to her. If only she could help him see how much he hurt himself by keeping everything inside.

Chapter Ten

Maintain, Cole, maintain, he coaxed himself. His hands shook and he gripped the edge of his desk so tightly his knuckles whitened. Complete frustration, unbearable helplessness, pummeled him. If only he could've done more or worked faster, more efficiently, a young man might still be alive.

He'd just returned from the morgue, where he identified a body. To make an already difficult ordeal worse, this was a fifteen-year-old boy, a street kid Cole had been working with, trying to get him the help he needed to kick his crystal meth habit.

A black despair, an immense sadness, made it impossible to breathe. Do *not* lose it, he told himself sternly. He knew what he had to do—separate himself from his cases, rebuild his fences and regain his perspective. He usually managed to direct his focus without much effort, yet for some reason, he had difficulty divorcing himself from his emotions this time.

He sat quietly and reminded himself that a good officer wasn't supposed to get scared, or saddened, or angry. How many times had his father, the Academy, told him that cops never show emotion?

Well, he never wept anymore. He hadn't cried for a long time, not even when Sarah died.

Sarah.

It hurt too much to even say her name out loud. Poignant memories of his daughter had stayed to plague him ever since he'd told Joely about her death the previous week. Not because he wanted to think about her. He always tried to avoid remembering because it opened a door he had carefully marked "Do not enter".

Images surfaced unbidden and he pressed his fingers firmly against his eyes, trying to prevent them from invading his aching brain. But his mind was beyond his control. Sarah, his sweet child, his beautiful little girl. Remembering her hurt unbearably, but try as he might, he couldn't banish her from his thoughts.

He had cherished Sarah, placed her before everyone and everything in his life, including his wife, but he hadn't been there to prevent her from climbing the tree in the schoolyard. He hadn't been there to catch her when she fell. He was there, though, to watch her die of a brain hemorrhage.

The doctor had tried to reassure him it was no one's fault. She was born with an aneurysm, it would've ruptured at some point, no matter what. So why did he still feel this overwhelming guilt that he'd let his little girl down? He'd failed her in a way he could never forgive or forget.

Anguish pressed down on his chest, choking him. Images flashed across his mental screen, vivid, painful. It frightened him that if he allowed himself to let go, it might break the string that held the package together and it'd be impossible to rise above his sorrow. He bent his head against the memories, squeezing his eyes shut.

The unexpected touch of a gentle hand on his shoulder rescued him from his tortured thoughts and he gazed up to find Joely standing beside his desk. The pain began evaporating at the sight of her. Spending time with Joely turned off a switch in his brain, shutting out the loneliness, the rage and frustration that tormented him since Sarah's death.

"Hi there. You sure were deep in thought. I have my Community Hours report for you." She gave him a loving smile as she slid into the chair beside his desk and put the file down in front of him. Crossing her legs, she propped an elbow on one knee. "Do you have time for an early lunch? I actually have an entire hour to myself before my next appointment."

"Sounds like a good idea. I need to get away from here."

Joely focused closely on him. He tried to smooth the tension from his face, but she was getting too good at reading his mood.

"What's wrong?" she prompted, reaching over to cover his hand with hers.

He brought her fingers to his lips and kissed them. "Tough morning, that's all. Let's get out of here."

* * * *

As they ate, Joely chatted about some of her cases. She prattled on for about five minutes before she realized Cole wasn't taking in a word she said.

Nudging him briskly with her knee under the table, she joked, "Hey, are you enjoying your trip?"

"My trip?" Cole replied, sounding as if he'd just woken up from a deep sleep.

"I don't know where you are, but it's not here."

Cole gave his head a brisk shake and his eyes lost their faraway look. "I'm sorry. I guess I am preoccupied. A street kid I knew died last night from a drug overdose and I had to ID him this morning. It makes me feel like a useless piece of crap when something like this happens."

Joely heard the throb in his voice and she sensed the grief that lay behind it. He was eating himself up because he hadn't saved a boy he barely knew. She suddenly understood what he'd been thinking so hard about when she arrived at the detachment. The circumstances behind his daughter's death remained a mystery to her, and Joely had decided not to bring the subject up again. He'd tell her when he felt ready. But however it happened, Cole had lost his child and it had devastated him. Now, he took it upon himself to save every other child in peril. When this didn't happen, he took it as a personal failure.

"That's so sad. It must've been awful and you have every right to be upset."

A fleeting trace of impatience crossed his face. "I'm not upset. I'm frustrated. I'm mad as hell, actually, and I'm trying to figure out what I could've done differently to prevent this from happening again. He was only fifteen, damn it, a boy Taylor's age. Somehow we as a society let this kid down, and now he's dead. It's not right."

She desperately wished he'd release himself from the torment of keeping all those powerful emotions, all that sadness, locked up inside.

"You work hard at hiding your pain, Cole, but I see it in your eyes. And you say a lot with the things you don't say. I wish you'd give yourself a break. You're an excellent police officer. You're gentle and compassionate, especially with the kids. You do everything humanly possible for them, but you're only one man and you can only do so much."

He waved her words away. "A boy is dead. My feelings don't really seem to be the point here." He picked up his glass, then set it back down without drinking from it. "Say, did you want to get together with some friends of mine next weekend? They're great people and I think you'll like them."

He changed the topic casually, but Joely recognized the determination behind it. She sighed and shook her head in defeat. How characteristic of him—disregard all emotions, if they weren't acknowledged, you didn't have to face them.

* * * *

The ball spun down the lane in a swift, straight line connecting precisely with the right side of the center pin. Joely raised her arms victoriously as all the pins collapsed in on themselves.

"Another strike? I'm starting to think you brought along a ringer, Cole," Michael Jamison complained loudly as Joely's score flashed onto the screen above their heads. For the third straight game, Joely was demonstrating her superior skills.

Michael was Cole's best friend and a fellow RCMP member in the Police Dog Service. Cole met him over fifteen years ago when they were stationed on Vancouver Island. He had already been a seasoned dog handler by the time Cole had started his career. The veteran had taken the rookie under his wing and before long they'd become closer than family. Shortly after Cole transferred to the lower mainland, Michael followed and he was now the principle dog handler for the surrounding detachments.

Cole smiled at his friend's jest, his gaze not leaving Joely's trim figure as she celebrated her fourth straight strike. Undefined emotions leapt in his chest as he watched her sway gracefully away from the lane toward the bench where he sat with Mike. Her infectious smile was sensual and sweet, both at the same time. It didn't matter how often he was around her, he always had the same reaction to that delicious smile.

Michael's wife, Anne, stepped up to take Joely's place on the lane and the two women exchanged friendly hand slaps, a bowler's ritual of passing on the good luck of the strike. Not that it would help Anne. She bowled with a lot more enthusiasm than skill and her balls spent most of their time in the gutter.

"I told you, Michael, it's all in the hip action," Joely quipped as she dropped onto the bench beside Cole. Her cheeks held a faint flush and her blue eyes sparkled with animation. Cole reached out a lazy hand and gave her shoulder a fleeting caress before sliding his arm behind her back and dragging her up close against him. Her nearness intoxicated him, creating an urgent, possessive pressure in his crotch.

"I thought you reserved your hip action for my pleasure only," he murmured against her ear and watched with amusement as the delicate rose in her cheeks blossomed into flaming red. He pressed his lips briefly against the heat of one soft cheek. She had skin soft as velvet and she smelled like a flower, only better. That elemental female scent, unique to Joely, drove him wild.

He fought a strong impulse to take her in his arms, right here and right now, and kiss her senseless. He met Mike's knowing gaze over the top of Joely's head, and Michael's hamster smile told him he recognized Cole's intentions. Cole had grown accustomed to his friend's ability to read his mind, and this time he knew Michael's mind, as well.

Mike approved of his choice in companions. Mainly because she was nothing like Debra, Cole's acid-tongued, strong-willed ex-wife, a woman Mike fiercely disliked. His friend had never forgiven himself, Cole knew, for inadvertently introducing the two of them at a party.

Mike had quietly made known his disapproval when Cole and Debra rushed into marriage, claiming they were too young and totally unmatched. His perception had unfortunately proved to be correct, and during the rocky years of Cole's marriage, Mike had provided him with an endless supply of steady, nonjudgmental support, while his family lovingly gave Cole a calm haven to retreat to whenever he needed a break from the war zone he called home.

It was exceedingly obvious that Joely and Debra were complete opposites. Joely knew her own mind and didn't hesitate to speak it, but she was very easy to be with. Where Debra would pout for days if she didn't get her way, Joely knew the power of compromise. Her temperament was sweet, her personality sunny and outgoing. Cole flinched inside as he recalled the way Debra had become more selfish and demanding with motherhood. Joely was a wonderful mother, and she and Taylor were absolutely dedicated to one another.

While Cole appreciated Michael and Anne's friendliness toward Joely this evening, on occasion their open interest bordered on shameless probing. In fairness to them, Cole figured they had a right to their curiosity. Until he met Joely and Taylor, the Jamisons and their children had been the only people who mattered to Cole.

"I guess I'll have to settle for another five," Anne moaned good-naturedly as she joined the rest of them on the bench. "I can't seem to copy Joely's hip action."

Cole had always considered Anne a combination sister and mother, and he loved her dearly. Edging gracefully out of her forties, she still had the same healthy, rosy-cheeked look she had when he first met her, all those years ago.

For a homely old bugger, Mike also looked impressive for his age. As good as Mike could look, at any rate. Deceptively powerful and sinewy hard, he was as lean and angular as Anne was round and soft. His short hair was still black and thick, with only a few fine wires of gray in it.

The sharp planes of Michael's engagingly unattractive face softened as he gazed at his wife, his adoration for her obvious. They were a couple of the lucky ones, Cole thought wryly. Somehow, they'd managed to beat the odds and make a good life together. If anything, their love for one another was stronger now than it had been in the early days. Not a common occurrence, he swiftly reminded himself.

"There's nothing wrong with your hip action, sweetie," Mike consoled Anne, as he patted her ample backside. "I'll take your cutey patootie any old day."

"Aren't you a doll," Anne cooed facetiously and planted a loud kiss on his large beaky nose. "Blind as a bat, but a doll all the same."

"I'll show you who's blind. A strike here we come."

He didn't get a strike that frame, or the one following, but he evidently decided if he couldn't impress anyone with his bowling abilities, he'd entertain them with his varied and imaginative bowling style. His hilarious antics kept them all crippled with laughter the entire evening.

When the time came to leave, they said goodbye in front of the bowling alley and promised to get together soon for dinner and drinks. Cole slung his arm around Joely's shoulders as they strolled toward his Mustang, parked further down the street.

"It looked like you enjoyed yourself tonight, angel."

"Oh, Cole. I just love Mike and Anne."

She abruptly stopped walking and leaned against him, coming up on tiptoes to catch his face between her hands, surprising him with a kiss. The press of her lips was incendiary and the fire in his veins blazed instantly. He wrapped his arms around her and slid his hands down the alluring curve of her back and over the more tempting curves that followed.

"And I love you too," she announced breathlessly when she pulled back. "I'm totally in love with you, Cole Dennison."

Cole raised a hand to caress her cheek. Then he sighed, dropped his hand and stared off down the street. An ache worked its way through his body, a terrible, wanting ache. Why did she have to ruin everything by saying those meaningless words? And why did that stupid, pointless, surge of hope rise up in him in response? He didn't want to have these feelings. He didn't want to hope anymore. It was senseless, because romantic love was nothing but an illusion.

True love and happy endings were something you watched in sappy movies. He lived in the real world, and reality was much harsher and not nearly as gratifying. In the real world, people hurt other people, even the ones they claimed to love. People died. Nope, true love was a rare creature and most endings were not very happy.

* * * *

Joely watched as a wistful dreaminess entered Cole's eyes making him look innocent and vulnerable, but it passed quickly and he stiffened in her embrace. He didn't actually move away, but

she felt him tense up and retreat into himself. Her stomach slid
sickly downward as she realized he didn't want to hear her words
of love, and she fervently wished to retrieve her hastily spoken
words.

Although she'd never imagined loving a man like this again,
she knew without a single doubt she was hopelessly in love with
Cole. She hadn't told him she loved him before, although she'd
been aware of her feelings for some time. She hadn't even meant to
tell him just now. Not this way. Not blurting it out right here in the
middle of the street. She simply couldn't help herself. On this
perfect evening, her love for him had overwhelmed her and the
need to share it with him had taken over her better judgment. Now
the mood was spoiled and she couldn't take back what had already
been said.

She anxiously searched his face for some response, but he
wasn't looking her way. She wanted to grab his shoulders and
shake him, to provoke some sort of reaction. She wanted to shout
at him, "Didn't you hear me? I just said I love you! Why won't you
talk to me?" Her chest burned with emotion and she felt tears
starting. Blinking hard, she refused to let them come. She eased
herself away from him so he wouldn't notice how badly she
trembled.

With silent consent, they resumed walking down the street.
After a few steps, Cole slipped his arm around Joely's shoulders,
drawing her a little closer. "It's late and I better get you home, or
there'll be hell to pay with young Taylor."

Taylor was spending the night at a friend's house and Cole
knew this, but Joely readily went along with his charade, relieved
to retreat from the awkward emotional ground. If he didn't want to
acknowledge what she'd said, he obviously wasn't ready to
proceed toward a commitment. She'd have to wait, be patient. She
just didn't realize his rejection would sting this badly.

"Did I tell you I have to work next Saturday?" Cole asked as
he shoulder-checked, then eased his car into traffic.

"You did. Taylor works too, then he's going to a friend's for a
birthday party. I guess I'll have a quiet day to myself."

"What a waste of a day we could've spent together."

"How about if I go to your place in the afternoon and get some

yard work done. Then I can put supper on before you get home."
She felt unreal, talking this naturally and calmly while a brutal
sense of dejection ate away at her insides.

With effort, she relaxed against her seat, watching the
streetlights pass by through the windshield, while her mind
wandered over the past couple of months since she first met Cole.
Initially, their relationship had been based on their intense physical
need for each other. Gradually the focus shifted and they started
doing more everyday activities with each other. When Taylor
wasn't home, Joely usually went to Cole's house. They spent hours
in his yard, gardening, relaxing in the hot tub and enjoying the
beauty surrounding them.

Stella and Maggie readily accepted them as a couple. Both of
them had told her they were thrilled she'd finally found a man
worthy of her love. Stella even invited them over for dinner to
meet her family. Joely hadn't been sure how Cole would react to
the young Carson girls. They were both dark and adorable like his
daughter had been, and Joely worried the resemblance might be
hard on him, but he had responded with incredible tenderness and
warmth to the girls' shy, giggly overtures. By the end of the
evening, there were at least two more females in the Cole Dennison
fan club.

The fact Cole wanted to introduce her to his friends made
Joely think he was ready to acknowledge they were officially a
couple and she was more than willing to accept this role in his life.

She had taken an instant liking to Michael and Anne. Anne
was like a plump little cushion, comfortable and round, with a
cheerful sort of face. And Mike had a heart as big as a truck. It
surprised her how much older they were than Cole, and it pleased
her to see their affection for him, treating him like the favored
younger brother.

"Have you and Mike been friends long, Cole?"

Cole flicked a glance at her, then returned his attention to the
road. "Fifteen years or so."

"I thought as much. You seemed very comfortable together."

He gave an ambiguous "hmm" answer. The traffic wasn't
heavy enough to prevent conversation, meaning yet another topic
not up for discussion. So, she dropped it.

Yet, it nagged at her. If she and Cole got along so well, why did he change the subject every time she tried to bring up his past or his feelings? His reactions no longer surprised her, nonetheless, his behavior made it difficult to gauge the seriousness of their relationship. To be honest, she had no idea how to describe her involvement with Cole. No type of commitment had ever been discussed by either of them.

She'd already admitted to herself she found the idea of marriage to him appealing. For the most part, they were so in sync they understood one another without the need for words, a touch or a glance often sufficed. And then, there was the intoxicating sexual fire constantly sizzling between them. They could never be alone for long without giving in to their desire.

But Cole's nature also had a dark side he kept her shut out of. This part of him prevented her from knowing what truly lie in his heart. And it was becoming increasingly difficult for her to accept their relationship on this level. She could never be happy settling for half measures, for half a man, the physical half who brought only his body to bed, not his heart. She needed Cole's love much more than she needed his lust.

Because she loved him, and was completely caught up in the discovery and marvel of that love, she hadn't stopped to consider whether he might feel the same for her. Maybe the commitment she took for granted, unvoiced though it was, didn't exist for Cole. Maybe she only imagined that she'd read in his eyes, in his gentle touch, a love that went beyond mere physical attraction. If he loved her, why didn't he just tell her? And if he didn't love her and wasn't looking for a commitment, she had the right to know.

* * * *

Joely listened to the hypnotic drone of the insects as she leaned back on her heels to survey her work. The sky was high and clear, the heat of the mid-June sun tempered by a soft breeze. If she kept up this pace, she'd have all the beds in Cole's backyard tidied up before he got home from work.

Today she found it difficult to derive her usual satisfaction out of working in the garden. Her preoccupation with Cole weighed heavily on her mind. She'd thought of little else since last weekend when he rebuffed her attempt to say she loved him. She wanted to confront him and make him answer her questions honestly. A part of her, though, mightily feared what those answers might be.

Impatient with her own self-doubt, she needed to stop skirting the issue and bring her concerns into the open. As she entered the house to wash the garden dirt from her hands, she decided today would be the day. Today Cole Dennison had to tell her exactly what his feelings were. And their relationship would either be made or broken by what he said.

Brave and noble intentions, she thought. She just hoped she could find the strength to follow through.

Cole arrived home as Joely prepared the grill to barbecue steaks. He nestled up close behind her, both of his arms circling her waist. "I like coming home and finding you here."

She turned in his arms to receive his warm kisses. "That's good, because I like being here. I feel like a wife getting her husband his dinner after a hard day at work."

It became very quiet and Joely glanced uneasily at Cole. He didn't say anything, he didn't have to—his grim look said it all. He didn't want her thinking of herself as his wife. A stinging heat rose in her face and she casually eased out of his embrace to busy herself with the barbecue. Losing her nerve for confrontation, she searched for a neutral topic to talk about, to get them off this dangerous ground.

"Guess what? Taylor received the second highest mark in his Biology class and the teacher says he has quite an aptitude for the sciences. His mark in Math has gone from a C at midterm to a strong B. I want to do something special to show him how much I appreciate the hard work he put into his studies. Do you have any ideas?"

She babbled intentionally in an effort to take the strained look off Cole's face. She felt certain he wouldn't be able to resist discussing Taylor and soon he started offering up one suggestion after another. He took over the job of grilling the steaks, while Joely set the patio table.

The warm day had turned into a balmy evening and the heady scent of blossoms filled the air, perfect for dining outside. Their conversation moved to other topics and it should've been an enjoyable time, but Joely covertly watched Cole's strong, handsome profile and worried about the closed mask he kept over his features. She doubted he said anything even vaguely relevant to the thoughts in his mind.

What are your true feelings for me, Cole? Do you even have any? The questions beat on her consciousness, upsetting her, spoiling her pleasure, the joy she usually took from being with him.

As they cleared away the dirty dishes, Joely couldn't bear the suspense of not knowing any longer and she voiced the question hammering at the corners of her mind.

"Did my reference to feeling like your wife upset you?" Painfully nervous and awkward, her stomach churned, and she felt absurdly close to tears.

"Come over here and let me feel you," Cole answered with a slow smile. "I'll tell you what you feel like."

Joely set the tray of dirty dishes clattering down onto the counter and stepped away from his reach. "Please don't do that."

He shrugged and folded his arms with vexing nonchalance. "What?"

"Attempt to distract me when I'm trying to ask a serious question. Why do you always avoid my efforts to tell you how I feel about you? And why won't you tell me how you feel?"

"I don't mind your need to spout all that lovey-dovey talk, just don't expect me to reciprocate."

The blunt statement nearly destroyed her, but there'd be time to cry over it later. Right now, Joely needed to know exactly where she stood with Cole.

"I guess what I'm trying to say is I'm at the point where I need to know where this relationship is going. What comes next for the two of us?"

Cole unfolded his arms and shifted his weight to lean against the counter. "Why does there have to be a next step? Can't we live for the moment? Take our relationship for what it's worth right now and simply enjoy it."

Her hand clenched tightly around the glass she was removing from the tray and she carefully placed it on the counter before it broke. "I'm starting to understand that you and I don't want the same things."

"What does that mean?"

"I love you, I want to be with you always. That's how I feel and no amount of not saying it is going to change my feelings. Now, you tell me what you want."

"I don't want anything. I like what we have just the way it is. I thought we had a mutually satisfying relationship." He smiled and he looked disappointed when the smile wasn't returned.

"I'm not interested in casual sex. If that's all you want, I'm with the wrong man, despite how I feel about you."

His smile got bigger. "There's nothing casual about our love life. It's damn hot."

And that, in a very neat, but very painful nutshell, was that. She obviously meant nothing more to him than a means of physical gratification. His blasé indifference showed clearly that he didn't care for her in the same deep emotional way she cared for him. Her love had little to do with the overwhelming sensual yearning that swelled between them from the first moment they met. It had much more to do with the type of man he was—his strong character, his compassionate personality, his quiet humor.

"I know you want me in a sexual way." She articulated slowly, picking her way carefully through her thoughts. "What I need is for you to want me in an emotional way. You never tell me how you feel. How can you be so composed, so controlled, so emotionally detached from me? How do you do that—just push your feelings away? Where do they go?"

"I was trained not to show my feelings," he replied, obviously impatient to end this uncomfortable conversation.

She refused to back down this time. "Then maybe it's time you learned. If you were able to share your feelings, maybe you could deal with them. How can I help you if you won't confide in me?" She held his gaze until he turned his back on her.

"You're trying to fix something that doesn't need fixing, Joely. You really don't know what you're talking about, so please save the homegrown psychology for your workplace." Cole's voice grew hard and Joely could sense the scowl she knew she'd find on his face. "Don't analyze me. What is this whole damn thing about anyway?" he continued loudly, rounding on her so suddenly that she jumped back. "Explain—we have feelings, so we have to *deal* with them? What does that mean—*deal with them*? I don't think it's necessary or important to share my feelings and discuss them all the time. Why can't you leave things alone? Why do you have to analyze everything to death?"

"I'm sorry if that's what you think I do. Unlike you, I don't have it in me to ignore how I feel. Besides, love isn't an emotion you can break down for analysis. It simply is. All you have to do is recognize it as that." Her throat filled with an exquisite bittersweet pain and it hurt too much to continue. "You know what? Just forget it, forget the whole thing. I can see I'm wasting my time."

Cole looked alarmed for the first time and his bristling assertiveness faded into restless dismay. "What are you saying? You're my lover and the best friend I've ever had." He leaned toward her and she tilted back, as if on a seesaw. "Do we have to label it? Why mess up the good thing we have with unnecessary words? Would it honestly make you feel better if I parroted back to you whatever you wanted to hear, even if I didn't mean it? Are you saying you want us to get married, knowing that isn't what I want?"

Joely shook her head with frustration. "No, that's not what I'm saying. I'm not in any way trying to coerce you into making a commitment you're not ready for. I don't want a marriage without love, anymore than I want loveless sex. I've already experienced both and I'll never settle for either again. When I get married, it'll be for keeps, so I have to know it's the real thing. I guess I hoped you felt the same way. It's painfully obvious you don't."

Her words totally confused him. It showed in the rigid set of his shoulders and his tightly knotted neck muscles. He had no comprehension of the importance of this to her. And if he couldn't understand her after all this time together, he never would.

"I'm going home now. There's no point in continuing this." Joely closed her eyes because it hurt too much to look at him. "Goodbye, Cole."

Please, if there was any justice left in the world, let her get out of there with a shred of her dignity intact. She could figure out how to survive this later. Right now she had to find the strength to leave before she broke down and let him convince her to stay.

Chapter Eleven

Joely looked as if she might push her way past Cole, so he quickly spanned her waist with his hands, not willing to let her leave with the way things stood between them.

"Wait a minute, Joely. You can't just say goodbye like that, like it's final." To his own ears, his voice sounded rough, edged with emotion. This situation scared him.

She wouldn't look at him. "I can't do this anymore. I don't want to get hurt and if I stay with you feeling the way we do, I will end up being hurt." She didn't seem angry, just resolute, and it almost killed him. He refused to let go of her and she steadied herself against him, giving him hope that if he held onto her long enough she might change her mind and stay.

"I don't know what to say to make this right," he murmured against her hair, holding her close so she couldn't see the agony that must show on his face.

"We've both said enough." She tried again to turn away and he clasped her tightly for the longest time, feeling as though his heart might burst in his chest. Finally, Joely shoved her way out of his arms, pivoted, and fled his house without looking back.

Cole threw himself into an armchair in the living room and closed his eyes, letting his head roll back. His shoulders shook and his breath came in shudders. How the hell had this happened? Everything changed too quickly. Joely left because of him, and he had a deep desire to take back his stupid, selfish words. He wished he could've said instead how important she was to him, how scared he was of losing her.

But how exactly could he explain to her what he didn't understand himself? He covered his head as though his hands could stop the thoughts tumbling about madly inside his brain. Some things he just couldn't face again. Opening himself up to the pain and heartbreak of loving someone placed high on his list of mistakes never to repeat.

Joely needed someone willing to share, to be open with her. That sure as hell wasn't him. He didn't know how to convey his wariness of commitment, or how to admit that his first marriage had been a living nightmare. He wasn't used to explaining himself or exploring his emotions. Joely made it look easy. She loved him and she told him, simple as that. She had no problem admitting exactly how she felt about anything. She didn't put limits on her love. And because of her openness, she couldn't understand how he withdrew into himself.

Emotional disconnection was a straightforward process he'd honed to perfection. Cut your life up into little pieces, and compartmentalize it. Keep each piece in its own section, only go into one section at a time and stay away from the ones that might be booby-trapped. Protect yourself at all costs.

And now, Joely thought she had to protect herself—*from him*. Her naked honesty when she'd said she didn't want to be hurt had floored him. How could she think never being together would be preferable, would hurt less, than being together some of the time? It made no sense to him. Somehow, he had to straighten this all out with her. He'd call her tomorrow, take a stab at being more forthcoming. They could make it work. They had to—he couldn't bear to lose her.

The tight muscles in his chest eased, and he began to breathe again.

* * * *

With a heavy heart, Joely sat quietly in her little yard, gazing up at the stars twinkling in the night sky and trying to sort through the jumbled mess of feelings inside her.

She'd begun to believe there weren't any men like Cole left in the world—strong, honorable, trustworthy men. The kind of man she wanted in her life. The kind of man she could have more children with. The kind of man to provide the stable family life she had always craved and never had.

The only problem was—he didn't want any of those things.

How could she have misconstrued their relationship this badly? It made her question her own judgment. She blamed youth and innocence for the trouble she got into with Brad, but she was now a mature, practical woman. Yet here she was, in love with a man she thought to be a perfect match for her, even though he didn't feel the same way about her. The time had come to give up what she obviously never really had. And it'd have to be a clean and complete break, anything else would be far too excruciating.

When Joely realized her decision meant never touching Cole again, never feeling his strong arms around her, never tasting the sweetness of his mouth, she ached with emptiness. She wondered how she could possibly survive the lonely agony that lay ahead for her. She couldn't stop wishing it might turn out differently—if only Cole loved her the way she loved him. If only…

She began trembling, shaking from the brutal pain that grew worse with each passing moment. Her shoulders heaved with tears, and the tears soon turned to sobs.

The garden gate creaked open, and through a film of tears she saw Taylor step into the yard.

He gave an exclamation of surprise. "Mom? What are you doing out here? It's chilly."

She hastily scrubbed the tears away from her face. She hardly ever cried and never in front of Taylor if she could help it. "You're home early, honey. How was the party?"

Taylor slipped into the chair next Joely's rocker, his attention focused on her face. "Okay." He leaned in closer. "Mom? What's up?"

Joely started to deny a problem, but when she opened her mouth a desperate little sob popped out. Tears returned to her eyes. She dashed them away, only to have them instantly reappear.

Taylor slid onto his knees beside her and hugged her close. "Did you and Cole have a fight?" His young voice shook with righteous indignation. "Did he do something to hurt you?"

He'd never openly acknowledged her relationship with Cole before and Joely wished she could rejoice in this first small admission, but it came too late. Her relationship with Cole was over.

She sniffed and shook her head. "No, Taylor, don't be angry with Cole. I've decided maybe I've become too attached to him and for my own sake, I need to stop seeing him. Cole doesn't want to break up, but neither does he want the type of permanent relationship I do."

Taylor tilted back on his heels and smoothed away a lone tear coursing down her cheek. "Well then, Cole's an idiot, isn't he?"

In reaction to her son's fierce expression, she somehow managed to dredge up a small smile from the wreckage inside her. "Don't judge him too harshly. He's such a good man and he's been quite the friend to you. As I told you from the start, I don't want our circumstances to affect the wonderful bond you and he have forged with each other. Promise me it won't or I don't know how I'll be able to bear this."

"You sure he wasn't being a jerk?"

"I'm sure." She rubbed her hands over her chilled arms. "You're right, it's cold out here. We should go inside and get some sleep." But she doubted a good night's sleep would be a possibility for her tonight. Or any night soon, now that Cole was out of her life.

* * * *

The jangle of the telephone woke Joely early the next morning. She had tossed and turned most of the night and the sky had already started to lighten before she finally dropped into a restless slumber. Fatigue fogged her brain and she fumbled clumsily with her tangled sheets as she searched for the source of the incessant racket. Just as she reached the receiver, the ringing stopped. With a grateful sigh, she sank sleepily back onto her pillow.

Taylor stuck his head in her room a moment later. "It's Cole on the phone. Do you want me to tell him you can't talk?"

She pushed up onto her elbows, blinking herself awake. "No, thanks, I'll speak to him. I don't want you in the middle of this." Taylor remained hovering apprehensively just inside the doorway. "Really, Taylor, it's okay. Leave me alone now, so I can see what he wants."

She waited until Taylor closed the door behind him before reaching for the phone. "Hello, Cole," she greeted him warily.

"Joely, I'm sorry," he apologized quickly, as though afraid she might hang up in his ear.

At the sound of his voice, a powerful longing filled her. She sat up more fully in bed and pushed her hair away from her face. "What are you sorry about?"

"Everything. This whole stupid mess is my fault."

A small thrill of hope flickered inside her, but she immediately quashed it. "What's changed between last night and now?"

"I had a sleepless night to think things through. I don't want to lose you."

"What does that mean? You want to continue seeing me on the same basis as before? You want to make a commitment? Get married? What?"

"I care about you, I want you to be happy. And I think I make you happy most of the time. But I'll never get married again. Can't we please work something out?"

Tears filled Joely's eyes and she bit back a sob. "The thing is, never is a very long time and I don't think I can wait around that long. Take care of yourself, Cole, and please don't call me again."

Joely managed to hang up the receiver before breaking down completely. Her heart clenched with unbearable pain and her face crumbled, tears spilling onto her cheeks. Taylor's arms went around her and she turned her face into his shoulder, unable to stem the sobs that wracked her body. Not even for Taylor's sake could she contain the ripping agony tearing her heart to pieces.

"It's okay, Mom," he whispered softly, gently rocking her. "It's gonna be okay."

His love and compassion gave her strength and gradually her tears dried up. "I'm all right now, honey," she tried to reassure him, even though she was far from all right. Her emotions felt raw and exposed, and the relentless ache inside her refused to leave. "Thank you for checking."

"What did Cole want?"

"He called to say sorry."

"Are you guys, like, back together again?" Joely recognized his confusion. She also sensed that he hoped she'd say everything was back to normal. She wished she could accommodate him. Oh, how she wished that. But she had no clue when she'd ever feel normal again.

"No, that's not going to happen. We care a great deal about

each other. Sometimes that's just not enough to work out the differences." She ruffled her hand through his hair and found a genuine smile for him. "Now give your momma a kiss and then you better get going or you'll be late for work."

After Taylor left, Joely roused herself, determined that busy hands helped tame a busy mind. Galvanized into action, she set about cleaning the condo from top to bottom. If she kept herself completely occupied, maybe she could lock Cole out of her consciousness. It'd be necessary for a very long time to fill every moment of her days so there'd be no time left for remembering.

* * * *

When the first Monday in July rolled around, Joely faced the dilemma of going to the police detachment herself or asking Maggie to do it for her. After careful contemplation, she decided not to risk seeing Cole. She knew it'd be disastrous to be around him. She missed him so much that if he made any attempt to renew their relationship, she might be tempted to settle for something less than the commitment she wanted.

Dragging her heels with dread, she went into Maggie's office to see if she'd go in her place. As she thought, Maggie wanted to know why, then before Joely could explain, Maggie guessed the reason.

"Wait a minute, don't tell me you and Cole are having troubles? Please don't tell me that. You're perfect together."

A terrible pain wrenched at Joely's heart, but she schooled her expression not to show the extent of her grief. "I broke up with Cole two weeks ago."

"What? Are you insane? Go fetch him back. Now! Work things out." Maggie practically screeched the words at her. She punched vehemently at the intercom button. "Stella, get in here right now."

Joely heard Stella's heels clatter across the tiled floor as she rushed to Maggie's office. "You didn't need to call Stella in like that, Maggie. She's probably thinking there's something seriously wrong."

"Something is seriously wrong. We have a crisis to solve."

Stella entered the room in time to hear Maggie's last few words. "What crisis? My goodness, what's going on?"

"Joely's ditching Cole and we have to stop her from making the biggest mistake of her life."

Stella turned to Joely. "Joely, sweetheart, are you all right? What happened?"

Joely sank into the chair Maggie had vacated in favor of pacing around the room. "I decided, for valid reasons, it's in my best interest not to continue my friendship with Cole. I want to know if one of you would please deliver my community service file to the detachment for me today. If not, even though it's best to go over the reports in person, maybe I could just email them this time. I'd rather not run into him right yet."

Maggie stopped pacing and stood before Joely with her hands planted on her hips. "Look, I *know* what I know and I *know* you still have feelings for him, big time. So why the decision to dump him?"

Joely gave a small, miserable shrug. "Things weren't working out. I've always thought honesty was the spine of a relationship and Cole seems to have a hard time with that concept."

Stella sat down next to Joely and leaned toward her, her face mirroring her concern. "I can't believe Cole's been lying to you."

"I don't think Cole ever lied to me. That's not in him. It's just…he keeps absolutely everything to himself. I love him, but the man's a disaster at expressing emotion." She felt drained and exhausted. "I really don't want to talk about it anymore."

Maggie smiled with affectionate commiseration. "Oh, now I get what you're doing. I've done it so many times, it should be called the Maggie Lapage syndrome. You just initiated the 'break up with him before he breaks my heart' strategy. Not necessarily a smart move, Jo. Is this what Cole wants?"

A slight, uncontrollable trembling coursed through Joely's body, a sure sign she couldn't take much more without breaking down. She'd kept the information about her split with Cole to herself because she knew Maggie and Stella would want to explore every little detail. Her emotions were too raw and her spirits too depleted for her to survive the two of them analyzing the situation.

"Never mind what Cole wants, Maggie," Stella admonished

with unexpected thoughtfulness. "This is obviously not a decision Joely made lightly and we have to respect her desire not to talk about it." She stood up and helped Joely to her feet, placing a protective arm around her waist. "Come on, honey, let's make a pot of tea and you can tell me all about Taylor's plans for the summer. Maggie will deliver your file right now, won't you, Maggie?" she suggested in a voice that brooked no objection.

"Sure I will, Jo. Don't worry, I'll take care of everything."

* * * *

Long after Maggie had dropped the reports off with Cole, their conversation stayed on his mind, like a poison eating away at him. He became increasingly irritable and restless as the day wore on. Several times, he barely caught himself from snapping the head off some hapless person whose only mistake was having the misfortune of speaking to him.

Lack of sleep played a part in his problem. He'd worked long hours the past couple weeks, not wanting too much time to spend alone with his mind. But even though he was physically exhausted when he went to bed at night, his busy brain didn't allow him to sleep. And the continuous sleepless nights had begun to wear on his nerves.

Not having the capacity to deal with all the emotions bombarding him was the other side of the problem. Every feeling he'd managed to lock away for the past four years had reappeared, battering away at him, and he had no idea what to do about it. He missed Joely more than he ever imagined he would and he couldn't get her out of his system. She'd hooked him like drugs hooked a junkie and he hated himself for being weak.

He'd been relieved it wasn't Joely who showed up with the agency file. After all they had shared, he didn't know how he could possibly maintain an impersonal business relationship with her. She'd asked him to leave her alone and he wanted to respect her wishes, but if he was anywhere near her, he'd be fighting a losing battle against taking her in his arms.

A large, furry bundle of enthusiasm nuzzled up against his arm abruptly interrupting Cole's introspection. "Hey Zeus, what are you doing here, boy?" He squatted down to scratch the German Shepherd behind the ears, in the spot where the dog liked it most. "If you're here, Michael can't be far behind."

"Right here, dude." Michael Jamison laughed as the huge dog nearly knocked Cole over while in the throes of scratching ecstasy. "Zeus, sit. Stay." He bent down and reattached the dog's lead. "You looked lost in your thoughts and I figured you could use a friendly greeting."

Cole grimaced under his friend's careful inspection as they both took a seat at his desk.

"Something going on you want to discuss with an old buddy?" Michael's statement was half question, half observation. "How's things between you and Joely?"

In no mood to be friendly, Cole knocked his fingertips against one another and tried to hang onto his patience. Mike could read him like a scoreboard so he didn't bother trying to fool him. Just like the dog obediently sitting at attention at his feet, Michael never gave up when on the trail of something he considered important.

"There is no me and Joely. I haven't seen her in over two weeks."

Michael's sideways glance with slightly raised brows spoke volumes.

"Don't give me that look," Cole growled irritably.

"What look?"

"That look—" Cole pointed an accusing finger. "—the one on your face. The one that says you think I'm an idiot."

Michael displayed most of his oversized rodent's teeth. "Have you been an idiot? What did you do exactly, to make Joely leave you, as though I have to ask?"

"If you didn't need to ask, why did you? Just leave it alone, Mike. The split's probably for the best anyway."

Michael's pleasantly homely face crinkled with concern. "You know, buddy, when Anne and I met Joely, we thought you'd finally found a good woman who could teach you how to love again. All you have to do is be willing to take the risk."

Cole pushed that notion aside. "I'm not good at risks."

"Whaddaya mean? You're a cop, you take risks every day."

"Well, I don't do those kinds of risks." His feeble attempt at being reasonable didn't manage to hide the edges of his frayed temper.

Michael nodded his head knowingly. "There's nothing quite like an angry bad attitude to save a man from serious depression, is there?"

"Lay off, Mike."

It was a tautly issued order, which Michael promptly ignored.

"You've always worked hard at being in control of your emotions. But there comes a time when you have to choose between self-control and pain. If the pain gets intolerable, then to hell with self-control. It's obvious you aren't happy right now, so why pretend indifference?"

Cole sighed and rubbed at the headache pounding away at his temples. "Let's not go there, okay?"

"No, we're going there, all right, because you need to go there."

"Look, I already said it was best Joely and I aren't seeing each other. She needs more than I can give. I had to let her down sooner or later, so it's better for both of us it came sooner."

Michael's weighty sigh conveyed his disappointment. "You really are a cynic, aren't you?"

"I'm a realist. Police work is a divorce-plagued profession. If we had ended up getting married, it never would've lasted anyway."

"Now you're just copping out, if you'll excuse the pun. Anne and I have been married for seventeen years. And you know how good I have it with her. You could have that too—with Joely. If only you weren't so scared to take the damn chance. Just step up to the plate, buddy, and give it your best effort."

Cole's lids dropped to hide the uncertainty in his eyes. When they lifted again, he made sure he'd buried all expression.

"Damn it, Cole, don't do that. Don't you dare do that to me. I know what's going on inside your stubborn head. Remember, I was there with you every painful step of the way. I know what you've been through and I know why you act the way you do. But you've hidden your emotions away for so long, denying you have any, you can't even recognize what you're feeling anymore."

"Mind your own damned business," Cole snapped, resenting

the personal observation that hit too close to the mark. "I'm not a discuss-my-feelings kind of guy and that's the way I want it. Joely, she has to dissect every little pathos that pops into her head. She's a social worker, you know. She's made a profession out of all that touchy-feely, psycho-babble stuff."

"If you'd stop for one minute and be honest with yourself, I think you'd admit you're the one with the problem, not Joely. Did you ever tell her how you felt about her?"

"No," Cole admitted reluctantly, then paused to take a deep breath. "I didn't because I don't know how I feel. I miss her like crazy. She's become a habit-forming drug, I can only make it so long without a fix, and I'm way overdue." He stopped abruptly, swallowing hard on the emotions he wasn't ready to face.

Zeus looked alertly at Cole, picking up on the despair in his voice. Michael patted the dog's head and murmured softly to him. When he returned his gaze to Cole, his eyes showed compassion.

"I understand why you're afraid to love again. After everything Debra put you through, who could blame you?" Michael pronounced the name of Cole's ex-wife as though it were a dirty word. "You think you'll be safe if you don't feel anything. But at some point, you're gonna have to face your demons, so you can put your past behind you and get on with your life. Sarah—"

"*Don't speak of Sarah*," Cole bellowed hoarsely. Zeus whimpered low in his throat, and Cole tempered his voice to a less forceful level. "Let's leave this conversation alone now, *please*, Michael."

Michael reached over and gave Cole's arm a sympathetic squeeze before he continued as though Cole hadn't interrupted him. "Sarah didn't die because you loved her or because you did anything wrong. It wasn't your fault. You couldn't've done anything to prevent it, yet for some damn reason you want to punish yourself. After all these years, you continue to punish yourself." He shot Cole a look that dared him to deny his words.

Cole leaned back in his chair, unable to say anything, lost in a huge dark pool of pain and guilt.

Mike stuck out a leg and nudged Cole's foot with the toe of his boot. "You know what Survivor Syndrome is, right?"

"The guilt war vets experience, and people who survive horrible catastrophes that their loved ones don't," Cole replied in a flat, wary voice.

"It's also what can happen to parents who outlive their children," Michael added softly. "Try to understand that, Cole. You have to find a way to forgive yourself and, heaven help you, you even have to forgive Debra in order to get past this."

Cole turned his gaze stubbornly to his desktop, rather than subject himself to his friend's shrewd scrutiny. He refused to say anything else until he thought this through.

They sat in silence. Cole could feel Michael's attention focused on him, but he continued to stare at his desk. Zeus watched him as well, pivoting his large head to alternately stare at Michael, then back at him. Eventually Michael's radio squelched and he brusquely acknowledged the call.

"I have to go now, buddy. I'll call you real soon and you'll have to come out to the house for dinner." He put his hands on his bony knees and heaved himself out of the chair. "Think about what we've discussed, please." Before leaving, he clamped a hand on Cole's shoulder in silent empathy.

Cole didn't look up as Michael and Zeus walked away. He stayed motionless for a long time, deep in thought.

Was Michael right? With all the anger and resentment he nursed over the death of his daughter and breakup of his marriage, was he only getting back at himself? Instead of protecting himself, he was actually screwing himself over?

* * * *

On his way back from lunch the next day, Nora Mercer stopped Cole at the front counter to give him one of those little pink message slips. Shock waves reverberated through his system as he read it. He reread every word carefully before calling the clerk over.

"Did you take this message, Nora?" he asked, trying, but failing, to keep his voice calm. How could he maintain calm with his heart slamming against his ribs and his blood drumming in his ears?

She glanced at the pink slip he waved. "Yes, I did, Corporal Dennison. You can see where I initialed it right there."

"When did it come in?"

"Could I have that for a moment, sir?" She took the slip and pointed at something she'd written on it. "The call came in at twelve fifty five." She consulted her watch. "About six minutes ago."

"And you took the call yourself?"

"I did, sir. I took the call," the clerk repeated with exaggerated emphasis, like a teacher with a slow student. "I thought it kind of strange because the woman didn't want to be forwarded to your voicemail and she asked me to be sure and hand the message directly to you."

"All right!" He snatched the message from her hand and kissed it.

Nora gaped at him as if she wasn't sure he had all his buttons, but he didn't care. Nor did he care that the call hadn't come to his cell phone directly. He was an uncharacteristic bundle of nerves and he didn't give a damn about that either. Because Joely had sent the message. Sweet Joely. Lovely, loving Joely. She wanted to see him at her office, which could only mean one thing. She missed him and wanted to get back together.

* * * *

"Joely, hi, I came as soon as I got your message."

Joely's gaze jerked up with disbelief at the sound of Cole's voice. It was him, all right, live and in-person, not just a figment of her needy imagination. Standing right there, as big and beautiful as ever, at her office door. Her nerve-ends quivered under the rake of his stare, the fire and intensity she saw consuming her. Her reaction irritated her into pretending an indifference she didn't feel.

"What do you mean, my message? I didn't call you."

Cole stepped into the room and closed the door behind him. "I had a message to come here and talk to you."

Joely recapped her pen and placed it on the desk, then closed the file. Her hands shook so she placed all ten fingertips on the desktop to steady them. It didn't take a genius to figure this out.

Her dear, busybody friend Maggie, had presumed to lend a helping hand. The woman meant well, but meddling came second nature to her.

"When you saw Maggie yesterday, did she happen to ask you any questions about us, about our breakup?"

Cole made a dismissive gesture. "She tried."

Considering Cole's reticence, Maggie wouldn't have gotten very far, so her crafty brain percolated a plan—if she forced Joely to talk with Cole, face-to-face, they might work things out. Then she arranged this by leaving a message for Cole, saying Joely wanted to see him. Rather devious, but it got him here.

Her brow creased at the audacity of Maggie forcing this unbearable situation upon her. "I think I'll have to put Maggie through the *meddle* detector on this one. Didn't it occur to you if I wanted to talk to you I'd simply call your cell phone or send a text? I'm sorry you wasted your time, because I didn't make that call and I have nothing to say."

Cole approached her desk and perched against it, near enough they almost touched. "Okay, maybe I should've recognized the setup." He shrugged. "Maybe I didn't care. So what if Maggie's pulled a fast one, I'm here now, so won't you at least speak to me?" He tried to take her hand, but she quickly stood and moved away from him.

She went over to the window and stared blankly outside, letting her hair fall forward to shield her face. The cozy whisper of rain sounded against the windowpane. Instead of relaxing her as it usually did, the gentle hum only served to emphasize her despondency.

"You're wasting your time," she repeated, hoping he'd just leave and let her start all over again, to try and get him out of her system.

Cole followed her over and stood behind her, his arm propped up against the window casing. "It's my time to waste, isn't it?"

He stood so close she could feel his breath warming her shoulder, so close that to move back an inch would place her against his chest. His nearness set off little tremors of excitement she found hard to control. Sensation tried to swamp her, but she resisted. She couldn't allow herself to give in to her desires. Her self-preservation depended on it.

Chapter Twelve

"Do you have any idea the hell I've been in these past few weeks? All I want to do right now is haul you into my arms and kiss away that frown. Resisting that urge is causing me real pain."

Cole's voice felt like the touch of fingers along the nape of Joely's neck, and her insides knotted with sweet agony. She forced herself to ignore the hunger, the need, that filled her every time he was near.

"That's sex talking," she replied bluntly, keeping her back to him. "I know the way you want me and it has nothing to do with love. You want one of those mature, sensible relationships where two individuals agree to spend allotted portions of their time together, sharing their bodies without sharing their hopes and dreams. That type of lifestyle is not for me."

"What do you mean? We've shared lots of things. We talked all the time."

"Sure we did. We've had conversations about our work, about Taylor's activities. We discussed any number of trivial things. But you refused to talk about anything important to you. Whenever I asked personal questions, you'd clam up tight and resent me for asking."

She turned away from the window and focused on him. "But I've seen the real man behind this facade you insist on presenting to the world. That's the man I love, the warm, sensitive, loving man you seem to think you shouldn't be." She tipped her head back to look fully into his eyes, checking whether her words made any impression at all. The unmistakable desire she saw there quickened her pulse. "I do love you, and it'd be so easy to forget everything and just kiss you."

Cole inched closer. His arm slid around her shoulders, pulling her to him, body to body. "Do it, kiss me."

Her hands splayed out in rejection against his chest. "Talk to me first. Tell me something significant about yourself." She stepped away from his arms and retreated to the safety of her desk. When Cole followed her, she motioned him into the spare chair to keep a necessary barrier between them.

He slouched down in the chair, releasing a sigh of frustration. "All right, I'll tell you about this past of mine you seem to find so fascinating." His expression showed serious concentration, then he adjusted his posture to sit straight up.

"You already know I grew up in Toronto. When I graduated from the academy, they stationed me in northern Manitoba for a year. Then I transferred to Vancouver Island. That's where I met Michael Jamison. I got married at twenty-four. I got divorced when I was thirty-four and I transferred around that time to the Burnaby detachment here on the lower mainland. I lived there until I moved to North Van about four months ago." He spoke in rote, as though reading off an old resume.

"You just spouted a bunch of facts. I want to know what you think, what's important to you. Tell me about your mom."

His jaw went stiff. "She died in a car accident when I was five."

"And?"

"And nothing. My memories of her are vague."

Joely didn't believe him, but she let it go. "Okay then, talk about your dad."

"My old man was a typical city cop—hardnosed, unemotional and dedicated. He wasn't home much. He's in his late sixties and lives alone, in an apartment in the same old neighborhood where I grew up."

Again, just bare facts.

"And the two of you didn't get along?" Joely nudged him toward a more personal area.

"Wrong. We always got along. Everything went my father's way, so he had no reason not to get along."

"Surely that was hard for you?"

Cole splayed his fingers out, palms up, in front of him, then leaned back and crossed his arms. "It was what it was."

The confession was reluctant and left a great deal unsaid. To get Cole to reveal anything personal, she'd have to do some persistent needling.

"You were married for ten years, that's a long time. Why did your marriage end?" She also wanted to say, "Tell me about your daughter's death," but she somehow knew that'd push him too far.

"My marriage was a never-ending root canal without any anesthetic," Cole protested with a reckless anger Joely had never heard from him before. "You don't need to hear the gory details. Believe me when I say it was horrible enough that I never want a repeat performance."

"You can't give up on love just because it didn't work out the first time," she insisted. She leaned forward, desperate to press her point. "Why won't you trust me? I love you. I'd never hurt you."

He stirred restlessly in his chair. She saw in his eyes the feelings that his stiffly held lips denied. She wondered if he even knew why he reacted the way he did, if he understood the emotions making him behave in such a manner.

"You can tell me anything," she said softly, wishing she knew how to reach him. "I won't judge you, I just want to help." She believed he loved her, if only he could acknowledge his feelings, but his silence said he wasn't willing to take the chance. Hopeless irritation surged through her. "You know what your problem is?"

"I'm sure you're gonna tell me."

Joely ignored his impatient tone. "You're so used to living outside your emotions, you don't even know what normal feelings are anymore. And the minute you think you might lose control and react with honest emotion, you shut down."

He said nothing and the stubborn set of his jaw told her everything.

Furious words filled her mouth and she wanted to hurl them at him, but this would only serve to hurt both of them, so she gritted her teeth and took a deep breath. "Please go. And please leave me alone from now on."

Cole's lips parted slightly in protest, but he remained silent. Joely turned her head away and squeezed her eyelids closed, willing the tears not to appear before he left the room. The crash of the slamming door had a permanency to it that vibrated through her body, releasing her tears.

* * * *

"Hey," Maggie said as she stuck her head in Joely's office. "Do you have time for dinner out tonight?"

"I can't," Joely replied.

"Oh."

The one syllable response made Joely look at Maggie with concern. She leaned against the doorjamb as though not certain of her welcome. Her shoulders had an uncharacteristic slouch.

Except for a brief discussion about personal boundaries after her disastrous meeting with Cole the previous week, Joely had not talked about what happened with Maggie or Stella. She'd been too wrapped up in her own pain and misery to care about anything else, and she realized she may have been abrupt with her coworkers.

Stella didn't seem to take it personally, and she went out of her way to comfort Joely and make her feel better. Maggie, on the other hand, had become quiet and withdrawn. It suddenly dawned on Joely she might feel partially to blame for Joely's rotten mood.

"I'd love to have dinner with you, Maggie, and we'll do it real soon. Right now I have to focus some attention on Taylor."

"Really?"

"Really. He's been restless ever since school ended and even his job at the vegetable stand doesn't seem to fill his days. He's bugging me to let him leave for Edmonton right away, rather than wait until the end of July as planned."

"Oh. I thought maybe you were still mad at me for asking Cole over here."

Joely went and got her, leading her by the hand into the room. "I was never mad at you. Like I said when it happened, I wish you hadn't done it, but I understand you acted with the best intentions."

"Have you seen Cole since then?"

"No, I haven't. I'll have to run into him eventually. It can't be helped. But he hasn't tried to contact me. Who knows, maybe now that he's had the opportunity to think it over, he might feel relieved to be set free. I'm sure plenty of women are more than willing to have a purely physical relationship with the likes of Cole Dennison."

"Don't even say that," Maggie wailed. "I can't imagine Cole with anyone besides you."

Joely found it impossible to picture Cole with another woman too, so whenever her thoughts drifted in that direction, she determinedly banished them from her mind. But she refused to encourage Maggie's illusions.

"Our relationship is finished, and Cole and I both have to get on with our lives. I love him and it's hard to bear the realization he doesn't want to love me back. He had an awful experience before and now he thinks love's not worth it. I almost agree with him. I don't know if I'll ever let myself care for another person as much as I care for him. It hurts way too much when it ends."

"You don't mean that. You aren't thinking straight because you're in pain. Once you're able to piece your battered perspective back together, you'll want to love again. That's the way you're put together. You need to love people. If not Cole, then someone even more wonderful."

She gave Maggie a heartfelt hug. "Thank you for saying that. I hope you're right."

Joely mulled over her conversation with Maggie as she drove home, and she decided she wouldn't allow her memories of Cole to hurt her anymore. She was glad she'd met him and had the chance to love him. Their time together had been magical, and from now on she'd do her best to remember him with love and delight, not sadness or regret.

* * * *

"How did your day go?" Joely asked Taylor at the supper table that evening.

He put the last bite of potato into his mouth and washed it down with the remainder of his milk. "Bor-ring."

"Boring? Why's that?" Joely stood and took her dirty dinnerware to the sink. She had an idea what came next and she didn't look forward to another disagreement with him.

"There's nothing to do. Can't I please go to Edmonton now?"

"Taylor, we've had this conversation way too many times and you know my position."

"C'mon, Mom. Dad wants me to go out there right now. Why can't I?"

"Because I want you to stay with me. Your job and your friends are here. Grandma doesn't get her holidays until the thirtieth, you know that."

"I only work four days a week. Besides, Mr. Ning has, like, five thousand relatives. He can find someone else to take my place. And I'm not a little kid who needs to be baby-sat. Grandma doesn't have to be home every day with me. It's not fair!"

Although Joely had been doing pretty good up to this point, she quickly became exasperated with the whining teenager. "Where in the world did you get the idea life was fair? I have already purchased your plane ticket for the end of the month. That's when you're going and not a day sooner. Now go practice some patience and leave me alone about this."

Taylor stomped out of the room and Joely began cleaning the kitchen. Taylor should be helping her, but doing the chore by herself was a good tradeoff if it meant getting a little peace and quiet. Barely ten minutes passed before Taylor returned with fresh arguments.

Joely quickly cut off his stream of contention. "I'm finding myself incredibly frustrated with you right now, Taylor. And I'm not prepared to engage in further verbal fisticuffs over this. If you keep trying to goad me into losing my temper, it will happen—and I warn you, you won't like the fallout."

"You're being mean for no good reason. You're, like, no I can't go, and I just gotta accept it. Dad wants to be with me and I want to be with him. You're the only one who doesn't want me to go, so why do you get to have the final say? You won't even give me a good reason why I can't stay at Dad's."

A slow-fired resentment grew and simmered inside her. She'd had it with always being the bad guy in her son's eyes when it came to Brad. All the years of pretending, of hedging around his questions made her tired. Enough was enough.

She rinsed out the dishcloth and folded it on the sink, then leaned back against the counter, needing support for her suddenly trembling body.

"You think you're mature enough to know my reasons? You really think you're ready to face the truth? Trust me, it's not pleasant."

Taylor's chin lifted confidently. "Nothing you say will change my mind about wanting to go."

They both fell silent. Taylor impatiently waited while she struggled to find the right words. She didn't know of a gentle way of saying it and she'd put it off too long already.

She took a deep breath and let it out slowly. Cautiously she searched her way through a minefield of dangerous memories, not wanting this to blow up on her and Taylor. "When you were a little boy and we lived with your dad in Edmonton, sometimes he'd hit you. Once he hurt you quite badly. That's why we left and that's also why one of your uncles is always with you when you see your dad."

Taylor's head jerked as though she'd slapped him, he shifted to face her more squarely. "You're lying!"

"No, sweetie-pie, I'm not lying. Your dad has a drinking problem and when he gets drunk, he often loses control of his temper. When I found out what he'd done, I took you away to keep you safe." She watched him carefully, knowing the battle going on inside him as he tried to comprehend this horrific news.

"Why are you telling such terrible lies about my dad? He'd never hurt me—*never*." She reached out for him, but he batted her hands away. "You're just saying that because you hate him, and you want me to hate him too."

"I know it's hard to believe, but I'm telling the truth. Your dad can verify this."

"You're not right! You're *not*," he screamed, tears streaming down his face. She grabbed him as he moved past her, but he shrugged her off and ran from the condo.

"Taylor, come back here!"

She followed him out to the yard, just in time to see the gate bang against the fence. With no chance of catching him, she decided to let him go off by himself to think things through. Her words came as a crushing blow to him and it shouldn't be a surprise he didn't believe her.

Only, she was surprised—and hurt. She closed the gate and went back into the condo, her thoughts thrashing furiously about in a cage of frustration. It worried her that she'd told him in the wrong way. If she hadn't broached the subject while arguing, he might've been less upset.

Minutes ticked by like hours and Joely tried to maintain her calm. Taylor was just out sorting through everything. He'd come home when the shock of what he'd been told wore off.

By eleven o'clock, Joely could no longer keep up the pretense that nothing was wrong. Taylor had left over four hours ago and her anxiety level rose ominously with each passing hour. She'd already phoned all his friends, including Nelson Baldwin. They all told her they had not seen Taylor this evening and they assured her they'd call if he showed up at their place.

There was only one other person Joely knew to turn to. One man she trusted to find her son.

* * * *

Scratch another wretched day off the calendar, Cole thought, as he parked his Mustang in the garage and entered his house. Knowing no one waited inside for him, no one to share the burden of his day, depressed him. The empty house didn't bother him. The problem was Joely wasn't here and would never be here again. Only her memory remained waiting for him.

He shook his head in frustration and sternly shoved his lonely thoughts into that back compartment, the one marked with all the do-not-enter warnings, to be ignored along with the rest of the unwanted feelings he had collected over the years. Now more than ever, he couldn't afford emotions.

Even though he wasn't hungry, he fixed himself something to eat and then automatically cleaned the kitchen afterward. Over the past few months, he and Joely had worked side by side to decorate the house. The boxes were all unpacked and artwork hung on the walls, books sat on the shelves. They'd even wallpapered the kitchen. Now everywhere he looked, he saw Joely.

Edginess out-warred exhaustion, denying him the blessed release of sleep, so he cracked open a beer and flipped on the TV. After surfing the channels for a few minutes, he turned the set off and tossed the remote. Mindless sitcoms didn't appeal to his mood and he had enough guns and drama in his real life, he didn't need to watch the pretend stuff.

He tilted his head back and shut his eyes, dropping his arm across them. The image of Joely flashed before him, vivid, beautiful and bittersweet. He wondered what she was doing right now. He wondered if she felt as miserable as he did or if she'd already put him behind her and moved on. If he hadn't been such a fool, he could be holding her in his arms this very moment. If only he could've told her what she needed to hear, she'd still be with him. If he admitted his feelings to her now, would she believe him? He didn't even know if he believed himself.

Did he honestly think he loved her or was he merely trying to convince himself because he missed her so badly? He only knew for certain he felt thoroughly wretched and had since the day Joely walked out of his house and out of his life.

And then there was Taylor. To Cole's infinite surprise, the boy had captured him completely, and not only did he enjoy their time together, he looked forward to it. Cole had only seen Taylor once since Joely broke off with him. Cole had asked about Joely and even though it hurt, he'd admired the fierce protectiveness that came over his young face. Joely had tried to keep the two relationships separate, but Cole understood Taylor's need to choose sides and, of course, he picked his mom. So, Cole had lost both of them. And he missed both of them.

His cell phone rang and he gladly reached for it, thankful for the diversion. He nearly dropped it when he saw Joely's number on call-display.

"Hey, Joely. What's up?"

"Cole, I'm sorry to call this late. I hope I didn't wake you. I need some help and I don't know who else to turn to."

He read the hint of hysteria in her voice and his heart rate accelerated with alarm. "Tell me what you need and I'm there."

"It's Taylor. We had a disagreement and out of frustration, I ended up telling him the truth about his dad tonight. He got terribly upset and took off. He's been gone for over four hours. He didn't bring a jacket or anything. His wallet's still on his dresser, so he has no money."

"Take a deep breath and calm down. There's probably a logical explanation for why he's been gone this long. Have you spoken to his friends? Perhaps he's just hanging out with a buddy until he feels better."

Cole squeezed his eyes shut as a couple of shivers chased each other up and down his spine. *Please don't let the boy be in serious trouble this time.*

* * * *

Joely pulled in a shuddering breath, but it did nothing to relax her.

"I talked to all of them," she told Cole. "No one has seen him. I know you can't file a missing person's report or anything, but I wondered if you could speak to the officers on duty and maybe they'd keep an eye out for him. I'm going out right now to look for him."

"You shouldn't be out alone this late at night. Let me go with you. I'll stop at the detachment first, then pick you up. Wait for me, okay?"

Relief made Joely almost giddy. If anyone could find Taylor, Cole could. He cared nearly as much for her son as she did. "Thank you. I'll wait, but hurry."

When the buzzer rang fifteen minutes later, Joely rushed outside to meet Cole. "I think we should check the Lonsdale quay first," she told him as they got into his car. "He hasn't been down there for quite awhile, but he was so angry, he might've decided to go back."

It took minutes to drive to the quay, but for Joely it felt like an eternity. Parking wasn't an issue that time of night and Cole found a spot right next to the market. Joely flung the door open as the car came to a rolling stop. She walked briskly down the pathway toward the open square, Cole followed a step behind. The market had long been closed and the square became the domain of local teenagers who used it as a hang out during the nighttime hours. The sound of voices carried to them on the wind and Joely strained her ears, hoping to hear Taylor's.

Cole touched Joely's fingertips and she grasped his hand, grateful for his presence. He squeezed her hand hard and didn't let go. As they rounded the corner, she saw a group of young people gathered on the steps by the fountain and she anxiously scanned every face.

She glanced at Cole in disappointment. "I can't see him, can you?"

"No, Taylor's not here. I think that Lionel character is, though. Do you want to talk to him?"

Joely nodded and walked resolutely toward the kids.

"Cops," Lionel announced, obviously recognizing Cole. "What's the problem, Officer? We aren't doing nothing wrong."

"Guilty conscious, Lionel?" Cole asked.

Joely didn't think being confrontational helped matters, so she smiled at Lionel. "I'm looking for Taylor. Have you seen him tonight?"

"Nope. Taylor ain't been around here forever."

Back in Cole's car, Joely couldn't decide where to look next. Worry muddled her mind and there were too many places to cover.

"If only I'd let Taylor have a cell phone, like he wanted, I might be able to reach him. At least he could call me if he was in trouble." Guilt crowded in with fear to fill her chest with agony. "Why didn't I think he needed one? Why did I have to worry it'd be an unnecessary expense?"

"Don't do that." Cole gave her a quick glance before resuming his scrutiny of the street to his left. "No sense beating yourself up. You said he didn't take his wallet, so he probably would've left a phone behind anyway."

What Cole said might make sense, but it did nothing to ease her torment. They slowly cruised up and down the length of Lonsdale Avenue, but with most of the businesses closed for the night, chances of finding Taylor were slim.

"Look," Cole finally spoke up. "Taylor might already be home. I'll drop you off and if he isn't there, I'll continue to look for him by myself. All right?"

"Of course, he's probably at home. I'm sure he is." Joely grasped eagerly at this suggestion. Much easier than facing the alternative.

When they pulled up in front of the building, Joely saw right away that darkness blanketed the condo. "Maybe Taylor's gone to bed. It's after midnight, and he's probably tired."

But Taylor wasn't home. Her temples grew tight as tears

formed behind her eyes. "I don't know what to do. I'm so afraid, I can't think straight."

Cole pulled her to him and she didn't protest. Right now, she needed his strong, calm assurance, to feel the circling protection of his arms around her. She leaned her head against his chest and relaxed in the gentle pressure of his embrace.

"Try to stay calm, angel. I'll check back at the detachment and then I'll look for him. I won't stop until I find him, I promise. I'll phone you if I hear anything. In the meantime, try to get some rest." His kiss was solicitous. There was compassion, not passion in his touch, and his lips were dry, seeking nothing, merely offering hope and comfort.

* * * *

Taylor headed for Lonsdale Avenue when he left home. He had no idea where to go, he just knew he had to get away from his mom and her lies. Although his tears stopped after a few minutes, he got angrier with every step he took. How dare she say his dad had hit him, had hurt him. He'd remember if that had happened.

A city bus pulled up to the curb beside him and on impulse he stepped into it. He dug in his pocket to pay his fare and realized he didn't have his wallet. He only had a small amount of change in one pocket, enough to pay his fare without much to spare. He got off the bus at Park Royal Mall, then crossed over toward Ambleside Park. Nelson's older brother, Kyle, worked at the theater complex next to the park and Taylor stopped there first.

"Hi," he said to the girl at the ticket window. "Is Kyle Baldwin working tonight?"

"Yeah, Kyle's working," she replied without bothering to look up from her cell phone.

"Well, um, can I talk to him for a moment?"

Her thumbs continued to fly quickly over the phone's keyboard. "Not unless you buy a ticket, you can't."

Taylor closed his eyes for a moment. Some real nice girls worked here, why did he have to get a snotty one? "Do you know what time he gets off?"

She shrugged. "Around midnight."

Midnight. If Taylor planned to wait around for him, he'd have quite a bit of time to kill. He planned to hitch a ride to Nelson's with Kyle. Nelson would put him up for the night without asking too many questions. Hopefully Mr. and Mrs. Baldwin would already be asleep so they wouldn't know he was there, because they'd call his mom and he wanted to let her worry a bit.

He instantly felt guilty at the thought of her worrying so he reminded himself of the whopping lies she'd told him. The only way he could put her through this, he realized, was to stay angry.

He entered the park and went straight to the beach. Balancing along the top of the logs scattered on the sand, he jumped from one to the next as he worked his way down the beach. He sat down at the end of the short pier and tossed pebbles into the water. The offshore breeze felt cool and damp, and he took in a big lungful of salt air. He loved this beach. For some reason, none of his problems seemed quite as bad when he was near the water.

Most of the seabirds were in bed for the night. Only a pair of scruffy gulls still scavenged along the rocky shoreline, and Taylor watched them for a while, entertained by how they fought over every little scrap of food they found. When he grew bored with this, he turned his gaze to the steady stream of traffic crossing Lion's Gate Bridge. Big, gray clouds hung so low in the sky, it seemed as though they almost touched the bridge.

Taylor shivered and hoped it wouldn't rain. He wished he had brought a jacket with him. And some money. If he had cash he could've caught a movie while he waited for Kyle, instead of freezing his butt off at the beach.

Normally he enjoyed watching the freighters working their way through the narrows, but tonight he didn't feel like it, so he left the beach. He noticed a pickup game of basketball going on in the park and decided to watch it from the concrete steps on one side of the court. The ball bounced out of bounds and rolled to a stop near his feet. He tossed it to the guy closest to him.

"Thanks," he said to Taylor. "Do you want to play?"

"Sure," Taylor agreed right away. If he kept busy, he wouldn't have time to think about his mom and the ridiculous pile of bull she'd tried to feed him.

When it got too dark to play and the park started to empty,

Taylor figured it'd be a good idea to head back to the theater. With any luck, he could talk to Kyle this time, and Kyle would probably let him wait in the lobby. Dressed only in a T-shirt and shorts, Taylor felt chilled, and nervous too, all by himself in the dark.

As he walked through the empty basketball court, three guys approached him. They seemed to have appeared out of nowhere.

"Hey, dude, can ya spare a buck or two?" one of them asked.

"Sorry, man, I don't have any money on me," Taylor replied as politely as possible and tried to continue on his way.

They moved so they stood shoulder to shoulder, blocking his path. Suddenly they looked mean and scary, and Taylor realized he might be in some trouble.

Chapter Thirteen

"C'mon, dude, what's a couple bucks?"

These guys weren't much older than Taylor, but there were three of them and only one of him. One guy was taller than him and skinny, the other two were shorter, with stocky builds. The shortest one in the middle did all the talking and seemed to be in charge.

"I'd like to help you out, but I seriously don't have any cash. I forgot my wallet at home."

The middle guy turned to his tall friend. "He forgot his wallet at home, how convenient."

Their laughter didn't sound funny and it scared Taylor. He couldn't stop himself from shivering with fear. He had never been in a situation like this before and he didn't know what to do. He stuffed his hands in his pockets and backed away from them, but they stepped toward him at the same time.

"Lemme see what ya got. Empty yer pockets."

Taylor hurried to show them his house key and a few coins. "That's it. That's all I have."

The middle guy pocketed the coins and let the house key drop to the ground. "What about that ring yer wearing? Fork it over."

Taylor's hand closed over his ring. "It's only worth something to me. It was my Grandpa's. It's not, like, expensive or anything."

They crowded closer and Taylor tripped against the stairs as he backed away. Losing his balance, he sat down hard, and the tall, skinny guy pulled him up roughly by the arm and spoke for the first time.

"You kin give over the ring or I kin take it away from you."

"It's just an old ring, please don't take it." Taylor tried to yank his arm free, but couldn't.

"It 'pears he wants ta do this the hard way, dudes," the first guy growled, cracking his knuckles. The third guy moved to the other side of Taylor and grabbed his free arm.

Even though he was terrified, Taylor tried to focus on the leader, tried to show no weakness.

"Say yer prayers, wise guy," the leader sneered, "and kiss yer butt goodbye."

* * * *

After Cole left Joely, he checked back at the detachment. As he expected, there was nothing reported in about Taylor. He then drove to every teen hangout he could think of in North Vancouver. He cruised past all the fast-food joints, convenience stores, the mall parking lots, high schools. With a lot of territory to cover, Cole was determined to check every possibility.

As a last resort, he drove over to Stanley Park. It'd be impossible to search the entire park, but Taylor often commented on his love for the water, so Cole thought he'd check out the beach area. Although the park was alive with night people, Taylor was nowhere to be seen.

Cole rubbed his knuckles under his nose to stifle a yawn. Discouraged with his lack of progress, he gazed with frustration at the sky as he climbed back into his car. The striated colors in the east announced it'd be dawn soon. He'd spent the entire night looking for Taylor without any luck and he was running out of options.

He decided to return to the detachment one last time, then go to Joely's. They'd soon have to consider the possibility Taylor had left town, perhaps hitchhiking to Edmonton. Cole knew Joely would be beside herself with worry and he wanted to offer her whatever comfort he could give.

The civilian clerk signaled him over when he entered the detachment. "I was just about to contact you. The West Vancouver police department called to say a young man fitting the description you sent over was found unconscious at Ambleside Park and they brought him to the Lion's Gate Hospital a couple of hours ago. He has no ID on him, and sir, he's in bad shape."

"Any idea what happened?"

Nora Mercer shook her head. "No, they didn't report that, just a teenaged John Doe. Unconscious, in serious condition. Sorry,

Corporal, I hope he'll be okay."

He nodded numbly. He didn't want to believe it could be Taylor, but it fit. Cole knew to look at the beach, he just picked the wrong one. Joely indicated Taylor left his wallet at home, so he'd have no identification on him.

Cole displayed his RCMP ID to the clerk seated behind the emergency desk at the hospital and asked to see the unidentified young man who had been brought in. She directed him to the far corner of the emergency ward.

He took a step to leave, then turned back. "Do you know what happened to him? How he became injured?"

"He must have struck his head, resulting in unconsciousness," the clerk told him with professional aloofness. "There's also indications he may have been in a fight."

Impotent anger swelled Cole's chest and he closed his eyes for a second to get a handle on his rage. Taylor wasn't a fighter. If the boy had been in a fight, someone had beaten him up.

Cole's steps dragged as he approached the curtained off area where he was certain he'd find Taylor lying injured and alone. He struggled to control the germ of terror spreading like a toxin through his body, making his chest ache and his knees tremble. His hand shook as he pushed the curtain aside far enough to look inside. One glance confirmed his fears—Taylor lie on the stretcher, hooked up to an array of tubes and monitors.

Cole shrank away from looking at the boy. A horrible feeling of déjà vu closed in on him. The hiss of the ventilating tube, the hums and beeps of the other machines, the hospital smell, all were too painful a reminder of when he lost his little girl. He remembered the overwhelming sense of helplessness. He remembered the sickening feeling of fear.

His heart thudded against his ribs and he drew in a breath so sharp it hurt his lungs. He had to force himself to enter the cubicle.

Good cops don't let their emotions prevent them from doing their job, remember?

"Taylor?" he murmured, moving toward the bed. The boy remained motionless. There was a bandage on his upper body near his armpit. A long tube, attached to some sort of canister, protruded from the bandage, the unseen end obviously inside

Taylor's chest. Cole didn't know its purpose, but it looked damn serious.

A doctor pulled open the curtains and stepped inside, startling Cole as he spoke. "Excuse me, sir. Do you know this young man?"

"Yes," Cole replied hoarsely, then cleared his throat. He showed the doctor his ID. "I've been searching for him all night. His name is Taylor Mills. What's the extent of his injuries? Will he be okay?"

The doctor noted Taylor's name on the clipboard hanging off the back of the bed. "We don't know his full prognosis yet. At the moment his condition is stabilized and barring complications, it should stay that way. We're about to transfer him to a ward upstairs. Do you know how to contact his parents?"

"I'll call his mom right now and then go get her. We can be back in fifteen minutes." Joely would be devastated and he wished he could do something, anything, to prevent her grief. But there was nothing, and he hated this helpless feeling.

* * * *

Joely managed to doze fitfully on the couch, but woke up every few minutes throughout the night thinking she'd heard Taylor come home. She'd had a shower and was about to phone all of Taylor's friends again, when Cole called.

"Cole, please tell me you found Taylor," she begged.

"I found him, sweetheart. Listen to me carefully, okay? Taylor's been injured and he's in the ER at Lion's Gate. I'm there now and I just saw him. He's unconscious, Joely, and I don't know how serious it is. I'm on my way to pick you up, so stay put. I'll be right there."

She stared at the phone in blind incomprehension. "What did you say? Taylor's where?"

Cole repeated everything calmly and slowly, and she told him she'd be ready to go when he got here, then hung up the phone in a daze.

She knew the symptoms of shock, how body temperature, blood pressure and muscle tone all crashed, yet her total paralysis amazed her. Her body completely froze, so did her brain. Cole had told her Taylor was seriously injured in the hospital, but she couldn't accept it. Not her Taylor, not her boy, he couldn't be hurt. She refused to let the thought settle on her mind.

When Cole rapped on the condo's patio door a few moments later, Joely continued to sit on the couch with her hand beside the telephone. She hadn't moved in the slightest since he'd called.

"Come on, baby," he whispered, wrapping his arms gently around her. "I'll take you to Taylor now. He's going to wake up any moment and he'll want his mom."

Joely didn't ask Cole a single question on the drive to the hospital and he kept looking over at her every few seconds. She knew her silence worried him, but it took too much effort to talk. Only one thought consumed her—Taylor had to be okay.

Cole brought her to the emergency ward and introduced her to the doctor he'd spoken to earlier. The doctor glanced at Joely with detached sympathy. "We've moved your son to a room upstairs. You can get the floor and room number from the reception desk."

"My son," she said in a barely audible whisper. "What's wrong with him?"

"Taylor has suffered a grade three concussion, which in itself is a serious injury. He also has a displaced rib fracture and a couple of cracked ones, a bruised kidney and a traumatic pneumothorax. The majority of the trauma occurred when he struck his head on some concrete steps. Facial contusions indicate the probability he was in a fight. It is likely he got kicked in the side while prone, causing the damage to his ribs and kidney."

Joely clung to the remains of her self-control. She wanted to scream, to rail against the injustice. This couldn't be happening. Not to Taylor. For a moment, she steadied herself against Cole, breathing hard so she wouldn't faint. It was even more horrible than she'd imagined, and she forced herself to focus on what she didn't understand.

"What's a traumatic pneumothorax?"

"A collapsed lung. Likely a result of the fractured rib puncturing the pleural cavity. We inserted a chest tube and the lung has resumed function."

Joely shuddered at the thought of an incision in Taylor's chest. Then her mind jumped to another concern. "Should we be worried because he hasn't regained consciousness?"

"I would certainly prefer if he woke up soon."

"What does it mean that he hasn't?" Cole asked, his arm circling protectively around Joely's shoulders.

"The longer he stays unconscious, the more concerned we have to be with brain swelling and comma. But it's too soon for serious worrying. The initial CAT scan came up negative for any bleeding, with no evidence of swelling at that time. Give it a few more hours and if nothing changes, the doctor in charge can order another scan to see if anything new is happening."

Cole thanked the doctor, then steered Joely into a nearby chair. It took mere moments for him to check at the desk for Taylor's room number and return to her, but the wait seemed unbearable to Joely. Only sheer willpower kept the fear inside her from mounting into hysteria. All the way up to the ward, she clung tightly to Cole's arm, certain she'd collapse without his steady support.

When they got to Taylor's room, she leaned against the doorjamb for several shaky moments before her legs found the strength to enter. *You have to be strong for Taylor,* she tried to persuade herself. Cole crowded in close, urging her on, but she stopped short when she saw her son lying on the hospital bed.

His chest rose and fell with each slow, shallow breath he took. An IV stand stood sentry over the bed and a nasal cannula snaked its way from behind his head. Its two clear, plastic prongs made a slight hissing noise as they vented oxygen into his nose. His left cheek and eye were swollen and discolored, so were his jaw and lower right cheek. His bare upper body had a tube running from a bandaged area near his armpit. The tube looked awful, but Joely understood it did an important job, draining air from his chest to allow his damaged lung to work.

Cole stood right behind her and she leaned back, bracing herself against his warm pressure. "I can't bear this, Cole. I can't stand to see my boy like this."

"Come on, sweetheart, let's sit you down beside his bed. Talk to him. It will make you both feel better." Holding her gently, he walked her toward the bed.

Joely perched on the edge of a chair and leaned forward, her elbows resting on her knees, her hands supporting her chin. She couldn't take her frantic gaze off Taylor. She watched every movement of his chest as though it might be his last. His face looked so young and the bruises looked so painful, and she tried not to think about what some horrible monster had done to him.

Finally convinced he wasn't about to stop breathing, she kissed her fingertips and pressed them against his pale cheek. "Hey, Taylor. It's Mom. I'm right here, honey. So is Cole. We want you to wake up, so don't keep us waiting too long, okay?"

Taylor didn't move at all, and Cole placed a reassuring hand on her shoulder. "Keep talking. Believe he can hear you."

She reached through the railing and picked up Taylor's hand. "Did you know you are God's gift to me, Taylor? Even when you're being a huge pain in the butt, you're still my perfect son and I love you so much. I want you to fight. You hear? You fight this and come back to me. I'm not ready to lose you."

She gently laid his hand back down on the bed and bowed her head, closing her eyes. "I failed him, Cole," she whispered. "I am his mother, I'm supposed to protect him and I didn't."

Cole hunkered down beside her. His brown eyes were pained beneath his lowered brows, his forehead creased with worry. "You can't blame yourself for what happened."

"Why not? I have to blame someone, why not me?" She trembled, wracked by the pain and guilt tearing at her insides. She'd sworn to always protect her son, to never let anyone hurt him again. And she'd failed. She'd failed miserably and what a horrendous price Taylor was paying for her failure.

* * * *

Cole glanced down at Joely's hands. She'd twisted them so tightly together the tips showed white from lack of circulation. He reached over and unclasped her fingers, rubbing them gently.

Grief was not a merciful emotion, and Joely was filled to overflowing with grief. Cole understood completely the thoughts going through her mind. He had felt the same way when he found Sarah like this. The first notion in your head was—*not my child, this cannot happen to my child.* Then came the guilt. *I am the parent and I couldn't protect my child, so this must be my fault.* It wasn't logical, it wasn't true, but it felt very real. And it hurt, and the pain was incredible.

"I understand what you're going through, but this is not your fault."

Joely rose from the chair and paced the short distance from the bed to the door and back again. Her gaze went from Taylor to Cole and her lips quivered uncontrollably. With a soothing motion, he drew her into the shelter of his arms and pressed her head against his chest just as the tears dammed up inside her found the release they needed. She cried deep wrenching sobs that tore at Cole's heart.

"I shouldn't have told him," she quavered between sobs. "I never should've told him. Or maybe I should've been honest all along. I wanted to protect him and I only ended up hurting him."

Cole smoothed the damp hair back from her face and kissed her brow. Shoulda, coulda, woulda. He knew that game inside and out. He held title as the world expert.

"Please don't play what-if and if-only right now, don't do that to yourself. There's really no way to win that game. You aren't to blame for this, some lowlife scum is, and I'll do my damnedest to make sure he pays. But that's not what's important right now. Taylor is. We have to concentrate on positive thoughts of him getting better."

Joely wiped the tears from her face and straightened her shoulders. "Thank you, you're right. I have to be strong for him."

She resumed her seat beside the bed and threaded her fingers through Taylor's. "Can you feel my hand, sweetie? I'm right here. Try to wake up, okay? Open your beautiful blue eyes for me, please, Taylor, please. I love you so much."

Taylor still didn't move and Cole felt Joely's despair grow in direct proportion to the amount of time passing.

A nurse quietly entered the room and asked Joely to go with her to fill out some necessary forms. Joely turned to Cole, he saw the look of panic in her eyes at the thought of leaving Taylor alone and he said, "I'll stay with him while you're gone. Don't worry about a thing, I'll be right here."

After she left, he positioned himself in the seat she'd sat in. He rubbed his fingers hard over his bristled jaw. Exhaustion weighed heavy and he must look a mess. He hadn't slept in over twenty-four hours.

He pushed his hands against the arms of the chair and unwound his body from its contours. Lowering the bed's side railing, he sat on the edge to get a better look at the boy.

He gingerly touched the welts on Taylor's face, then picked up one hand and then the other, examining them closely. As he suspected, his hands were unmarked. Taylor hadn't hit anyone. He hadn't even defended himself.

Unexpectedly, as he watched and worried over this young man, he began to experience a remarkable change within himself. Deep inside, his guts twisted and tightened with the sensation. He wondered for a moment where it came from. The emotion felt new to him, or at least it was something he hadn't felt for such a long time it seemed new. Confusing, painful—yet at the same time, good. He didn't know if he should be frightened or simply thankful.

He lifted Taylor's hand again and as he did, he thought he detected a slight movement in the boy's fingers. "Taylor, open your eyes and look at me," he urged in a low voice that commanded obedience. The boy's eyelids fluttered slightly. "Come on, Taylor. Wake up."

Taylor's eyes flipped open, then immediately closed again. He whimpered softly. "Mom?"

"It's Cole, partner. How're you doing? You gave us quite a scare."

Taylor turned slightly on the bed and moaned. "It hurts."

"What hurts, Taylor?"

Taylor's eyes opened again and he gave Cole a dazed look. Cole imagined the pain in his head must be excruciating and his bruised body probably ached beyond endurance. Years ago while working a case, Cole had fallen from the roof of a building and broke several ribs. He remembered how each cautious breath had sent agonizing pain shooting through his chest. Taylor's injuries were much more severe and the pain must be proportionally worse. Poor kid.

Taylor tried to moisten his parched lips, but it was obviously difficult to move his jaw. He whimpered again and Cole placed a soothing hand on his shoulder.

"Take it easy, little buddy. You're going to be okay."

"Mom? I want my mom."

"She's down the hall. You lie still and I'll go get her."

Cole quickly raised the railing back up on the bed. He couldn't wait to see the expression on Joely's face when he told her Taylor was awake.

* * * *

As Joely hurried along the corridor, she saw Cole leave Taylor's room. "Cole? Where are you going? You promised you'd stay with Taylor."

A wry smile lifted the corner of his mouth. "I know, but the dang kid wants his mom."

A flash of pure joy electrified her. "He's awake?" She shouldered past Cole in her haste to get into the room. "Oh Taylor, Taylor." Joely eagerly reached out to him and kissed his face, his ear, his hair, then his face again. Touching him reassured her he was really all right.

Taylor tried to smile, but the attempt looked pitiful. He lifted his hand and his eyes filled with tears. "They took Grandpa's ring. I'm sorry, Mom." His words slurred with painful effort.

"Hush now. The ring doesn't matter, honey." Joely heard the soft swish of the door and looked up to see Cole enter with a young doctor by his side.

"I'm Dr. Halliwell," the doctor told Joely as he shook her hand. "I'll be taking care of Taylor during his stay at the hospital. It's good to hear he's decided to wake up." He stepped up to the bed and gave Taylor a friendly grin. "How are you feeling, Taylor?"

"My head sorta hurts and it's kinda hard to breathe," Taylor said with a sideways glance at Joely. She understood instantly how he was downplaying the extent of his pain for her benefit.

The doctor nodded perceptively. "I'd be surprised if that's your only discomfort. You broke a rib and cracked a couple more, so I'll hold off on the jokes for a while. Laughing won't be much fun. If you can hang tough for a few minutes, I'll have a nurse bring you something for the pain."

While he talked, he efficiently checked Taylor's vitals. Then he took a careful look in each eye and asked Taylor to squeeze his fingers. "I'm pleased with the progress so far. I need you to promise me one thing, though. No getting out of bed by yourself. Besides the tube you're sporting that you don't want to mess with, you have a grade three concussion, which is about as bad as it gets. If you even sit up, you'll become dizzy and nauseous, and we don't want you doing any face plants, okay?"

After the doctor left, Cole approached the bed. "Do you know who did this to you, Taylor?"

Taylor touched his forehead and squinted, then grimaced as he shook his head. "Naw, it was three guys I've never seen before. I kinda remember what they look like, though."

Although nothing changed in Cole's expression, Joely sensed an added alertness about him. "I know you hurt, little buddy, but if you could tell me what happened, I can get my men looking for these guys. Will you do that for me?"

They waited in silent anticipation while Taylor slowly pulled the details from his pain-clouded mind. He told them everything that happened from the time he left the house right up to the point where he lost consciousness.

"After the two dudes grabbed me, the leader guy swung at me. I saw the punch coming and I tried to turn away, but he got me on the side of my face. The second blow came up from under my chin and everything went black. The next thing I remember is waking up here in the hospital with you, Cole."

"Did the punch knock you out, Taylor?" Cole asked patiently.

"I can't even remember being hit. It's like his fist came up at me sorta slo-mo, then nothing. I must have one of those glass jaws they talk about in boxing, huh, Mom?"

Unshed tears ached behind Joely's eyes as she listened to him talk of his ordeal, but that's where they'd stay. If Taylor could put up a brave front for her, the least she could do was return the favor. She reached over to touch him lightly on the chin where the bruise darkly marred his fair skin.

"I guess you do. You did a real good job remembering everything, honey. When someone gets a bad concussion like you did, they often can't remember anything."

"I remember it like a dream. It doesn't seem real." He gave a soft laugh, then winced and closed his eyes. "It hurts like it's real, though."

"You'd make a great detective," Cole told him seriously. "You were very observant, even in such a scary situation. Your excellent description of those hoodlums will help us a great deal in locating them. You take it easy. I have to go to the detachment for awhile, but I'll be back."

Joely's throat tightened with love for him when he bent over Taylor and smoothed an affectionate caress across the top of her son's head. He turned and kissed her brow before he left. She realized afterwards she hadn't even thanked him for everything he'd done.

Taylor reached over and touched her hand. "I'm sorry, Mom."

Joely squeezed his fingers. "I'm sorry, too."

"What you told me about Dad, it's the truth, isn't it?"

She nodded sadly. "We don't have to discuss that right now, honey. You need rest."

Taylor stared at the ceiling and Joely could almost hear him thinking. Very quietly. Trying to remember. "I know Dad used to hit me and I used to be scared of him. But I'm not anymore and I'm not mad at him. I still want to go see him."

Joely bit down on her trembling lip. "Just because you find out something disappointing about someone, it doesn't mean you have to stop loving them. Your dad has some serious problems in his life, but I can assure you, you're not one of them. I know he loves you very much and he is so very sorry for what he did to you."

She squeezed his fingers again and gave his hand the tiniest of shakes. "And about Grandpa's ring, I don't want you to feel guilty about losing it. There was nothing you could do. You'll miss having it though, won't you?"

Taylor nodded his head and winced again with the pain. As though on cue, the nurse returned to the room and adeptly administered a painkiller. She took Taylor's pulse and inspected the IV drip, then smiled and winked at Taylor before leaving.

"Close your eyes, honey," Joely urged him. "I'll be right here beside you when you wake up." She sat quietly, her fingers linked through her son's and watched him fall into the blessed release of sleep.

Chapter Fourteen

"Good morning, sunshine." Joely leaned over the railing to kiss Taylor's forehead. Although his bruises were a darker, uglier shade of purple, she thought he looked much better. His bed was slightly elevated, the nasal tube had been removed, and hospital pajamas covered the tube in his bandaged chest. "Did you have some breakfast?"

"Nah, I might get some mushy stuff later. My jaw hurts and my stomach's kinda woozy so the doctor said I gotta just drink fluids."

Knowing what a healthy appetite he had, Joely offered him a look of commiseration. "I'll bring you a chocolate shake later. Have you seen Cole?"

"Um-hmm. He came in a little after you left last night. He told me his watch commander put out a BOLF report on those guys who stole my ring. That means 'Be on the look-out for'. I also talked to a West Van police officer. Everyone will be searching for my ring. I just know I'll get it back."

Joely didn't share his confidence, but she didn't want to discourage his optimism, so she changed the subject. "The doctor thinks you might be able to go home tomorrow. It's only a maybe right now, depending on when they're able to remove the chest tube, so don't get your hopes up too high yet. You have some serious injuries there, sport." She lowered the railing and settled comfortably on the edge of the bed. "I phoned Uncle Harry last night, and he let Grandma and Uncle Rick know what happened. He and Aunt Carolyn will probably come see you after work this evening."

"I hope Grandma doesn't worry too much. She'll feel real bad I lost Grandpa's ring," Taylor added morosely.

Joely rubbed a hand over his tousled blond hair, before sliding it down his cheek, turning his face toward her. "I didn't mention the ring to Uncle Harry because it's not important. The only important thing is for you to get better. I know you treasured that ring. It made you feel connected to your grandpa and I'm sorry it's gone, but everyone loves you way more than they do any old ring. Believe me, no one will blame you for losing it. It wasn't your fault."

Taylor nodded slightly, showing his understanding, if not his agreement. "Does Dad know I'm in here? Maybe I should call him and tell him I'm okay."

"I'm sure Uncle Rick already called your dad. If it makes you feel better, you can phone him when you get home."

After visiting with Taylor most of the morning, Joely felt confident enough in his recovery to go to the office for a few hours. It horrified Maggie and Stella to hear what happened and they both took time off during the afternoon to visit with him. Maggie brought the chocolate shake Joely had promised, along with a selection of magazines. Harry and Carolyn came after dinner, with a new handheld video game for Taylor to play. When Joely left the hospital that evening, she felt content Taylor had plenty to keep him amused.

She hadn't heard from Cole since he left the hospital the previous day. She probably should phone and thank him for all his help, but she held back because even though she owed him a huge debt of gratitude, it wouldn't be right to use it as an excuse to contact him. Nothing had changed between them and she didn't want to start back up with him, not until he admitted he had feelings for her. It was too easy to forget her resolve when around him, so she decided a nice thank you card might be a better option.

* * * *

Cole had just returned to the detachment after spending the afternoon in court, when Trip Wilson came by his office. Trip had been back to work for about a month, and although he and Cole weren't particularly friendly, they maintained a polite working relationship.

"Corporal, I've been looking for you. I brought in a couple of persons of interest you might wanna talk to. They match the description on the BOLF the watch commander put out this morning. Interested?"

Tension twanged inside Cole like a wire drawn too tight. "Very. How'd you come across them?"

Trip heaved his powerful frame into the spare desk chair. It creaked in protest as he pressed his broad shoulders against the back. He explained how he'd been cruising around North Vancouver and was about to head back to the detachment when he caught a peripheral glimpse of the subjects as he drove by.

"There were two of them. A tall one, a real bone rack, and a short one with a boxer's build. I U-turned and cruised by again, nice and slow-like. The shorter dude stared me down as I rolled past. I thought he acted a little too cool and he gave me too much of an I-got-nothing-to-hide look.

"I checked the rearview mirror after I was by 'em, and sure enough, the little rat flipped me the bird. So, I parked a short ways away where I could observe their movements yet continue to maintain physical cover. They were verbally harassing every person who walked by, so I turned around again and pulled to the curb beside them. I got out of the cruiser and suggested they accompany me to the detachment, that we were interested in having a conversation with them. Naturally they weren't as interested as I was, but I managed to convince 'em."

Cole didn't comment. He wasn't sure he wanted to know what kind of persuasive tactics Trip deployed to convince them. "I can't believe you just happened across these guys, Trip. That's some piece of good luck."

Trip ducked his head, but not before Cole caught a glimpse of his pleased smile. "Actually I spent the entire day doing nothing but looking for those little creeps. If I didn't find them today, I woulda spent all day tomorrow searching for them and the next day too, for as long as it took. I wanted to do it for Joely, I mean, Ms. Sinclair and her kid. They didn't deserve the bum deal they got and I wanted to help 'em out. Ms. Sinclair was quick to help me when I needed a favor of her, even after the shabby way I've treated her. I figured I owed her. I'm pretty sure I got us two of the thugs who hurt her boy."

"I'll be sure to let Joely know what an upstanding job you did for her. She'll certainly appreciate your efforts. Now, which interview room are they in?"

"They're in separate rooms, one and two. The skinny bones," Trip consulted his notepad, "one Roger Kevin Lorency, doesn't have much to say. He's nineteen years old, has a juvy record for B&E, assault and possession of narcotics. He's quite nervous and appears to be high on an unknown substance, although there were no narcotics on his person.

"The other is Gerald John Michaluk, goes by Mick. He's twenty-one years old. The dude's all bravado and smart mouth, wants to see a lawyer. I made some inquiries on this guy, and word on the street is he's one mean little bugger, a regular walking reign of terror. His rap sheet's peppered with assault charges. The last charge stuck and he did some time. My take is he's got a drug habit, steals to pay for the narcotics, then gets his jollies beating on the vics after they've handed over their cash."

A powerful bolt of rage roared through Cole, making it hard to concentrate. He couldn't shake from his mind the image of Taylor's crooked half-smile. It was a boy's smile—a boy struggling hard to be a man. He was a good kid and he didn't deserve what happened to him.

Cole took his time getting a pad of paper from his desk drawer. By the time he stood up, he was back in business. "Thanks for the good work, Trip. I hope these are the perps I'm looking for. I think I'll start with Roger Lorency."

When Cole entered the interview room, he saw right away what Trip meant. The young man sat quietly with his head hanging down and he didn't acknowledge Cole's presence until he sat next to him. His small eyes, when he looked up, were a bit vacant, going in and out of focus. His narrow face, badly pockmarked with acne scars, was void of expression.

"All right, Roger, we know all about what you and your buddies have been up to. The drugs, the assaults, the robberies. You're in a fine mess of trouble but things might go easier for you if you're willing to cooperate."

The steel in his voice would've frightened tougher men than the one before him and Roger's hands shook visibly as he clenched them together. His vague gaze transformed into one of fear. "I don't know nuttin'. Ya gotta talk ta Mick," he muttered, refusing to make eye contact with Cole.

"Mick? You're referring to Gerald Michaluk?"

"Yeah, Mick. I ain't sayin' nuttin' 'less Mick says so."

"It's a real shame you don't have the backbone to stand up for yourself, Roger. But then why should I expect different? You're obviously a coward. Only a coward would hold a person so he can be beaten while he's helpless to defend himself."

Roger's sharply protruding Adams apple bobbed up and down nervously. "I ain't sayin' nuttin'." He licked his lips, then wiped his mouth on his shoulder.

"All right, I'll go see what Mick has to say. You sit here nice and comfy. I won't be too long. At least you better hope I'm not long. You seem to talk the talk pretty good, but I think your walking's got no legs. Judging by the way you're shaking and sweating, you must be about due for your next fix. You might not be quite as comfortable when I get back, then we'll see if you still have nothing to say."

He left Roger to think about that while he went to speak to Mick Michaluk. The short man was pacing pugnaciously about the room when Cole opened the door. The description Taylor gave him matched this fellow right down to the small, white scar on his chin. He was powerfully built, his nose pressed flat against his face and his deep-set eyes shone aggressively at Cole like two polished marbles. The smirk on his face was familiar to any cop. It was the look of a man who thought he was getting away with something.

"Mr. Michaluk, please take a seat. I have a few questions I'd like to discuss."

"I ain't got nuttin' ta say," Mick answered belligerently.

"I said take a seat."

Mick grabbed a chair and twisted it around, straddling it backward. Cole sat on the one at the other side of the table.

"You like flexing your macho little muscles, hey Mick? That's okay, tough guy, go ahead, see how far it gets you. We get lots of tough guys in here. And they generally end up talking sooner or later."

"I ain't talkin' 'til I see my lawyer."

So, he wanted to play it that way. That was fine. Cole had broken far tougher prospects than this one in his time. He leaned forward, closing the distance between their faces. "It's okay, you don't have to tell me anything. I already know what you did Monday night and I'm going to see you pay for it. You're going back to jail, pal."

Clamping his lips shut in a wide smirk, the young man responded by moving even closer to Cole. It became a game of nonphysical aggression. "What you know? You don't know squat."

Cole scowled and raised his voice. "You think *you're* me? You're asking *me* the questions now? All right, I'll tell you what I know and you see if it's squat. I know you approached a young man at Ambleside Park, soliciting him for money. I know when he told you truthfully he didn't have any, you had your two flunkies hold him while you hit him with your fists."

Cole's voice rose even louder in anger and loathing. "I know that after the boy was knocked out and lying helpless on the ground, you put the boots to him and then left him there, not caring whether he lived or died." He dropped his voice dangerously low. "And I know if anything happens to that boy, I'm gonna be on your heels all the way to hell."

Completely unperturbed by Cole's outburst, Mick crossed his arms casually along the back of the chair and Cole followed the movement, noticing the scraped and split condition of his knuckles. Fighter's hands to match his fighter's face. Cole's gaze came to rest on the ring Mick wore on his pinkie finger. It was a signet ring and Cole's mind instantly flashed back to when he had seen a ring like that before.

The first time he'd taken Taylor to basketball, the boy had been wearing a ring and was told he couldn't play with it on. Taylor worried he might lose the ring if he took it off. He said it had belonged to his grandfather and because they shared the same initial, his grandmother had given it to Taylor for his birthday. Cole had kept the ring in a zippered pocket for him and as soon as the game ended, Taylor promptly asked for it back. Losing his grandpa's ring had upset Taylor more than the beating he took.

"That ring you're wearing, Mick. Let me have a look at it."

The kid's room temperature IQ clicked on and he sat up, putting his hands in his lap. "It ain't mine. A buddy owed me money, so he gave me the ring ta pawn. I ain't got round ta it yet."

"Hand over the ring, or I'll call in a couple of members to assist you in removing it."

Mick twisted the ring off his finger and tossed it in Cole's direction. The initial T gleamed golden in the gemstone. Cole had no doubt the ring belonged to Taylor. His temples throbbed with pure fury. He wanted to reach across the table and do to this kid what he had done to Taylor. Instead, he carefully took a small baggy out of his pocket and placed the ring inside.

"I think it might be a good idea for you to call that lawyer of yours now."

* * * *

"Cole, hi!"

Joely was surprised and more than a little delighted when she answered the sharp rap at her patio door and found Cole standing there with a pleased grin on his face. With effort, she managed to put on a convincing show of casual nonchalance and invite him in. Once they settled into the living room, Cole told her everything that had transpired with the two young men Trip Wilson picked up that afternoon.

"I had to give the ring to the West Vancouver city police. Because the attack happened in Ambleside Park, it's in their jurisdiction. Taylor will get it back once the case is settled. It's as good as over anyway. As soon as Roger Lorency knew we made the connection with the ring and I told him we had a witness who could ID them, he folded like an umbrella. He said a person by the name of Wade Jackson was the third guy with them. The West Van police are picking him up as we speak. I think we'll be able to connect these three to a whole slew of unsolved assault cases in the lower mainland area. And it's all thanks to Trip Wilson, if you can believe that."

"Sure I believe it. Under all that bravado, Trip's a decent person. I'll make a point of thanking him as soon as possible. Taylor will be thrilled to have his ring back. I don't know how to thank you for all you've done."

"I know how you can," Cole responded, flashing her one of his perfect smiles.

Joely's head jerked up and she gaped at him, not willing to believe what he was implying. "What's that suppose to mean?"

His sidelong glance caught her startled look and his smile got even wider. "I'm starving. If you'll fix me one of your famous Denver omelets, I'll consider your debt wiped clean. Whaddaya say? Could you spare a couple of eggs for a hungry, hardworking cop who missed his lunch?"

Joely relaxed and smiled back. "You don't have to lay it on so thick, of course I'll feed you. Come sit in the kitchen and keep me company."

It only took a few minutes for Joely to whip up the omelet and it took Cole even less time to inhale it. She gawked in amazement at how quickly the food disappeared from the plate.

"You really were starving, weren't you? I should've made you something more substantial. That won't hold you for long."

"No, this hits the spot. Thanks." Cole pushed back his chair and extended his arms behind him. "I guess I should head home. I've taken up enough of your time."

Joely watched the play of bicep muscles as he stretched and her mouth went dry. "You don't have to rush off," she assured him. "It's been a bit too quiet and lonely around here without Taylor. Why don't I dish up some ice cream and we can see if there's anything good on TV?"

That suggestion was probably a huge mistake. She shouldn't be anywhere near this man, especially not while feeling so vulnerable and obligated to him. Her brain might be telling her one thing, but her heart spoke of something entirely different. The yearning rising up inside her swept away logical thought and her firm resolve along with it.

A fleeting shadow passed over Cole's face, then resolved itself into a smile.

"Why not?"

Joely could think of several good reasons "why not", but not one of them seemed to matter at the moment. She didn't want him walking out the door just yet.

* * * *

Cole had been so lonely for Joely's company, what harm would there be in spending a few hours with her? He could behave himself for that short length of time. He'd do it for Joely, because she asked him to stay, even if it'd be damn tough keeping his paws off her.

"Do you have Mocca Almond Crunch?"

"You know I do. Why don't you check the TV listings, while I dish up the ice cream?"

Fighting an urgent impulse to flee, Cole sprawled out on a corner of the couch and tried to concentrate on the newspaper guide. He kept telling himself to leave, to get up and walk out. The barrier he'd so carefully built around himself had developed serious cracks, leaving him defenseless and exposed, and conflicting emotions warred with one another inside his head. It scared him and he wanted to be alone to regroup. But his yearning to be with Joely outweighed his fear and this frightened him even more.

Before he'd finished battling it out, Joely returned with the ice cream. She set his bowl on the coffee table in front of him and sat herself down beside him.

"Find anything to watch?" she asked, shifting her weight and tucking her feet beneath her.

Cole dropped the guide onto the table and picked up his dessert. He couldn't look Joely's way because she sat close enough for him to smell her scent and it stirred up his senses. Coming on to her in any way whatsoever would be very bad form, so he focused on pushing the ice cream around the bowl instead.

"This might not be such a good idea. I should eat my ice cream and go." He cursed himself for speaking when he heard the tremble in his voice.

Leave, this moment, get up and leave now. The words pulsed through his brain in warning. But another plea, this one coming from his heart, rang even louder. *Stay, this is where you want to be, so just stay put.*

* * * *

Joely took a small bite of ice cream, holding the cold

sweetness in her mouth as she studied Cole's profile. His beautifully sculptured mouth pursed slightly as he stared down at his bowl and her heart stirred in her chest. She'd never be able to look at his lips without recalling the magic of them on her body.

"I don't want you to leave," she objected bluntly, urgently. Common sense told her she shouldn't have said that, but common sense had nothing to do with the fire leaping from pulse to pulse, turning her body hot and restless.

A traitorous excitement built in her system and it was no longer important that he only wanted her body, and not her heart. It didn't even matter that he could give her only a part of himself. She wanted that part and she needed it right now.

Let tomorrow take care of tomorrow. Just give me one more night with the man I love.

"Please stay with me tonight."

Cole carefully set his bowl down and turned to her, his fathomless brown eyes searching hers, as though unable to believe she wanted this. The smile he gave her showed traces of tiredness, wariness, mingled with pleasure, and he reached across to gently caress her cheek with his fingers—the strong, capable fingers she loved so much.

"I'll stay. If you aren't comfortable making love, that's all right with me. I'm happy just to hold you…touch you." His fingers slid up through her hair, before settling back on her cheek, his thumb tracing the outline of her mouth.

She shot him a look that promised to charge his batteries, then stood and pulled him to his feet, slipping her hands down his back, feeling the play of muscles in the marvelously constructed body beneath the thin cotton shirt.

A low, husky groan rumbled through Cole's chest. He lowered his mouth onto hers in hard possession. Her lips willingly parted under his. Their kiss was long and probing. When it ended, they were both left shaken. Taking up his hand, Joely led him to the bedroom.

They wasted no time in ridding each other of their clothing, then tumbled onto the bed, kissing, tasting, caressing, trying to make up for the time they had lost.

* * * *

Cole's sated body relaxed as they lay quietly in each other's arms. His mind roamed back in time, focusing on his past and how it had always held him back from truly loving anyone. He forced himself to acknowledge the sadness and regret that existed inside him because of everything he once had and then lost. Sarah, his precious little girl, wasn't coming back and he could do nothing about it. But there were others who loved him and needed him in their lives. Joely and Taylor were just waiting for him to let them in, if only he could allow himself to do it.

His throat ached with emotion and he cradled Joely more securely in his arms. He felt the strength of her love flowing into him. All the lonely, painful circumstances of his life came rushing up to swamp him and his surprising need to share it with Joely grew so acute, nothing could dam the words.

"Do you remember the first time I came to your place, to speak to Taylor?"

Joely murmured her acknowledgment with a small puzzled sound.

"It made me incredibly jealous when Taylor came in the room and kissed your cheek, and you touched his face with such love. I felt green with envy because he got to kiss you and not me. Mostly, I envied the loving relationship between the two of you, as a parent and a child. It painfully reminded me how I once had a connection like that with my daughter, but it was now gone forever and I missed it so much.

"It also reminded me how I had never shared that type of love with my own father. I can't remember ever sitting on his lap, not even as a small child. When he told me my mother died in a car accident, I started crying and I tried to wrap my arms around his neck for comfort. Instead of giving me the security I needed, he pulled my arms away and insisted I stop crying. In my family, showing vulnerability is showing weakness."

This confession wasn't easy for Cole. Pulling the words out hurt more than pulling teeth, but with each admission it got a little easier. Maybe Joely was right and he could handle this whole dealing-with-your-emotions thing, after all.

Chapter Fifteen

Jocly didn't move so much as a muscle, stunned by Cole's revelations and this unexpected willingness to discuss himself. Curiosity and questions consumed her, but instinct told her to keep quiet and let him tell her, in his own way, what he was finally ready to say.

"My father never liked it when my mom cuddled me or kissed me too much. Said I'd grow up to be a sissy. But when we were alone, she always held me in her arms and made me feel safe and loved. Then one day she vanished, no warning, no goodbyes. My father said she died and that meant she was gone for good."

Cole fell silent and Joely searched for something to say, scared of saying the wrong thing. She yearned to reach out and help him carry the pain he shouldered, but she didn't want him to turn away, to close that door on her again.

"It sounds like your mom loved you a great deal and she would've never wanted to leave you. You're such an easy person to love—" She abruptly cut off the flow of words. She wouldn't burden him with professions of love until she was certain he wanted to hear them. He'd allowed her inside his armored walls and if she intended to stay, she'd have to use the greatest care and delicacy.

"Easy to love?" Cole gave a bark of laughter. "I doubt Debra would've agreed with you."

Joely turned slightly in his arms, moving her head from his chest to his shoulder so she could watch his face. He looked down at her, his gaze naked and vulnerable.

"Debra?"

He took a shuddering breath. "My ex-wife. There wasn't a lot of love in my marriage, which was both our faults. I realized almost from the start the restless passion I felt for her had little to do with real love. She was physically beautiful and extremely strong-willed, and I thought I needed that type of woman—the opposite of my gentle, submissive mother.

"Didn't take long to discover the shallowness of her beauty. She was totally selfish—selfish and self-absorbed. The entire world had to revolve around what Debra wanted or didn't want. And she wanted much more than a rookie cop could provide. And she didn't want children. More than anything, I craved a family, and we fought constantly about it. I was about ready to admit defeat and end our marriage when we found out she was pregnant. For me, her pregnancy was the luckiest of accidents.

"Once Sarah came into my life, I became so busy falling in love with my baby, Debra's constant demands ceased to exist for me. I'll never forget the day the nurse handed me that warm, wiggly little bundle. It felt like holding a tiny miracle in my hands."

He cupped his hands together in front of him, and Joely easily envisioned him cradling a small baby. Carefully, adoringly. Proud and protective. If possible, that image made her fall in love with him a little bit more.

She nodded and whispered, "I know what you mean."

Cole gave her a tender smile. "I had no clue it was possible to love another human being as much as I loved my little girl. And the real miracle was how she loved me back—completely and unconditionally. She was my little princess, my angel, and Debra constantly complained about how I spoilt her. After Sarah died, our sham of a marriage couldn't survive all the bitterness and guilt between us. I haven't heard from her since, except for the divorce papers in the mail."

He grew quiet, and Joely held her tongue, giving him time to sort through his memories. When he began to speak again, it was as though he were alone in the room, talking to himself, reminiscing. He looked at nothing except the ceiling above them. He explained that as much as he disliked and resented Debra, he couldn't put all the blame for their breakup on her. He'd completely shut down, had been capable of nothing more than the barest of survival motions, not wanting to remember, to think, to feel. He had nothing left inside to give his wife—he hadn't wanted to give her anything. He didn't want to love her. He didn't want to love anyone, and it had been a relief when she left. It allowed him to completely cocoon his feelings and emotions. To feel absolutely nothing.

"When I allow myself to think about Sarah, I miss her so badly, I can't breathe. She was such a lively little girl, and smart too. From the time she was tiny, those big brown eyes took in everything around her with intelligent curiosity. She wanted to experience everything and had no natural fear. She especially liked to climb."

He stopped talking again, swallowing hard. With tears burning her eyes, Joely braced herself. She almost couldn't bear to hear what she knew must come next.

* * * *

The events of the day his daughter died, long buried, but never forgotten, came charging out at Cole and he nearly choked on the agony of it.

"One day, Debra paged me at work to say Sarah had fallen out of the big maple tree in the school yard, and Debra wanted to know if I could pick her up from school. She sounded annoyed that her schedule would be disrupted if I didn't go. I got to Sarah's school at the same time as the ambulance. My little girl died three hours later of a cerebral hemorrhage. She had just turned eight years old."

Cole could feel Joely trembling, and she pressed her face against his shoulder. Her tears warmed his skin, and he envied her the release those tears brought. Pain radiated from his body. His throat burned and his chest ached, but his eyes remained dry.

Joely softly kissed his shoulder and tightened her hold on him. "Oh, Cole," she whispered. "What a terrible, terrible tragic accident."

"I couldn't reach Debra so she didn't get to the hospital until it was too late. I just couldn't forgive her for that. For a brief time before they took Sarah into surgery, she was conscious and she stared at me with huge pain-wracked eyes that begged me to make it better. Daddy always made everything better, except that time I couldn't. I've never felt so helpless in my entire life.

"The doctor explained afterward that Sarah had been born with an aneurysm. It was a miracle, he said, she'd lived for eight years. I was supposed to feel lucky I had her for that long. Well, I didn't feel lucky, I felt as dead as she was. I'd lie in bed and see her face, hear her voice. Her happy little giggle is forever imprinted on the inside of my eardrums. Then I'd torment myself wondering what kind of mischief she would've been up to that day if she were still alive."

Joely laid her hand against his cheek in a warm caress. He covered her hand with his, and turned his head to kiss her palm.

"I can't imagine the horror it must have been for you. I don't think I'd make it if that happened to Taylor."

"You'd make it because you have no choice, but it's absolute hell. That's what seemed so unbearable to me—life just *went on*. A parent should never outlive their children. It's much too cruel. And the sadness never goes away, you merely get used to carrying it. I could only cope by refusing to acknowledge my grief. If I denied its existence, I thought I might have some hope of surviving."

His voice took on a quaver and turmoil churned in his stomach. What the hell was he *doing*? What would Joely think after seeing him at his most vulnerable? Then he forced himself to relax and for the first time since Sarah's death, an inner spring of tension began to gradually unwind. He refused to damn himself for opening up his heart, especially not with this wonderful, compassionate woman who loved him.

To hell with his beliefs that he'd only be strong if he didn't care about anyone. Loving Joely didn't make him weak. It strengthened him. Yes, he needed her, but that wasn't a weakness. That was love. And he wanted it, very much. If Joely wanted him too, no way would he risk losing her again.

"When my daughter died, I died. I mean in a very real way, everything I was or thought I was, died with her and I felt completely alone. I was lost. Until you found me." He sought out and found Joely's eyes and he knew the pain would finally stop because he read clearly in her loving gaze that she wanted to take another chance with him. "You have a beautiful heart, Joely, and you've somehow managed to unlock mine. A stubborn, scarred-up, old heart that's been closed to everything for a long time."

She opened her arms to him and he moved his body to cover hers. Her kisses were sweet and poignant. There was no urgency to their movements this time, only a slow, sure rhythm that was healing as much as it was pleasing. The new certainty they felt with each other twined around them and brought its own special magic to their lovemaking. Then, locked in the warm circle of each other's arms, they finally slept.

* * * *

The sound of a ringing phone penetrated Joely's dream and her subconscious ordered her to ignore it. She snuggled closer to the warmth of Cole's body, but when he moved out of her reach she opened one bleary eye to look at him. He sat on the edge of the bed and spoke quietly into the phone. Joely's brain had barely reached a level of functioning that allowed her to wonder who would be calling at the crack of dawn. Cole always woke up completely alert and she gave thanks the phone was on his side.

After he hung up, he turned on the bedside lamp and touched Joely gently on the shoulder. "Joely, honey, are you awake?"

She squinted up at him. "What time is it?" Leaning up on one elbow, she rubbed at her eyes. As she took her hand away, she caught a good look at Cole, and what she saw shocked her wide-awake.

The expression on his face was pure, naked anguish.

"My goodness, Cole, what is it? Who was on the phone?" Iciness crept over her skin and she sat up, pulling the duvet protectively around her.

Cole looked upward, blinking, and he took a deep breath, then shook his head. "The hospital. They've had to move Taylor to ICU. It's serious and they want you to get there as quickly as possible."

Seconds slipped by as her mind tried without success to grapple with what he'd said. "No, they're mistaken. Taylor's coming home tomorrow—today. He's okay. He's better now."

Nothing could be wrong with Taylor. She shook her head over and over again with increasing agitation. She couldn't believe it, wouldn't believe it. It simply wasn't a possibility.

Cole caught her face up with his hands, holding her still. "Listen, honey. You have to get dressed and I'll take you to the hospital. We have to leave right now. Do you understand? Taylor

196 Joyce M. Holmes

needs you."

"Did they say—" Joely gulped back a sob. "Did they say what happened?" She slid off the bed and started dressing, her motions stiff and mechanical.

Cole gave a brief negative shake of his head. "No, they're running tests to figure that out." He pulled on his clothes as he spoke. "The nurse I talked to said he's in acute pain and he's breathing with extreme difficulty. The doctor should have some answers by time we get there."

Joely went into the bathroom to splash some water on her face and run a comb through her hair. The drawn colorless face looking back at her from the mirror appeared to be that of a stranger's. A stranger who had just been told her son was dangerously ill.

A sick churning began in her stomach, prompted by waves of fear. One thought stuck in her brain, circling tirelessly—Taylor couldn't die, she couldn't bear it if he died. The thought of losing her child was insufferable, but the fact was there to be suffered all the same.

They made the short trip through the dark, quiet streets in tense silence. When they arrived at the hospital, Joely stared at the building with dread. Intuitively understanding her reluctance to enter, Cole eased his hand onto her back and half guided, half pushed her toward the ICU where Dr. Halliwell waited for them.

The doctor solemnly explained they had located a blood clot in Taylor's lung that had suffered the pneumothorax. "The pulmonary embolism has severely cut off the blood supply to the lung. He needs to have surgery immediately to remove it."

A cold hand closed around Joely's heart and squeezed. She drew a deep tortured breath, reaching out a shaky hand to grip Cole's fingers.

"What are the risks to this surgery?" Cole demanded.

Dr. Halliwell looked seriously from one to the other. "The thrombus must be removed in one piece. If it breaks apart, there's the possibility of serious complications. We'll take every precaution to ensure that doesn't happen."

Joely squeezed her eyes shut and swayed against Cole. Fear strained her breathing and she had difficulty comprehending what she heard. Some things were too awful for the mind to accept.

"Isn't there something less risky you could do? Blast it with a laser or shrink it with radiation or something?" Even though she knew her words sounded frantic, crazy probably, she couldn't stop herself from asking.

The young doctor grimaced sympathetically and shook his head. "At this point, surgery is our best option. There are drugs we could administer in hopes of dissolving the thrombus, but I'm afraid we don't have the luxury of time. We must move expediently."

"So, you're saying if he goes to surgery, he could die and if he doesn't, he could die also?" Cole choked out in disbelief. "That's great, we've got a couple of great options." He took Joely in his arms and held on for all he was worth. She could feel him trembling and she hugged him back before turning in his arms to listen to what else the doctor had to say.

"I must repeat, time is an important factor here." He spoke patiently, but Joely read the urgency in his body language. "We want to get him into the OR right away to remove the blood clot before it causes any further damage. I need your permission before I can proceed."

Knowing she had to make up her mind in a hurry, but filled with uncertainty, Joely debated the best course of action. "We have to chance the operation," she said finally. "I want to see him first. Is he awake?"

"Yes, although I must warn you, he's in pain and it's difficult for him to breathe. He won't be able to say much."

"It's enough he knows we're here for him."

After signing the necessary paperwork, Joely went into the ICU room by herself. It took her several seconds before she got her emotions under control so she could look at Taylor the way she thought she should look at him. One glance revealed his world of hurt.

All natural color had drained from his face, the bruises stood out in stark relief against the whiteness of his skin. His eyes were glazed with pain and fright. A light film of sweat dampened his forehead and upper lip. The nasal cannula was back in place, feeding him the oxygen he badly needed to help him breathe. Electrodes from a heart monitor decorated his bare chest.

She kissed his cheek and sat beside the bed, taking his hand in hers. "Hi, sweetheart. I don't want you to worry about this, okay? It's just a small setback. The doctor says you need a little operation and you'll be fine afterward. I'll wait right here. As soon as you wake up, I'll be here to see you, I promise."

"Mom," he gasped, his hand tightening in hers. "What's wrong with me?"

Joely refused to tell him the gravity of the situation, the riskiness of the operation, but she needed to explain the facts in simple terms to ease his mind. She'd do all the worrying for the both of them.

She dredged up a convincing smile and made herself speak confidently, even though she questioned the accuracy of her information. "Don't try to talk, honey. Save your strength and I'll tell you what I can. When you were injured, when your rib broke, it pierced your lung. Somewhere, probably at the site of the puncture, a blood clot formed. That clot is now blocking the blood supply to your lung. That's why it hurts to breathe.

"The doctor has to remove that little clot and everything will be back to normal, you'll be able to breathe again. I'm sorry you have to go through this pain, but I want you to stay calm and put your trust in the doctors to make you better. I love you, Taylor, remember that."

It relieved her to see some of the alarm recede from his eyes.

The door opened and two orderlies rolled in a gurney. They efficiently lifted Taylor and his multitude of tubes over onto the gurney and silently rolled him back out. Joely reached out a hand to the place on the bed where Taylor had just laid, her fingers spread out against the warmth that lingered on the sheets. She rested her forehead against the chrome railing and closed her eyes, praying for a miracle.

A hand squeezed her shoulder and she looked up to see Cole standing beside her. Their eyes met, gazes filled with so much grief and suffering, they couldn't hold the look for long.

"Come on, you don't need to sit in here. It's too depressing. Let's go into one of the lounges for awhile." Cole's voice sounded hoarse, as though he had a cold.

"I can't leave. I told Taylor I'd wait here."

"We'll let the ICU nurse know where to find us. Taylor won't be back for hours."

They found a quiet corner of the visitor's lounge and Joely sagged against Cole's strong body as they searched for comfort on the hard couch. He turned her toward him, pulling her into the incredible gentleness of his arms, stroking her hair as he pressed her cheek against his chest.

"Try to empty your mind of all your worries and just relax. Get some sleep if you can."

The touch of his hand in her hair and the soft crooning of his voice soothed her and she snuggled closer, closing her eyes in the safe harbor of his embrace. Amazingly enough, she did fall asleep. For a moment, a brief wonderful moment, when she woke up she thought it had all been a nightmare. The moment didn't last. Recollection crashed through her and she pushed her way out of Cole's arms.

He lightly brushed the hair back from her face. "I wish you had slept longer."

His face was drawn, his eyes haggard and his jaw darkly stubbled. Joely doubted he'd slept at all. "I wonder why we haven't heard anything yet?"

"It hasn't even been an hour. You'll probably feel better if we get some food into you. How about we go to the cafeteria and grab something quick?"

Reluctantly Joely agreed to go with him. But once there, she found she could do no more than push the food around on her plate. To placate Cole, she took two bites of the toast and drank the orange juice, not tasting any of it.

Cole cleared his throat uncomfortably, and Joely shifted her empty gaze from her plate and turned it up to him.

"I have to go to the detachment for awhile. I need to rearrange my schedule if I want to spend the rest of the day here with you. Will you be okay without me for a short time? Can I phone Stella or Maggie to come and sit with you?"

She reached over to give his arm a reassuring squeeze. "Thanks for the offer, but you go ahead. There's nothing you can do here and I'll be fine by myself. I'll wait a little longer, then I'll make some phone calls." She pressed her fingertips into her forehead and rubbed them across her brow. "I left my cell phone at home on the charger. We were in such a rush…"

It took real effort to swallow down the huge lump of pain and terror lodged in her throat as she remembered the panicked early morning trip to the hospital and the reason behind it.

Cole got to his feet and pushed his chair in. "I can swing by your place and get it for you."

Joely stood as well, and they started back to ICU. "No, you go do what you need to do. I'm sure I can find a payphone in the lobby. It just means I can't keep you updated with texts."

"Don't worry about that, I'll get back here as soon as I can."

No news, good or bad, waited for them at ICU and Joely braced herself for a long, tense day. She knew Cole was delaying. He hugged her over and over again, trying to convince her Taylor would be okay, offering reassurances they both knew he had no right to make. When he finally said he had to go, she pressed her forehead against his shoulder, wishing he could stay. With his arms around her, she found the strength to believe everything would come out all right. She wasn't sure she could keep it together without him by her side, but she also understood he had other responsibilities. If she asked him to stay, he would, even if he shouldn't. So, she put on a brave face and didn't mention how being alone terrified her.

Once he left, she had nothing to do except wait. But she found herself incapable of just sitting and doing nothing. She moved back and forth from the closed double door of the Intensive Care Unit to the chairs designated for family members. She drank black coffee and watched the clock. Several times, the ICU nurse came out to talk to her. The news remained the same—surgery was running long, and Taylor continued to hold his own.

For what felt like the hundredth time, Joely closed her eyes and leaned her head back against the wall. She heard the ICU door open and a uniform rustled. She sat forward and looked up expectantly at the nurse standing in front of her.

Despite her professional air, the nurse's observant eyes held a gentle quality as they swept over Joely's face. "I just got word from surgery and I knew you'd want to hear right away. Taylor is in recovery now, he'll be back up to ICU soon. I can't tell you any more than that, but the doctor will be up to speak with you shortly."

Taylor was okay! He made it!

The words sang joyously in Joely's brain. Overwhelmed by her sense of relief, she could do little more than murmur her thanks to the nurse. It all suddenly became too much for her and she put her head in her hands and began to sob. Footsteps came from down the hall, then someone sat in the chair next to hers. Her intuition told her it wasn't Cole, so she ignored the person.

A hand touched her arm. "Joely? What happened to Taylor?"

Joely's head jerked up at the sound of panic in Brad's voice. "What—what are you doing here?"

Tension was written all over his face and a muscle leaped along his jawline. "I came as soon as I could arrange it after Rick called. Why are you crying? Has Taylor taken a turn for the worse?"

She twisted toward him, her teeth bared in anger. "Taylor and I have been through hell and back the past few days, and it's all your fault," she hissed, shoving him away from her. "*Your* fault, Brad Mills. If you would've told Taylor he couldn't visit you, if you were honest with him instead of encouraging him to defy me, none of this would've happened."

Joely raged on and on, venting all her fears and frustrations on the man sitting next to her. Ignoring the flinch that altered his expression, she told him in vivid detail everything that had happened to Taylor since the night he'd found out the truth about his dad. Several times Brad opened his mouth to speak, but each time he closed it again. Finally, a sliver of rational thought returned to Joely and she managed to stem her angry eruption. She turned abruptly away from Brad, drawing several deep breaths to calm herself.

Out of the corner of her eye, she saw Brad avert his head. He put his hands over his face and began to weep. These weren't his usual tears of self-pity, they were the deep wrenching sobs of a man in mortal agony.

"Oh, Brad, no, don't cry," she stammered, instantly full of regret, ashamed of her outburst. "I'm sorry, I shouldn't have hurled all those terrible things at you. It's not your fault. I've just been so scared I might lose Taylor."

Brad looked over at her with self-condemning eyes of anguish. "No, you're right to blame me. I've made such a mess of my life. Of all our lives. When I saw you sitting here crying, I thought Taylor had died, or something awful, and I wanted to die too."

"I was crying with relief. He's been in the OR for hours. The surgery carried many risks, but I just heard he's in recovery and I'm certain he'll be fine. I can't believe you flew out here. Why didn't you tell me you were coming?"

Brad scrubbed hard at his face, then dried his hands on his pants. "Because I didn't want you to say I couldn't see Taylor. Rick sounded vague when he called, he just said Taylor was hospitalized because he had been beaten up and he had a concussion. I phoned your place this morning from the airport. When I didn't get an answer, I came directly here."

"I'm sorry I laid into you. I've been overwhelmed with guilt myself since this happened, so I needed someone else to blame. I guess you were the easiest target. I'm actually glad you're here. It'll make Taylor feel much better to see both of us when he comes up."

Brad reached out and tentatively took Joely's hand. "I want to tell you something else. After I left here in May, I joined AA. I haven't taken a drink in two months. I'm back in counseling and I think I'll be able to do it this time. I want to straighten up and be the kind of dad Taylor can be proud of."

Joely bit her lower lip. She had heard that line too many times to get excited by it. Although joining AA was a very positive step, and not an insignificant one. Two months without a drink was a long time for Brad. She had no doubt he spoke the truth.

"I hope it works for you this time. I really do. You understand, don't you, that Taylor knows what happened between the two of you when he was little?"

Brad closed his eyes against the tears welling up. "I'll talk to him. I can never excuse why I did what I did, but I can say how sorry I am and tell him how much I love him." The tears wouldn't be contained and they slid down his cheeks.

Joely's battered heart broke for him, for all of them, and the pain they'd endured. She slipped her arms around his heaving shoulders. They held on to each other and cried.

* * * *

Cole rushed back to the hospital as soon as he could, anxious to see Joely and check on Taylor's condition. It had bothered him all morning that Joely might get word about the surgery and he wouldn't be with her when she needed him. He knew how it felt to sit and wait alone, not knowing if the child you loved would live or die.

He clearly remembered the frustration, the helplessness and absolute anguish he went through. Losing a child had to be the deepest fear of a parent. He hadn't wanted Joely to face the possibility by herself.

He worried about how Joely would survive if Taylor didn't pull through. She wouldn't die if Taylor did, but a part of her most assuredly would. He had firsthand knowledge of how hard it was to function when such an important part of you was dead inside. A nasty feeling deep in his gut told him if anything happened to the boy, Joely wouldn't be the only one not to recover. He didn't think he could go through that agony again and come out as a whole person a second time.

As he approached the ICU, he saw Joely embracing a man he didn't recognize. He hesitated in his stride until he realized they were both crying.

Taylor!

Something happened to Taylor! Terror blindsided him, his breath ripped painfully from his body.

"Joely!" He knew his voice came out too loud when they both jumped and moved away from one another. Joely's eyes were bruised and darkened by anxiety, her entire ordeal written in the dark circles under her eyes. Pushing aside his dread, Cole attempted to compose himself and try again. "Taylor—is he out of surgery? Have you heard anything?"

Joely sprang from her chair and threw herself at him, clutching him tightly. "I'm so glad you're back. Taylor's in recovery. He made it through the surgery." She used both hands to wipe her face free of tears. "I'm afraid I lost it there for awhile and Brad took the brunt of it, but I'm okay now. Especially now you're here."

Cole eyed the tall blond man standing a few feet away, swiping furtively at his eyes. So this was Brad, the man who had caused such misery for Joely. He wanted to hate him, but he didn't—he felt pity. He pitied him because he had been married to a wonderful woman and had fathered a great kid, and through his own shortcomings, he'd lost it all.

Brad's loss was his gain. He had plenty of shortcomings of his own, and he was so grateful for Joely's willingness to give him a second chance. He didn't plan to ever lose her again.

"Brad." Joely motioned him over. "Come and meet Cole. You remember the police officer Taylor has befriended?"

Brad stepped stiffly up to Cole, and Joely watched the only two men she had ever loved as they shook hands. They were of much the same height, but all resemblance ended there. Cole was powerfully built, dark and ruggedly handsome. Brad was lean and lanky. Although he was a couple of years younger than Cole, he looked older. Still an attractive man, his golden good looks had dissipated slightly over the years. His face was softer and creased, showing the effects of too much hard drinking.

Joely almost smiled at the way they cautiously took each other's measure. An ears-back, watchful sort of look male dogs give each other before deciding whether it was worth fighting.

Then Brad gave a shaky smile. "It's nice to finally meet you, Cole. I understand you're someone pretty special to my son and I want to thank you for spending time with him." He took a quick, audible, breath and began speaking again before Cole could respond. "I missed seeing you last time I came out because I needed to get drunk instead. For the record, I haven't had a drink since that day. Hopefully, I'm on the road to becoming a recovering alcoholic."

Cole looked a little taken aback by the impromptu confession. He glanced briefly at Joely before answering. "That's good to hear. Taylor also thinks a lot of you. He'll be glad to know his dad cares enough about him to get sober."

As Joely continued to observe the two together, she realized she didn't hate Brad anymore. She could finally leave the memory of their life together in the past where it belonged. If Taylor was willing to forgive him and move on, then so could she.

She spotted Dr. Halliwell coming toward them from down the hall and she introduced Brad as Taylor's dad.

"When will Taylor be back in his room?" Brad asked the doctor, showing his impatience to see for himself that his son was all right.

"I just left him in recovery. His vitals are stable and he's awake, so they'll bring him up shortly. We had a little problem with the thrombus rupturing during surgery, however, we're confident we found all the pieces and the bleeding was minimal. He'll have to be closely monitored and we'll keep him on blood thinners for a while. You can all stop worrying now. Taylor will make a full recovery."

When Taylor was settled into his room, they were told only two people at a time could go in to see him. Cole volunteered to wait so Joely and Brad could be with him first. Taylor was lightly drowsing when they entered the room. Joely bent on tiptoes over the railing. She rested her cheek against the top of his head and closed her eyes with relief.

"You did real good, my son," she whispered and kissed his pale cheek. His eyes fluttered opened at her gentle touch.

"Hey, Mom," he said weakly.

"Hi, baby. Look who's here." Joely stepped back to let Taylor see his dad.

"Dad!" His voice contained a lot more enthusiasm this time.

"Hi, sport."

Joely sensed the apprehension in Brad and she decided to give him some time alone with Taylor so the two of them could sort things out.

"Tell you what, Taylor, Cole's waiting outside for his turn to see you. I'll go keep him company and you can visit with your dad for a bit, then Cole and I will come check on you, okay?" She smoothed a hand over his cheek and leaned down to kiss him again.

Brad nodded his appreciation when she turned to him. "Keep it light, and don't tire him or upset him," she whispered in warning before leaving them alone.

Chapter Sixteen

Brad wiped his hands nervously on the front of his pants and cleared his throat, trying to figure out what exactly to say to his son.

"Your mom says you've been through quite an ordeal these past few days. I'm real sorry about that, and I guess I have to take some responsibility for what happened."

Taylor didn't say anything for a moment. He stared levelly at Brad and his jaw firmed. "Mom told me why she'd never let me see you alone, but I don't think what just happened is your fault. I got mad at Mom and I did some stupid stuff. I've had to grow up a lot this week and I know this was no one's fault."

Brad sat tentatively on the chair beside the bed, leaning forward with his forearms on his thighs. "I don't know what to say, Taylor, how to explain my past behavior to you. I'm an alcoholic, and I have been for most of my life. That's not an excuse for my poor behavior when you were a little boy." He leaned closer, desperate to see some sign of forgiveness on Taylor's impassive face, wanting it, but knowing he didn't deserve it.

"So, I won't try to excuse myself. I'd like to tell you about my life back then. I don't know if it'll help you understand me any better or not, but I want to tell you anyway. Okay?"

After a long hesitation, Taylor's blond head nodded imperceptibly. Not an encouraging gesture, but Brad didn't expect more. He covered his face with his hands and breathed deeply several times, then focused back on Taylor.

"I was always real popular back in school, you see. Then I graduated, barely, and suddenly I had to face the real world. Not only was I no longer Mr. Popular, I was an unskilled, uneducated goof who didn't know the first thing about hard work. When your mom and I found out about the pregnancy, my parents told me I had two choices, marry Joely or hit the road. I chose to marry your mom, but I felt forced into it and I resented it.

"Joely didn't approve of my lifestyle, and we ended up fighting all the time. I had a lot of frustration inside me to contend with. You were a great little kid, Taylor. I just didn't know anything about raising a child. Every time I turned around, you were into something and it got me so crazy."

Brad stopped talking when he realized Taylor was silently crying. His tears slid down the sides of his face into his ears, but he didn't try to wipe them away. It destroyed Brad to watch this, knowing he caused those tears.

"I'm listening to myself speak and I can't believe how selfish I sound." Brad mocked his own words. "Poor me, poor Brad. Had to marry a beautiful, sweet girl. Had to become the father of a terrific little kid. Man, that was really tough. What an incredible jerk I was. I'm sorry, Taylor. So sorry."

Taylor licked his dry lips. "Do you love me, Dad? Or do you look at me and feel guilty for what you did to me?"

Brad swallowed hard. Taylor was right. He had grown up, and he deserved the truth.

"I look at you and feel guilty." Taylor flinched and Brad hurried to continue. "I feel guilty and I regret how I missed watching you grow up. Because I love you so much, and I'm very proud of the young man you've become, despite having me as a dad. I've made lots of mistakes in my life, and I'm sorry for them all. Except the one that created you. It's too late for your mom and me, but I hope it's not too late for you and me. I'm going to try real hard not to drink anymore. I know myself well enough not to make any big promises, but I'll do my best to never let you down again. Now all I need to know is whether you can forgive me?"

"I already have." Taylor reached his hand through the railing and Brad scrambled to his feet, eagerly grabbing it. "And I'm glad you want to quit drinking, because even though I love you, I won't be around you if you aren't sober."

That love, Brad knew, was all the motivation he needed to keep him on the path to sobriety.

* * * *

Joely went looking for Cole when she left Taylor's room. She hadn't had a rational moment to think about the two of them since they'd made the early morning dash to the hospital. Cole hadn't said he loved her last night, but she felt sure he had finally admitted it to himself. It wouldn't be long before he told her.

She knew the past several hours must've been particularly hard for him, first opening up about his marriage and his daughter's death, then having this terrible scare with Taylor. She had been in such a bad place herself, she was unable to think about what he might be going through or offer him any form of support. She cringed inside as she pictured the blaze of absolute terror showing on his face when he arrived at the hospital a short time ago, because he thought her tears meant something had happened to Taylor. She'd be strong for him now, as he always was for her.

She found Cole leaning against the wall in the hospital corridor, his shoulders hunched, his hands shoved deep into his jeans' pockets. As she approached him, his gaze lifted to meet hers.

"I'm sorry. I couldn't face going in there just yet. This whole thing with Taylor, it reminds me too much of Sarah—" He made a choking sound and couldn't go on.

Joely reached out her arms to meet his tentative step forward. "Everything's okay now. You, me, Taylor, we're all going to be just fine." His arms clutched her to the taut line of his body and she held him fiercely.

"I've been an absolute idiot. I thought if I didn't admit, not even to myself, how I felt about the two of you, if I refused to say the words out loud, I couldn't get hurt, but I was wrong. I was so scared, so miserable, when you left me. And I can't describe how terrified I've been about Taylor. I've already lost too much in my life, I don't know what I'd do if I lost you and Taylor, too."

His eyes held back tears and as Joely watched, one of them escaped and trickled down his face. Her hand trembled as she traced a finger softly along his cheek where the tear left a wet streak.

"You haven't lost us. We're right here and we aren't going anywhere. You just try to get rid of us."

They clung tightly together. "Never leave me, Joely," Cole whispered hoarsely against her hair.

"I won't," Joely promised, trying to absorb the shudders that vibrated through him. "Not ever."

"Since my daughter died, I've lived my life without love and I thought that's the way it'd always be. Until I met you. I love you so much, and I want to marry you, I really do. I want you, me and Taylor to be a real family. The sooner the better."

"Sooner's definitely better. I'd love to give Taylor a little brother or sister, maybe both." They smiled at one another and kissed, their mouths tasting each other, loving each other. "Now I think the young man waiting down the hall will be thrilled to hear our happy news. Do you want to tell him?"

* * * *

Cole entered Taylor's room tentatively, not wanting to disturb a private moment between the boy and his dad. Brad stood beside the bed, holding Taylor's hand as though it was a very precious package. He turned when the door opened.

"If this isn't a good time, I can come back," Cole told him.

Brad smiled down at Taylor. "I'll let you visit with Cole, but I'm not going far, okay? I'll be back as soon as I'm allowed." He kissed Taylor's forehead before leaving.

Taylor looked exhausted. He had been through such an ordeal, and his eyes were heavy with pain and the aftereffects of the anesthetic. Cole lowered the railing on the bed and perched himself carefully on the edge. Tears left streaks on the boy's cheeks and Cole used a knuckle to wipe them away. Then he touched Taylor under the chin lightly with the tip of his finger.

"You all right?"

"Uh-huh. I am now."

"You have a good talk with your dad?"

Taylor nodded. "Did you have a good talk with my mom?"

"Yup." Cole nodded back.

"I'm real glad."

"Me too."

Taylor's fingers searched for Cole's right hand and he pressed it weakly. Cole covered Taylor's hand with his left hand and squeezed back.

They smiled at each other in silence, a warm understanding flowing between them that had no need for further words.

* * * *

The beginning of August had already rolled around. With the wedding less than three weeks away, it was past time for the invitations to be sent out. Joely had been after Cole for days to give her a list of people he wanted to invite and so far, had gotten nowhere with him.

They sat outside on Joely's patio, sharing a glass of wine after dinner and enjoying the last rays of sunshine before the sun rounded the west corner, leaving the yard in shadows. Their talk naturally centered on the upcoming wedding, and Joely mentioned to Cole, yet again, that if he wanted to invite anyone to the wedding, she needed the list.

Cole handed over a folded paper with a dramatic flourish and a bashful smile. "Sorry it took so long."

Practically snatching the sheet from his fingers, Joely scanned it eagerly. The very short list contained the names and addresses of a few people he worked with. "Wait a minute, Cole, I don't see your father's name."

"I thought you wanted to know who I'd like at our wedding?"

"That's what I asked for," she agreed.

"And that's what I gave you." He leaned over to tap the paper in Joely's hand.

"I see, but your father's name isn't on it," Joely repeated in case he'd misunderstood her the first time. "I'll need an address to mail the invitation to. We should courier it, maybe, to give him a little more notice. Or better yet if you phoned and invited him yourself."

"Hold on there, Joely. I don't want to invite my old man."

She pulled her head back to give him a look of puzzled disbelief. "That's just not right—he's your dad. He'd want to be here. And I'm looking forward to meeting him."

"Firstly, he would not want to be here. Second off, I don't want him here, and third thing, I don't want you to have to meet him."

Joely glanced toward the open patio door to where Taylor played a game on the computer in the far corner of the living room, and she made her voice go soft and reasonable. "Why not? We're celebrating a very special occasion and our entire family should be here to celebrate with us. He's your father."

"Adam Dennison may have fathered me, that doesn't necessarily make him my father. I spent my entire childhood trying to please that unyielding man and never succeeded. The day I walked out of his house to be on my own is the day I stopped trying to prove worthy of his love. He chose not to attend my graduation from the academy, and he didn't bother to come to my first wedding, so what makes you think he'd come now? There's no law saying you have to stay in touch, just because you're related."

Joely saw beyond Cole's armor of prickly indifference to the fear of rejection his father was still capable of arousing in him. Although Cole had become much better at expressing his feelings in the past few weeks, some things were harder for him to deal with than others. In most of their previous discussions, Cole had not admitted any bitterness toward his father, putting the blame squarely on himself for what he perceived to be his shortcomings in his father's eyes.

After countless conversations, Joely thought she had convinced him at last that it was normal and perfectly acceptable to feel hurt, or scared, or tender. He'd talked at great length about his daughter, even showed Joely the only photo album he had of her. It had been the first time he was able to look at her pictures since her death.

Joely had cried while she studied the photos of the precious little girl who looked so much like her daddy. And Cole had expressed both sadness and pleasure at the memories the pictures brought back to him. By finally acknowledging that Sarah's death was not his fault, he'd found a measure of closure. He could now remember her without the debilitating hurt and rage that previously accompanied her memory.

However, his father was alive and therefore still capable of making him feel inadequate as a man. He might be more accepting of himself when around Joely and Taylor, because their love made him feel safe. But if faced with his apathetic parent, who rejected any display of emotion, Cole might revert back to the need to hide his feelings.

Joely understood completely why Cole felt this way without him having to tell her. She even shared some of his fear of regressing to his former self if confronted by either rejection or condemnation from his father. But she'd also learned a few things over the past few weeks, and the most important of those lessons was that facing your fears with truth and courage was the best option for everyone involved.

She'd spent the past eleven years hiding the truth about his father from Taylor, thinking she was protecting him and preserving the love he had for his dad. Where in reality, she had simply enabled Brad to continue with his destructive lifestyle with no fear of repercussions with Taylor because she went to great lengths to make sure Taylor didn't know.

Once the truth about Brad's abuse and alcoholism were out in the open, Taylor was able to forgive his dad and this in turn gave Brad the strength to stay sober. Taylor also finally understood why Joely hadn't let him spend time alone with his dad, and that source of friction between mother and son was now gone. Facing the truth, scary as it was, turned out to be less harmful than hiding from it.

Surely the same held true for Cole and his father. Cole wasn't a scared little boy anymore, seeking security from a man incapable of giving it. He was a grown man, much loved and badly needed. He knew this and he loved back with all his heart. In this safe, loving environment, maybe he could finally make peace with his father. Or at least he could come to terms with the fact that just because they were two very different people, it didn't make Cole any less of a man.

Cole waved his hand in front of Joely's face. "Joely, do you hear what I am saying?"

Joely smiled and brought her attention back to him. "I hear you, honey, I just don't happen to agree with you. Your dad is getting older, and you've told me he lives all by himself. Maybe he's lonely. After such a struggle and a tremendous amount of pain, you're finally at a happy place in your life, don't you want to share that with your dad?"

She felt a ripple of impatience go through him. "If I thought my father wanted to be here and share in our happiness, I'd call him right now, but I know he wouldn't." He slung an arm over Joely's shoulder and pulled her against him.

"The only important thing to me is marrying you. I'd be happy to go to a Justice of the Peace with only Taylor in attendance if it meant you'd finally become my wife, but I know the ceremony holds more meaning to you. I want our wedding day to be perfect in every way, because you deserve it. A sour, disapproving old man is not someone who could add to our happiness. I'm trying to be cooperative, but all cooperation ends at the mention of inviting Adam Dennison to our wedding. Please don't expect that of me, okay?"

Joely gave him a quick kiss before disentangling herself from his grip. The determined set of his jaw left no doubt he'd made up his mind, which meant the next move was up to her. She smiled as a thought formed.

"Did you want to go over my list?"

Cole chuckled. "Why would I want to do that? You can invite whoever you like."

Joely nodded with satisfaction. In effect, Cole had just given her permission to add his father's name to her list. And he'd even inadvertently provided her with the man's name.

* * * *

"Cole, it's Taylor."

Cole had just arrived home from their place, so it surprised him to hear from Taylor again this evening. "Hey, buddy, what's up? You sound upset."

"Desperate is more like it. Mom's driving me crazy."

"And what's your mom doing to drive you crazy?"

"She's mothering me to death. I just asked if I could go to the beach tomorrow and she said no. I want to do the things normal fifteen-year-olds like to do, but the only place she lets me go without her is your house. She even phones from work twice a day to check up on me. Will ya talk to her for me? *Please*?"

Cole swallowed down his laughter at Taylor's plaintive tone because the boy was serious. Taylor had spent a week in the hospital after his surgery and although he'd been home for two weeks now, Cole saw how Joely still worried and fussed constantly over him. The doctor assured Joely that Taylor's fatigue and headaches were to be expected. In fact, he'd told her the boy had less adverse side effects than many other people with similar injuries. He said if Taylor used common sense, he could slowly start resuming normal activities. But when it came down to letting Taylor go off with his friends, Joely couldn't do it.

Cole commiserated with Taylor because he also faced challenges with Joely. He spent all his free time at their place because she wouldn't go out and leave Taylor home alone. He and Joely had spent every night with each other while Taylor was in the hospital, but since he'd come home, they hadn't had a single private moment together. Cole tried to be patient, but it was getting to be too much.

"How about if we have a chat with her after breakfast tomorrow? Maybe between the two of us, we can get her to see she's smothering you. I'll take you and your friends to the beach tomorrow, I promise. Get a good night's sleep and I'll see you in the morning."

* * * *

Joely placed the last breakfast plate in the dishwasher and closed the door, then punched the button to turn it on.

"Hey, Mom, do you have a moment? I need to talk to you about something that's bugging me."

Taylor looked peaked, and Joely quickly moved to his side, feeling his forehead for any sign of fever. "Are you not well? Is it another headache? Are you dizzy?"

He pushed her hand away. "Mom, honestly, you have to stop. I'm not sick. That's what I want to talk to you about. I'm, like, bored out of my head. You don't let me go anywhere or do anything. I'm going crazy."

"It's a parent's prerogative to worry about their children. Besides, it's for your own good. You were very ill, and you have to take it easy if you want to make a complete recovery."

"No, I think you're doing this for your own good, not mine. I've done everything the doctor told me to do, and I'm way better

now. I know it was real scary for you, but it's over. I survived, but I
don't know if I can survive much more of your smothering."

Joely looked from Taylor to Cole, standing just behind the
boy's shoulder. His expression told her she should expect no
support from him.

"What is this? A conspiracy? The two of you are ganging up
on me?"

Taylor reached out a hand in appeal. "We don't want to fight
with you. We just want to make you realize how impossible you're
becoming. Cole's taking me and my friends to Ambleside today.
We're gonna laze around on the beach, maybe check out the hot
chicks. If there's a basketball game going on, we might play. And
I'm gonna sit on those steps I cracked my head on and prove to
myself and everyone else that I'm okay."

His jaw stiffened and he lifted his chin, but it continued to
tremble. Cole placed his hand at the base of the boy's neck and
gave it a squeeze.

When Joely started to shake her head, Cole spoke up. "I *am*
taking the boys to the beach today, Joely. It's a beautiful day and
there's no reason to keep Taylor cooped up inside." He glanced at
Taylor and smiled affectionately. "He won't be playing any
basketball, but he *is* going, and those chicks he referred to will be
wearing bikinis, not feathers. It's time, sweetheart, you have to let
him go."

Joely's bottom lip quivered helplessly. Right or wrong, she
had the strongest need to wrap Taylor in cotton and keep him safe
in her pocket. "Why Ambleside, Cole? Take him somewhere else.
Why does he have to go back there?"

"He wants to go to Ambleside, so that's where we're going."

"I have to, Mom," Taylor pleaded for her understanding. "I
can't hide from there, pretending nothing happened. That beach is
one of my favorite places and I won't let those thugs take that away
from me." He licked his lips and plunged on. "I can't let you do
that to me either. I know you love me and you worry about me, but
you can't lock me up to keep me safe. It won't work."

Joely heard the truth in his words. After an instant of silence,
she nodded. "Oh, Taylor, forgive me. I have been a little crazy,
haven't I?" She closed her eyes for a second as a choking fear

welled up inside her. She determinedly pushed it back down. "You go to the beach, honey. You have a good time with your friends. But no basketball and don't sit in the sun too long. Cole, if he starts to get a headache, I want you to bring him straight home and—"

"Mom!"

"Joely!"

"Oh look, I'm doing it again, aren't I?" Joely laughed at herself. "Have patience with me, please, Taylor. I'll try not to mother you as much. Feel free to set me straight if I forget."

"You can bet I will. Thanks for seeing things my way." Taylor gave her a quick hug. "I'll use the phone in your room to call the guys and set up a time to go."

After Taylor left the room, Joely smiled coyly at Cole. "Come here, you." She grabbed a handful of his hair, playfully pulling his head down. "Will you be ogling the cute girls in bikinis too?"

Cole slipped his arms around her waist. She felt the curve of his grin against her brow. "Why would I want to do that when I have the most beautiful woman in the world right here in my arms?"

"Thank you for saying that." She kissed him deeply, her lips searching for a fulfillment only he could provide. Breathlessly, she twisted her mouth away when he showed no sign of letting up. "And thank you for coming to Taylor's rescue yet again. I love you so much."

Cole's hands roamed down Joely's backside, pulling her against him. "I love you too, baby. You know how much." His touch ignited fires deep inside her and she felt the answering fires in him.

With her arms around his neck, she leaned her head against his shoulder. "I'd like to make a date with you for this evening. We need a little time by ourselves."

Cole rested his chin on her hair. "I'm glad you realize that, because I didn't want to push you, but damn I've missed you."

"I've missed you, too. Taylor can have friends in tonight and we'll go over to your place." She kissed him quickly, then stepped away as his hands became persistent. "If we don't stop this, we might forget Taylor is down the hall." She winked at him and grinned. "Save your strength for tonight. You'll need it."

* * * *

With the guys at the beach, Joely decided it was the perfect opportunity to try to reach Cole's father. She carefully went over all her misgivings about whether she was doing the best thing for Cole, and she kept coming to the same conclusion. Cole needed to see his father and talk to him and have his father see his happiness. Given his father's unbending attitude, it'd be a long shot whether she could convince him to come out, but she'd give it a good try.

She checked on the computer to get a phone listing for Adam Dennison. There were three A. Dennison's in the greater Toronto area. Joely carefully wrote down all three numbers. As long as he didn't have an unlisted number, the process of elimination should connect her with the right person.

The first number rang busy. The second one went to voicemail with a woman's voice giving the message. A man answered at the remaining number, but he sounded young and not the person she wanted.

Suddenly edgy and dry-mouthed, she dialed the first number again with shaking fingers. She didn't know what she'd do if it wasn't the right number, and she wasn't real sure how to proceed if it was.

"Hello?" a male voice answered.

"Hello, is this Adam Dennison?" Joely asked, encouraged by the lack of nervous quaver in her voice.

"Yes. Who's this?" The voice sounded abrupt, distrustful.

"My name's Joely Sinclair, Mr. Dennison. Do you have a son named Cole?"

"Cole, yes." Still no warmth or curiosity.

"Good. Sorry for sounding mysterious, sir. I just wanted to make sure I had the correct person. The reason I've called is to let you know Cole and I plan to be married in a few weeks. As a surprise for Cole, I'd like to invite you out here to North Vancouver, for a visit before the wedding, so we can get to know each other."

Only audible breathing crossed the line for a moment. "You have the wrong person. My son's already married. He lives on the island in British Columbia with his wife and daughter."

Joely's breath was knocked from her body as surely as if he punched her in the midriff. Cole had never told him Sarah had died and his marriage had ended! Forcing herself to calm down and start breathing, she realized the reason was obvious. If Cole was unable to discuss Sarah's death with anyone, he definitely wouldn't have told his unresponsive father.

"Mr. Dennison, when did you last speak to your son?"

"Oh, going on six years ago. They came out for my retirement party."

How could they have not been in contact for so many years? It was beyond Joely's comprehension. Rarely a week went by without her talking to her mom or one of her brothers.

"Mr. Dennison, sir, I hate to be the one to tell you this." Joely sucked in a deep breath for courage. "Sarah, Cole's little girl, died four years ago. She had an aneurysm. Cole has had a difficult time dealing with her death. I'm sure he wanted to tell you, he just couldn't find the words to discuss it with anyone. His marriage ended a short while later."

Some muffled coughing sounded in the background and when Adam Dennison spoke again his voice was hoarse. "Cole lost his little girl? Is that what you said? That little girl?"

"Yes, I'm very sorry to tell you about your granddaughter like this over the phone, sir. It was a terrible tragedy."

"My granddaughter, yes, well," he said it as if it just occurred to him she had been his granddaughter. "And Cole's divorced, you say, and he's marrying you?"

"Correct. Cole has been an absolute blessing in my life. He's an exceptional human being, and my son and I love him very much. We're getting married on August twenty-seventh and we'd like you to be here to share in our happiness."

"I don't know," he said without much interest. "British Columbia is a long ways away. I don't know if I have the time."

As a retired police officer, time off work wouldn't be a consideration. Maybe he couldn't afford it. He was a proud man, and she'd have to be careful not to insult him. "I know we practically live on opposite ends of the country, but it's not such a bad trip. If you'll accept my offer, I'd like to send you the plane tickets. It would be a gift from me to my husband, to have his father in attendance when we get married."

Adam Dennison snorted loudly. "I don't need your plane tickets. I can get my own."

"That's fine, however you want it," Joely quickly assured him. "I'll leave the arrangements up to you. If you will please call me after you've booked your flight, I'll make sure someone's available to pick you up at the airport. I hope you can get away early enough so we'll have some time to spend together before the wedding."

Joely knew he hadn't actually agreed to come, so she rushed her words, not giving him a chance to speak. She gave him her phone numbers, both at home and at work, as well as her cell, making him repeat them to confirm he had actually written them down.

"Now remember, this is a surprise for Cole, so please don't say anything to him," she reminded him before hanging up. She intended to tell Cole long before the wedding day. However, she'd have to prepare him first. It wouldn't do to have his father phone him ahead of time and ruin everything.

Chapter Seventeen

"The phone's for you, Mom," Taylor called to Joely from the patio door. He followed Joely from the yard back into the condo. "He said his name is Adam Dennison. Who's that? Cole's dad or something?"

Joely shushed him quickly. "I'll tell you about it later." She took up the receiver, then noticed Taylor watching her curiously. "Go away, Taylor." She made a shooing motion with her hand, her anxiety making her abrupt.

Taylor showed no sign of offense as he shrugged and went outside. Only then did Joely answer the phone. "Mr. Dennison, I'm sorry for keeping you waiting. How are you doing, sir?"

"Fine, just fine."

Joely smiled at his brusque tone. He might not like what Cole referred to as "all that touchy-feeling stuff", but she wasn't about to stop trying.

"Good to hear. I hope you were able to arrange your schedule to give you a few extra days with us? I look forward to getting to know you."

"I got a flight out there arriving on the evening of twenty-fifth and I fly back home on the morning of the twenty-ninth. Could you book me a motel room? Nothing fancy."

That gave them a day before the wedding and a day after, not as long as Joely had hoped for, but perhaps a short first visit might be best. If everything went as well as she expected, there'd be plenty of visits in the future.

"I'm sure Cole will want you to stay at his place, Mr. Dennison. Don't worry about the details, I'll take care of it. Let me grab a pen so I can write down the flight information. I'm very happy you're able to come out," Joely prattled in nervous excitement. She carefully copied down the flight times and numbers on a piece of paper. As she hung up the phone, she heard the patio door open and close.

"I'm sorry if I sounded impatient with you, Taylor. If you want to come here, I'll explain about that phone call."

"Taylor went over to a buddy's house. Perhaps you want to tell me about the call."

Joely whirled around at the sound of Cole's voice. She hurried over to him and reached up for a hug. "I didn't expect you. What a nice surprise."

Her smile faded when instead of hugging her back, Cole grasped her wrists in his hands and held her away from him. "Who were you talking to?"

"It was about the wedding." Joely swallowed hard, wondering how to tell him his father actually agreed to come out. She definitely didn't plan on him hearing about it like this.

Suspicion sharpened on his face. "Taylor seemed to think you were speaking to a relative of mine. I only have one relative, and it makes me wonder how my old man got your phone number when I haven't talked to him in years, and he knows nothing about you. How did that happen, Joely?" he asked, a trace of disbelief and hurt coming through the firm tone of his voice. He let go of her arms, lightly pushing her away.

Joely tried to smile, but one look at Cole's face and she gave up the attempt. His eyes were hard, his expression stern.

Tread carefully here, she warned herself.

"Come sit down and let me explain." She lifted a placating hand, but he shook his head in warning and stepped back.

"So you admit you called my old man, even after I asked you not to? Even after I told you I didn't want him here?"

"I remember what you said. If you'll please come in, I'll explain. I believe I had good reasons. And, your dad—he wants to attend our wedding." She started toward him again, but he flung out his arms, stopping her.

"There's nothing further for you to explain. I don't want my old man out here. I don't want to see him. I don't want to speak to him. I thought I made my feelings clear."

Joely got a scared, sick feeling in the pit of her stomach. He really meant what he'd said and she'd badly misread the situation.

She pressed the palms of her hands together in an urgent gesture. "Please, don't be upset. We can work this out. Let me explain why I invited your dad out, why I didn't tell you right away."

His expression didn't change except for a slow, deliberate compression of his lips. "I've heard all I want to hear. You intentionally went behind my back to invite the one person I least wanted to attend our wedding. I hope you two have a merry old time together. But you'll have to excuse me if I skip that particular ordeal." With those ominous words, he wheeled and walked out.

The power of her emotions stunned Joely into immobility. Something heaved in her chest, something hot and painful. Her breath caught and she felt lightheaded. Turning slowly, she sank into an armchair and folded her arms around herself. What in the world had just happened? She desperately tried to comprehend how and why Cole had walked out of her house and possibly out of her life.

Because you betrayed him, that's why, a stern little voice in her head chastised brutally. She took his fragile trust and thumbed her nose at it, determined to do what she wanted to do, telling herself it was for his own good, when in reality, her actions caused more harm than good.

At some level, she always knew Cole's angry reaction could be a possibility, but she refused to acknowledge the dangers. Because she was the professional, right? And she knew Cole had to face his unresolved feelings for his father before he could truly be happy. If he wouldn't do it on his own, she'd force him to, even if it meant going against his strongly voiced wishes.

Now, thanks to her meddling, she may have lost the man she loved. A single tear washed down her cheek and spilled onto her shirt. She impatiently swiped at her face, determined not to waste a single moment indulging in self-pity. She had to figure out a way to make things up to Cole, to regain his trust. She loved him far too much to give up without a fight. She'd beg, plead, do whatever it took, to redeem herself in his eyes. If only he'd give her another chance.

And that scared her beyond belief—what if he refused to see her, what if he didn't want to forgive her?

As Joely tried to visualize the impossibility of never seeing Cole again, he suddenly appeared at the patio door. At first, she thought he might be a mirage, invented by her overwrought mind, but when he called out her name and stepped inside, she knew he was real and he'd returned by his own volition.

She moistened the nervous dryness of her lips with a quick sweep of her tongue. "You...you came back?" she managed to stutter, her heart pounding with both fear and hope.

He drew a deep, very audible breath. "I got in the car and then I just sat there and thought, 'I can't do this. I can't leave Joely.' I can't walk out on you—on us." He came over to where she sat and pulled her up, his strong hands under her elbows, so she stood close to him. She saw her pain mirrored in his eyes. "If I left you, something inside me would be lost forever. You mean everything to me. I love you, Joely. I want to marry you and nothing else matters." He held her so tightly her ribs nearly cracked.

She burst into tears of relief and clung to him, her face pressed against his, her tears running down his cheek as well as her own. "I love you too, so very, very much. I'm sorry, oh sweetheart, I am really, really sorry. I'll fix this mess somehow. I'll phone your dad and make some excuse so he won't come out here." The rest of the words she wanted to say got stuck in her throat and she swallowed down hard on her sobs.

"Hush now, it's okay, don't cry anymore." Cole brushed her hair back from her face and bent down to kiss away her tears. "I'm sorry too. I'll never walk out on you again."

His lips traveled from her cheek to her throat and then down her neck. His hands ran slowly up over her hips, pressing her snugly against him, offering her proof of his desire. A delicious shiver ran through her and she moaned softly when his mouth moved back up to cover hers, firmly, persuasively.

"Umm, remember Taylor," she whispered reluctantly against the sweet taste of his lips.

"Taylor's out and he'll be gone for hours," Cole assured her with a throaty whisper. She didn't protest when he lifted her into his arms and carried her to the bedroom, closing the door firmly with his heel.

* * * *

"Cole, we have to talk about your dad," Joely nervously pointed out, as she snuggled closer to him on the couch. They had just left her bedroom and the residual glow of their lovemaking still enveloped them, making Joely reluctant to bring up the touchy subject, but she knew it couldn't be ignored. Although making love was a delectable way to show someone forgiveness, problems were worked out by talking.

"Look," Cole sighed heavily and leaned his head back against the couch. "I'm not happy you invited the old man out, and I'm astounded he accepted the invitation, but I don't want you to take back your invite. Maybe you're right, maybe I do need to see him. It's about time."

Joely looked up at his strong profile, at the small frown creasing his forehead and she wished her love was enough to heal all his troubles.

"It's totally your decision whether your dad attends or not. I'm sorry I did what I did, the way I did it. Not even Maggie has attempted such a terrible case of meddling and believe me, she's pulled off some lulus."

Cole smiled tolerantly, but Joely kept her face solemn. "Even though I do think you and your dad have some issues to work out, it's not my place to force it on you. I should've tried harder to discuss my concerns with you and if I wasn't able to convince you, I should've backed off. I'm sorry and this will never happen again. Honesty and trust are what I want for us, and I promise to never trim the truth with you again."

Cole pressed his cheek against the side of her head, rubbing it against her hair. "I know you'll always have my best interests at heart. Even if it stings a little bit. It's just that my father has a way of making me feel inadequate. When he finds out how badly I messed up, it'll only confirm what a failure I am, and he won't hesitate to tell me exactly what he thinks. I don't want to go back to seeing disappointment in his eyes every time I look into them."

Joely sat up straight, pulling away from his arms and turned sideways, facing him on the couch. "How can you say that?" She smacked him lightly on the shoulder. "You take that back right now. You are not a failure. You never have been. What happened to Sarah was totally out of your control and you know it. You were a wonderful father. And you're great with Taylor and his friends. They all adore you. As for your marriage, it takes two to make a relationship work. It wasn't just your fault. Debra holds some blame, too. She didn't appreciate what a treasure she had."

Joely came up on her knees and leaned into Cole. "I happen to know firsthand how sweet—" she nuzzled his cheek "—and warm—" she rubbed the tip of his nose with hers "—and passionate you are." She kissed him full on the mouth.

Cole's laughter rumbled against her lips and he pulled her onto his lap. The playful kiss deepened and became serious as the ever-present spark of passion ignited between them again.

"Ah-ha!" Taylor called as he walked into the condo. "Caught in the act." Joely and Cole turned flushed and smiling faces toward the boy. He grinned back mischievously. "I gotta admit, you two make a cool couple—for old people."

"Old people!" Joely leaned forward on Cole's lap and gestured with her arm. "Come here and I'll give you old."

Taylor plopped down on the couch next to them. Cole pretended to put him in a headlock before settling his arm across the back of the couch behind Taylor. His other arm remained possessively around Joely, keeping her on his lap.

Joely watched the two loves of her life with a tender gaze. "I don't know about you guys, but I think we make an awfully cute family."

"*Cute*, ugh." Taylor scrunched his face up in disgust and pretended to gag.

"Cute or not, we will be a family, Taylor," Cole told him seriously. "I don't presume to take your dad's place, but I'd like to be some sort of father figure to you. You okay with that?"

Although Cole's demeanor didn't change much, Joely sensed how he hung on Taylor's reply. His quick and positive answer deeply gratified her.

"Are you kidding? It'll be so cool to have you as a dad. You're, like, the best. I mean, I love my real dad and everything, but it's okay to want Cole for a dad too, right, Mom?"

"Most definitely, sweetie. We're going to be very happy together." Her arms encircled both of her guys and she hugged them close. Now more than ever, she believed this to be true. She knew if they were honest and worked together, they could surmount any obstacle in their path. With any kind of luck, that even included the formidable Adam Dennison.

* * * *

While Cole waited for the plane carrying his father to disembark, it surprised and pleased him to discover he didn't have any feelings of dread. He was only mildly apprehensive. If anything, he mostly felt curious. It had been many years since he last had contact with Adam and he speculated on how the passing of time might have affected his old man—would he be even more cantankerous or could he have mellowed with age? Remembering the stern, unyielding father of his childhood, he doubted the latter was possible.

Up to this moment, Cole hadn't tried to analyze his feelings for his dad or figure out how to act when the old man arrived. He just knew he was tired of playing the role of perfect son. He had never been successful at it anyway. He'd simply be himself and react honestly to whatever Adam tossed his way.

As the crowd thickened with the new arrivals, Cole spotted Adam amongst the group heading for the luggage carousels. He stepped forward, pushing away from the wall he leaned against.

"Hey, Pop, hi."

Adam turned and moved out of the crowd toward him. "Cole, it's good to see you. I hoped you'd be here. It'd be mighty difficult to meet up with someone without knowing what she looked like." He clenched Cole's outreached hand and clasped him briefly on the arm before they joined the tail end of people moving to the carousels.

"Joely wanted to be here, but with all the wedding organizing, she's finding out there aren't enough hours in the day. She says hello and she'll see you in a couple of hours for dinner. How was your flight?"

"Long."

They spoke very little during the drive across town. A sudden down-pouring of rain combined with heavy traffic to take up most of Cole's attention, and Adam never engaged in small talk if he didn't have to.

It wasn't until they were seated in Cole's living room with a cold beer in hand that Adam cleared his throat and pursed his lips to indicate he had something important to say. He stared evenly at Cole until Cole felt compelled to speak.

"You have something on your mind, Pop?" Cole assumed the admonishments and recriminations would start now. He settled back in his chair, prepared to listen to a litany of his faults. However much he dreaded the ordeal, he reckoned they might as well get it over with.

"I haven't heard from you for a long time." Adam's voice sounded more puzzled than castigating. "I tried calling you once, but the number I had was out of service."

Cole shrugged. "I moved. Don't tell me an ace inspector with the Metro Toronto Police Service couldn't track down his own son? It should've been a walk in the park for you."

Adam took a long pull on his beer. "And it would've been, if I'd tried, but I didn't. I figured you'd call eventually. As time went by and I didn't hear from you, I guess I got a little stubborn. I wanted you to make the first move."

"What a surprise! And so out of character for you."

A strong thread of mockery ran through his reply, and Cole knew Adam picked up on it right away. First, he looked shocked by the comment and then a reluctant smile appeared briefly on his craggy features before he turned serious again.

"I didn't know what you were going through, son, or I would've made more of an effort to reach you."

An awkward silence developed. Cole picked intently at the label of his beer bottle and wondered where his father was going with this conversation. So far, it sounded more like an apology than a reprimand. He expected Adam to be querulous and blustery, that type of behavior he understood.

This person sitting before him looked like his father. He had the same salt-and-pepper-colored brush cut, maybe a little more salt now than pepper. He was still tall and fit. His face had aged, there were more creases than before, but his hazel eyes were as alert as ever, and he was still gruff and blunt. But the slightest thread of apologetic gentleness in his manner was a totally new experience, and Cole didn't know how to react to it.

Adam cleared his throat again and he sounded so uneasy that Cole glanced over at him with concern. Never in his memory had he seen his father look this uncomfortable.

"Sorry to hear about your little girl, son. Real shame. Shouldn't have happened. She reminded me of you when you were a boy, dark eyes full of spirit and sass."

Pain tightened Cole's throat. He swallowed with great care and forced himself to breathe naturally. "I guess I should've let you know, but it was a tough time and I didn't really talk much about it, about her, with anyone."

Adam nodded. "Your lady friend, Joely, told me as much. I bet you didn't expect to get much sympathy from me either. I don't blame you. And I'm glad you got rid of that Ice Princess. Never understood why you'd marry such a spoilt brat."

A rush of bitter anger threatened Cole's self-control, but he squashed it. He wanted to give his father some real truths and he didn't want anger to get in the way. "I married her because I thought she was the opposite of my mother. She was strong-willed and self-possessed." Deliberately, he decided to put the old man on the spot. "I thought you of all people would approve."

"Nope, never liked her. You are your mother's son, Cole, and that's not a bad thing. You are who you are. And I am who I am. I can't change that, but I can see how maybe I made some mistakes. My father had no idea how to show love, and he raised me much the same. Then I tried to make you that way too, because I believed it was the only way to be. Life's a lot easier if you don't have to take the time for emotions. Funny thing is, sometimes you feel things even when you don't want to."

Cole didn't allow the shock to show on his face. "Don't tell me you've been lonely, old man? Have you come to realize there's lots of empty hours in the day when you have no friends because you've driven everyone away?" Cole had almost, almost, ended up in the same position, himself. Maybe he had some of his father in him, after all.

Instead of the angry rebuke Cole expected, Adam gave a circumspect shrug, and he felt a sudden compassion for his father as he watched him grope for words. For the first time in his life, he

saw Adam Dennison as a human being, not some unfeeling
machine.

"I don't blame you for feeling bitter. When a man gets older,
he feels his own mortality, and he begins to question himself and
doubt his previous convictions. I've always held strong opinions,
no one knows that better than you. Some of those values I've
upheld at the expense of others that should've been more
important—like the happiness of my own son. I've wasted too
many years, sacrificed too much that should've been precious—all
in the name of pride and stubbornness."

It was Adam's turn to become overly interested in his beer
label. "I've been keeping time with this wonderful lady, she's made
me see a whole new side of life. Her name's Pauline, Pauline
Towers. She convinced me to come out here and see you. She
rightly pointed out that you're my only son and I should let you
know in person how badly I felt when I found out your daughter,
my granddaughter, had died. Family's real important to Pauline.
She has two grown children, they live out this way, in the
Okanagan. She often speaks about moving west to be closer to
them. I find I don't much like the idea of her moving away."

Adam Dennison had fallen in love, Cole thought
incredulously. He wished he could feel resentful. He wished he
could yell, "Why couldn't you've been that way with my mother?
Why couldn't you feel something for me when I needed you?" But
he felt no resentment. Because he understood. Joely had shown
him how to love and how to be loved. He gave thanks someone
was able to do the same for his father.

Something sharp inside that had jabbed and poked away at
him all his life began to dissolve, and he felt at peace. In two short
days, he was marrying the woman he loved more than anything,
and he looked forward to starting a new life with Joely and Taylor.
They'd be a real family and hopefully, he'd soon have more
children of his own. There'd be room in that happy family for a
grandpa, if that grandpa showed an interest.

The smile on his face was as genuine as his words. "I'm happy
for you, Pop. Pauline sounds like one heck of a good woman. Do
us both a favor and don't let her get away. You have family out
west too, you know. There really isn't anything holding you in

Toronto now that you've retired. Maybe the two of you could make the move together. The Okanagan Valley's a pretty nice place to grow old."

"Thank you for saying that. You have no idea how much it means to me."

With suddenly trembling hands, Cole carefully placed his beer bottle on the coffee table. He swiftly knelt beside his father's armchair and grasped him in a rough hug. He wasn't sure what to expect in return. He just knew he wouldn't accept rejection this time. If Adam tried to push him away, he'd refuse to let go.

To his immense pleasure, his father wholeheartedly hugged him back. Cole closed his eyes and savored the novel experience.

This was right. This was real. And he'd do whatever it took to make sure it stayed this way. Because he had finally learned love was a strength, not a weakness, and love could heal anything if you were willing to give it a chance.

* * * *

"Mom, are you ready? They've started the music." Taylor's apprehensive voice came through the door of the small room Joely shared with Stella and Maggie at the church.

"Come on in, Taylor. I'm just about finished here." She gave the small flowered headpiece one final adjustment. It would have to do. Ready or not, she was about to get married. Her breath caught and her stomach tensed.

She was actually getting married.

Through the reflection of the mirror, she saw Taylor enter the room. He'd been staying with Cole since her mom arrived, so Joely hadn't seen him yet today. She thought he looked dashingly handsome in his tuxedo, even though his face was drawn with nervous excitement.

Stella handed her the gorgeous bridal bouquet of orchids and baby's breath. "What do you think of your mom, Taylor? Isn't she beautiful?"

Stella's words embarrassed Joely, but she did feel beautiful in her sleeveless gown of ivory satin and antique lace.

"You really are, Mom. You look fantastic." Taylor's smile lit up his face and his eyes shone brilliant blue. Then the worried expression returned. "But, like, we gotta go. Everyone's waiting for us in the church."

"Wait!" Maggie bawled. "I nearly forgot to give Joely something." She rushed over to her purse and fumbled through it. "Here you go, Jo. This should cover all the bases."

She handed Joely a delicate blue hankie.

"Thanks, Maggie, but I won't need a hankie. I don't plan to cry today."

Maggie made a small, rather rude, noise that let Joely know she didn't believe her for a moment. "It's something old— belonged to my grandma, but it's new to you. It's something borrowed—I'm lending it to you. And it's blue."

"All right." Joely tucked it down the front of her gown. "I'll accept it for tradition's sake. But I'm not going to cry. I'm the happiest woman in the world."

"We know you are," Stella told her and the three women gathered into a group hug.

"*Come on*," Taylor complained impatiently. "We gotta go now."

Maggie started down the aisle first, then a few steps behind her, Stella followed. Joely took a deep breath and tucked her hand into Taylor's offered arm.

"This is it, sweetheart. Today you, me, and Cole become a real family. Ready?"

"I've been ready for*ever*."

As they moved slowly down the aisle, Joely surveyed the happy faces turned their way. They were all here. Everyone she loved was in this room today to share in this blessed event, and it meant so much to her. There was Stella's husband, with a firm hand controlling each of their adorable little girls. Next came the Baldwin family. Nelson and Kyle looked self-conscious in their suits, poor guys.

Several friends from her condominium building smiled as she passed them. Then she spotted Rick, Karen and the girls. Cindy and Stephie looked beautiful in their new dresses. Her nieces were growing up way too fast. Harry and Carolyn beamed at her, and Harry tossed Taylor a wink.

Joely's mom was crying, as Joely knew she would. Joely's throat tightened with emotion and she gave her mom a tremulous smile, then turned her attention to the other side of the aisle before she succumbed to tears along with her.

Her gaze landed on Anne Jamison, her happy round face glowed proudly, as though she was the mother of the groom. Then Joely saw Adam Dennison. Was that actually a smile on the old man's face? She grinned back at him and his smile grew larger. He was coming around. Maybe with love and perseverance, Joely would, one day, have the father she'd always wanted.

Suddenly they were at the altar and Taylor leaned down to kiss her cheek. His eyes shone suspiciously as he backed away from her.

Don't you dare cry, Taylor Mills.

Joely knew if he broke down, she would too, and she didn't want to cry. He gave her hand a squeeze, then moved to the other side of Cole and Michael, to do double duty as a groomsman.

Cole reached out a hand to draw her beside him. She raised her gaze to his—her handsome hero, her knight in shining armor. In a few minutes, she would become his wife. To have and to hold, to love and to cherish for the rest of her life.

An indescribable euphoria filled her heart as she continued to gaze into his eyes. Dark eyes full of love and peace and certainty. She adored this man with her entire being.

Cole took her shaking fingers in his large, warm hand and raised them to his lips to slowly kiss them. Then he grinned and mouthed the words, "I love you, angel."

Joely fumbled for the hankie Maggie gave her. What the heck. It was her wedding day. She was entitled to shed a few tears.

THE END

About The Author

Joyce Holmes lives with her husband and very small dog in the beautiful Okanagan region of British Columbia. An empty-nest mom, she treasures family time, especially with her two precious little grandsons. Hiking, biking, boating and photography are pursuits she enjoys when she's not dreaming up stories in her head or planning her next great adventure.

http://www.JoyceHolmes.wordpress.com

Secret Cravings Publishing
www.secretcravingspublishing.com

Made in the USA
Charleston, SC
04 January 2013